the itinerant indian

edited by aruna nambiar

alex joseph
anthony koithra
aruna nambiar
deepa ravi
john mathew
mahendra rathod
mathew chandy
m r shetty
nikhilesh dholakia
preethi d'sa
rahul rao
raja ramanathan
sarita mandanna
vidya k baglodi

illustrated by n c unni

Published by: **Unisun Publications**
Unisun Technologies (P) Ltd,
Kodava Samaja Building,
7, I Main Rd, Vasanthnagar,
Bangalore 560052, India.
Phone : 91-80-22289290 Fax: 91-80-22289294.
e-mail : info@unisun4writers.com
website : www.unisun4writers.com

First printing March 2005
Copyright © Individual Authors

Typeset and printed by WQ Judge Press
Residency Rd, Bangalore 560025.

£ 7

€ 9

$ 12

Special Indian Price: Rs 295 only

All India Distribution:
Prism Books (P) Ltd
#1865, Cross 32, 10th Main, Banashankari II Stage,
Bangalore 560 070.India.
Phone-91-80-26714108 e-mail: prism@vsnl.com

Chennai, Delhi, Hyderabad, Kolkatta, Kochi, Mumbai, Pune.

ISBN 81-88234-09-5

Unisun dedicates this book to

All those who travel by air, water and land... and of course those who travel comfortably seated in their armchairs...

foreword

Be honest now – have you picked up this book to learn what the entrance fee is for Disneyland? Or where you can find a vegetarian menu amidst the smorgasbord of carnivorous delights in the Far East? Or how tall the Eiffel Tower is and when it was built? Forewarned is forearmed. Whisper to yourself, "LET'S GO find another book," quietly return the offending piece to that gap in the dust, back away carefully from the shelf, and head FO-the-DOR's.

Lest you labour under the misapprehension that this book is not of academic importance however, let me assure you that it contains a treasure-trove of information. You will learn, for instance, that shovelling shit can be fun – if you're on a reserve in South Africa. That slurping of noodles is not just expected in a Japanese ramen restaurant, but is also a highly efficient noodle consumption technique. That it is an honour in Australia, to be able to trace your background to a convict transported from England. That the longest beach in the world is a little 'worse – for wear'. That the Children of Gandhi live in Brazil, not Porbandar.

If you have ever been stuck in an alien land, hot or homesick, uncomfortable or unemployed, frozen or famished, or generally out of your depth, you will find ample company in misery as you turn these pages. If you are a jaded traveller who has sampled all that the world has to offer, only to discover surprises closer to home, you will find your wonderment echoed in these writings.

But it's not just about travel. It's about nostalgia; it's a chance incident in a far off place transporting you back to a time when you were still a naughty kid reading comics in class; it's reminiscing about the good old days when Chennai was Madras and booking railway tickets was a day-long adventure. It's about discovering that the world really *is* a small place; that you can talk about chole bature with a cabbie in New York; that the obsequious Indian salesman is inescapable whether you're in London, Abu Dhabi or Singapore. Most of all, it's about identity – that thing which makes us see the world through desi eyes; where a risotto is but an Italian khichdi; when you can't stop hankering for vendakkai sambar – even after a quarter century outside the homeland.

As our writers touch down at the North Pole or wade in waist-deep snow in Antarctica, buy harem pants in Istanbul and chocolat in Paris, it may also dawn on you that, while vested interests babble on about the evil 'Globalisation of India', there's another insidious phenomenon silently sweeping the world – the 'Indianisation of the Globe'. So much so, that curry can be found in London and palak paneer in New York, just as croissants and pasta have entered the desi lexicon. Is there really any thing like a 'foreign' language anymore?

We're no longer restricting our travels to shopping trips to Dubai and conducted tours of the Statue of Liberty either – we're dancing the samba in Salvador and chatting with the Queen at Buckingham Palace; we're being chased by lovesick animals in Oman and irate landlords in Bahrain; we're wrestling with the language in Bavaria and teaching 'ratbag' students Down Under; we're even meeting old friends in Nivati.

Nivati – where's that, did you ask? Well, read on, won't you? And yes – do enjoy the ride...

Aruna Nambiar

the itinerant indian

VII

Comfort Food

Sarita Mandanna

It had been pouring all day, water dripping off gables and pounding at shuttered windows, overflowing from gutters in the narrow, cobbled streets near the University of Milan. Now the wind had picked up, blowing our umbrellas inside out and sending gusts of icy water down our necks. We were cold, miserable and starving. Food, we decided, we needed something hot and steaming to cheer us up. As one man, or woman in this case, we vetoed the thin, crusty pizza we had been nibbling on ever since we had arrived. Weather like this begged sturdier fare – something closer to home.

Bedraggled but determined, we waylaid bemused-amused-locals, asking for recommendations. And so it was that we squelched our way to Café Fiamma. It was tiny, no more than six tables and a blazing fireplace, the word RISOTTO scrawled over a blackboard. We collapsed by the fire, shivering and exhausted. The café owner fussed and clucked over us, bustling out with two heaped servings of

1

risotto. It was hot, she warned, fresh off the stove. The rice was perfectly cooked, with a mouth-watering steam thickly redolent of mushrooms, and the tiniest hint of truffle curling gently upwards from bright yellow plates. We dribbled hot pepper flakes over our portions; I sprinkled extra cheese on mine. Our shoulders relaxed, we forgot our jeans clinging wetly to our legs. And then there was silence, broken only by little oohs and aaahhs of pleasure as we spooned what seemed like hot, undiluted sunshine down our throats.

We ate incredibly well that spring. Fresh catch in the fishing villages of the Cinque de Terre, truffle omelettes and lentil soups in San Gimignano, blood oranges drizzled with olive oil in Siena. And yet, among the smorgasbord of delights as we waddled our way across Italy, it is the humble meal of risotto that I most remember. An Indian and a Sri Lankan, homesick for rice one blustery evening in Milan, grinning contentedly over two plates of Italian khichdi.

It is an enduring pattern. No matter where in the world I might be, when the chips are down and my back is to the wall, it is the familiar tastes of home that I gravitate towards. Take Bangkok. I was staffed on a complicated deal and ended up staying there for a straight month, a blur of consistently great food the whole way. My client's assistants took the overworked Indian waif under their wings. Thrilled when I told them I loved Thai food, these wonderful ladies took it upon themselves to stuff me silly.

"Special order for you," they would whisper as they brought in our lunches. There we would be, discussing strategy over our working lunches, the rest of the team eating cold sandwiches while I tucked embarrassedly into duck pad thai.

There were the frequent, epic meals with our client, an avid foodie who took it upon himself to introduce us to restaurant after flagship restaurant. Cigar in hand, he would expound on the delectable food Bangkok had to offer as we tucked into meal after fantastic meal.

There were so many options, each surpassing the other in quality and variety. And yet, dinner was on autopilot. I would wrap up from the office and head back to the Sukhothai well past midnight, brain aswirl in spreadsheets and pitches.

"Prawn choo chee goong," I would tell room service. "Green chillies in fish sauce. And yoghurt. Yes, that's right. No, not vanilla. Unflavoured. Sawadee kha!"

The hotel staff doubtless thought me eccentric, the way I insisted on mixing dinner with breakfast yoghurt, but what a meal! Succulent jumbo prawns awash in a spicy yellow gravy, curds over hot rice, a dash of salt and a splash of green chillies. My mind would still as I ate, the tiredness slowly ebbing away. My dinner, a faithful imitation of the many happy times at Mahesh Lunch Home in Bombay – prawn gassi, a glass of cool majjige tangy with ginger and green chillies, and Sundar the maître d', plying us with food.

Flash forward to school in Philadelphia, and desperate all-nighters scrambling to get submissions in on time. Oatmeal just did not cut it those mornings. Low on blood sugar and with 8 am class looming large, I would make my bleary way to Vinod and his breakfast cart. He was a cheerful, enterprising Punjabi who did brisk business in toasted buns, omelettes and eggs sunny side up. For the desi students though, there was an off the menu special – freshly scrambled eggs with jalapenos, ginger, tomatoes and coriander, tomato ketchup optional. We would drift in to class, clutching our various fixes – Starbucks lattes, donuts, Coke, blueberry muffins, leftover pizza. And one warm tortilla filled with a spicy, tongue-tingling anda bhurjee just the way Mom used to make it.

Before I knew it, school was done and we were on our way to Africa for a graduation hurrah. Included in the itinerary, a week of climbing Kilimanjaro. What do you get when you put a couch potato and the largest freestanding mountain in the world together? A very unlikely mountaineer indeed! Add to that a freak viral that I had barely shaken off before the hike and a woefully inadequate sleeping bag that had me lying awake night after night, shivering despite layers of insulating clothing. Sleep-

3

deprived and exhausted (a bad-workswoman *will* quarrel with her tools), I trekked for four seemingly endless days. One of us had a mild pulmonary oedema and had to be rushed off the mountain, two others dropped out midway. The rest of us made it.

I started the descent in a kind of catatonic trance. Stopping only to pick up a souvenir (a lava-stone pitted and brown), talking to no one, concentrating only on placing foot after foot. When we reached camp, a friend took one look at me and insisted I borrow her sleeping bag, equipped as it was for sub-zero temperatures. I protested only feebly as she bundled me in and fell deeply asleep almost immediately, cocooned in blessed, forgotten warmth.

They woke me for dinner, insisting I had to eat. It had been a protein-rich diet so far, roast meats and fried eggs to fortify us for the climb. Mostly, I had been too cold and tired these past days to pay much attention to what I was eating.

That night though, the cook had made a celebratory dinner. It was a thick stew of minced meat and bitter greens, with a kind of flat bread to mop up the sauce. I sat cradling the hot bowl, still bundled up in the sleeping bag, completely befuddled to realise I was eating parathas with methi kheema.

That stone I picked up lies on my dressing table, proud memoir of my mountaineer days. I pick it up and am instantly transported. The bright blue sky and the snow-capped peak of the mountain. The flat, black lava lands. Sub-zero temperatures at night, shards of ice in the drinking water. A cook who somehow, somewhere, learned to make Indian khana. The sensation of that meal, bite after blissful bite sliding into my stomach, the best methi kheema I have ever had.

Here in New York, I am spoiled for choice. You could try a different restaurant every day of the week, and still have places left to discover after a year. What's your pleasure? Italian, French, Turkish, Korean, Greek, or Sushi? Ethiopian, Croatian, Swedish, Indian, Chinese, Brazilian or

Thai? Fusion, cutting edge or just like grandma used to make? It's all here, served 24/7, more cuisines served in more variations than you can imagine.

And yet, in this abundance of riches, I am still a creature of habit. At the end of a particularly long day, when I don't have the energy to deal with deciding what to have for dinner, it is a familiar number I dial.

"Hellooo, CurryandCurry, mayIhelpyou?" It's a little dive just north of the stretch of cabbie joints collectively called Little India, the kind of place you wouldn't be caught dead in. But the paneer is soft and the palak thick, and the cook spices it with pieces of fresh ginger.

(As an aside, we nearly parted ways some months ago, the palak paneer and I. Baffled at my weight gain, I finally called the restaurant.

"Hellooo, CurryandCurry, mayIhelpyou?"

"Do you put butter in the palak paneer?" I asked.

"Naa ji naa!" exclaimed the indignant owner. "Butter bilkul bhi nahin hain, bas thoda creamy sauce dalte hain ji."

Needless to say, the mysterious creamy sauce has since been banished from my palak, and waistline and good relations are both restored.)

When the weather is foul and the City grouchy under grey skies, I revert to my South Indian roots. Rain equals rice in my equation, low-carb be damned. I head for Little Korea and a meal of dolsot bibimbop. The rice, heated in a stone wok, is cooked through on the top and deliciously crunchy at the bottom. Julienned vegetables are mixed in, along with minced tofu, meat or shrimp and a healthy swig of hot sauce. An egg yolk is cracked on top in a final masterstroke. The heat of the rice cooks the yolk into a kind of Asian hollandaise sauce, indiscernible yet binding the ingredients together into an entirely comforting mass. Korean khichdi anyone?

It isn't just me, you know. The City is swarming with us, folks who clone foods into dishes we have loved in the past. There is the Kashmiri friend and

5

fellow rice lover who hoards the hot sauce she buys from a little restaurant in Chinatown. It is the ultimate picker-upper she claims, this sauce mixed into hot rice. There is the friend who chose his building specifically because the Ethiopian restaurant he loved was opening a branch next door. The injira and chicken curry reminds him of appam and stew.

All of this makes me wonder: if we are what we eat, might it also be that we eat what we were? That we choose our favourite foods because they remind us of where we have been, of who we were? Take a recent visit to Argentina. So much for our preconceived notions of parrilla and more parrilla. Yes, there was steak and a lot of it, but there were also fabulous little restaurants serving reasonably priced, innovative and utterly fantastic food. We haunted the Palermo Viejo area, downing thimble after thimble of mulled wine with cinnamon and orange rind, wild mushroom tarts and brochettes of game. There was Patagonian braised lamb, wild boar pâté and elaborate chocolate desserts. We ate, we drank velvety Malbecs, we ate some more. And yet, the thing that stands out most clearly in that period of happy gluttony? Empanadas picante, spicy turnovers filled with cheese, spinach or minced meat.

"Samosas," reflected a friend as she chowed down, "basically, these are excellent samosas."

What's more, the phenomenon is universal. A friend took a year off after school to travel around the world. He talks about China, the wonderful, delicious food, and how he eventually got completely sick of it. He booked himself into the nearest five-star, budget be damned and ordered lunch. Ignoring the vast menu, he asked for a simple tuna sandwich and a glass of chocolate milk. It was the best thing ever, he says, reminded him of home. Another recently spent the better part of a month in India and the Middle East on work. He was on an expense account and ate like a king. "The food was fantastic, but truth be told," he confessed, "by the end of my trip, all I could think about was a good cut of meat grilled in my backyard."

6

There is a reason we have favourite foods, dishes that we instinctively turn towards when the chips are down. There is a reason why no trip to Dubai is complete for neither my sister nor I without the puffs from a little bakery at Karama. The puffs are good, but certainly not the best we have had. But it is a ritual, something that started casually one holiday and has now settled into an enduring pattern. Come what may, we have to get those puffs, our memories of Dubai intrinsically linked with a fluffy little triangle of pastry. Therein lies the real appeal of comfort food, its ability to conjure up memories of times we have shared with those we care about.

There may be more to this theory however. My sister was visiting New York, and I had chalked up a slap up schedule, choc a bloc with good eating. There was my favourite, award winning Mexican restaurant with the great guacamole; the neighbourhood French bistro that served the best onion soup in town. We would go to tapas bars and Latino lounges and the new Thai restaurant down town. I took her to Chinatown for a dimsum brunch. "This is the real thing," I said enthusiastically, "just like in Hong Kong." I pointed out the hole-in-the-wall joints selling almond tea, pork buns and red bean cakes, the red lacquered restaurants serving Sichuan, Cantonese and everything in between. I was waxing poetic on the sheer variety of food you could get here, when she cut in.

"When are you cooking for me?" she asked.

I have to admit, I was completely blindsided. Cook, in a city like New York, the food capital of the world? Why on earth would she want to eat at home when she could choose from virtually any cuisine on the planet? She was adamant. Fish curry, she said, she wanted my fish curry.

Silly girl! Shaking my head, I bought fresh tilapia from one of the stalls in Chinatown. We headed midtown to the Indian store, where I picked up fresh ginger, a sprig of curry leaves and a knob of tamarind. I cooked that afternoon, meen moilee with mustard seeds and coconut milk. There

were Vietnamese noodles steeped in water, milk, pepper, bay leaves and pearl onions. She likes potatoes so I fried some, tossing them in salt, turmeric and chilly powder. There was rice of course, and curds.

We sat down at the table. Noodles excepted, it was a familiar menu for both of us, deep-rooted memories of Mom cooking us fish curry and rice. We ate in companionable silence, passing dishes back and forth, happily absorbed in our lunch.

That's when it hit me. There is a reason we all have wish lists when we go home, dishes we want our mothers to make. If love is the language of a utopian world, then food must surely be its medium. Eating out and ordering in is all very well, but the very best kind of comfort food? Anything really, cooked especially for us – with love. The stuff that memories are made of.

Railway Reminiscences

Raja Ramanathan

Yesterday I visited the website of the Indian Railways. Given the size of the network and the geographical spread of the country, the website is a technological accomplishment of unparalleled proportion. Surfing through the site, I realised that sitting here, a few kilometres behind Toronto's Lester Pearson International Airport, I could book tickets for travel three months ahead, on the Gummidipundi Passenger that would depart from Madras (sorry, Chennai) Central's Platform Number 8. How things have changed!

Booking tickets for visiting uncles from Calcutta (before it became Kolkata) was one of the chores of my teenage existence. Uncles would land up for the summer holidays and, a few days after their arrival, we would have to book their return tickets. Somewhere in 1965 or 1966, Uncle J and his family consisting of his wife and three kids, and Uncle S and

9

his wife and four kids, landed up at the same time, in what was then Madras.

Uncle J, being the junior of the two, was assigned the task of getting eleven second-class three-tier tickets for travel between Madras and Howrah. I was appointed chief sidekick to Uncle J. My attempts at trying to wheedle out of the assignment by pleading that I had a test the next week were effectively put down with three arguments:

- That, in the first case, I never did study for my tests.
- That if necessary, I could take my textbook to the station, and be coached by Uncle J, who was an Economics Honours graduate.
- And that, and this was the clincher, the railways issued only six tickets to a single buyer.

The next morning Uncle J and I woke up at 4.30 a.m. My mother had made coffee and Uncle J magnanimously offered to buy me breakfast at the station. Uncle J got on the pillion of my bicycle and we cycled 'doubles' to a friend's house near Adyar Main Bus Terminus. Having successfully avoided early-rising cops looking to fill their monthly quota of criminally-minded people riding 'doubles' illegally on bicycles, we reached my friend's house, deposited the bicycle there, and made our way to the bus stop to catch the first Number 5 bus to Parry's Corner (the old colonial name of the new Paarimunai).

The bus started off its perilous journey at 4.55 am and, with the grace of our ancestors, we reached Madras Central around 6 am. Off we got from the bus and made our way to the booking counters, which opened at 8.30 am.

About ten people had already queued up ahead of us in front of the Howrah counter. This was not bad. At the peak of the summer travel rush, people slept overnight to be in a vantage position when  the counter opened. Uncle J and I positioned ourselves in this line-up of the faithful who wanted to travel to Howrah ten days from then (bookings opened ten days ahead of the travel date and generally were sold out by around 10 am). Uncle J told me to go and get the booking application form.

I wandered off ogling the pretty young girls who stood in the ladies' line-up to the left of the main queue. Indian women's liberationists had ensured separate queues for women. The girls were clutching their student concession forms, and I had half a mind to ask them if they had got them stamped by the Station Superintendent's office. If they hadn't, I wished to tell them, they would not be able to buy the tickets and would lose their vantage position. I was even willing to volunteer to take their forms and get them stamped by the almighty Station Superintendent.

I caught Uncle J's eye, which was telling me, non-verbally but sternly, to move on and get the reservation application forms. After sauntering around aimlessly for a while, I finally got the forms. As I came back, I noticed that some other busybody had approached my pretty friends and was getting their forms stamped by the Station Superintendent. Oh, if only I had come alone, without Uncle J!

The forms were duly filled by Uncle J, while I bent over so that he could use my back as a desktop. And thus began the two-hour long wait for the counter to open.

Madras Central, at 7.30 am was a live and bustling place, an epicentre of enterprise that could make an interesting case study for any top business school, what with several thousand people converging there purposefully each day.

Every two minutes or so, some train or the other would leave or arrive and announcements would be made about this impending event in Thamizh, English and what was allegedly Hindi. After 1965, when Madras decided to say No to Hindi, the Hindi announcements were dropped. But pre-1965, every few minutes you would hear of the impending arrival of a train in a stretched-out drawl: "Dillise ...yaanewali...Girandu trunk express... abhi thodihi dermein... platform number yek par aayegi..."

If you listened carefully, you would decipher that it

was some good Dravidian soul getting even with the Aryans for centuries of oppression, by writing down the announcement in the Thamizh script and massacring the pronunciation.

The Thamizh and English versions did not require the same exercise of collective social vengeance. Though the British had left only recently, they had left behind the railway system and that merited the English language a kinder treatment. And in 1966, Thamizh, slowly but surely getting de-Sanskritised, was well on its way to supremacy.

The oracle-like pronouncements in Thamizh served as a backdrop for myriad other sights and sounds; the jasmine flower vendor, a heavenly sight for the hormone-filmed eyes of a sixteen-year-old; the rushing, red-clad porters (do they have a more socially correct title now?); the calls of "murukku, masala vadai, vadai, soda, tea, coffee, biskit", all jammed together into a single, polysyllabic sound.

Once in a while, Uncle J would decide to wander off, letting me hold the place in the line that would have, by then, grown to fifty or so, the last ten having no chance of getting a ticket. Then he would return, and allow me to meander away. Once I took a little longer than I usually did: having had to stand in the early morning queue to perform ablutions at the Madras Central public washroom. On my return to the queue, Uncle J looked at me somewhat quizzically and apropos my somewhat long absence said, "If you want to smoke, you can do so in front of me. Where were you this long?"

Uncle J's comment opened up a new world of adventure for me. At sixteen, I had been sorely tempted by the tobacco industry's attempts to win my mind. Ads of damsels falling for the guy who lit his cigarette and blew swirls of smoke in the air held tremendous promises of the flesh. Till then, however, I had never smoked. It had been too risky a venture with several family wellwishers in the Adyar area only too willing to report back home on such 'immoral activities'.

However, Uncle J's comments were my trigger to try out this new experiment.

So when I got my turn to wander off from the

booking line, I made a beeline for the cigarette stall, and asked for a Wills Filter. The cigarette then cost 8 paise for one and 15 paise if you bought two. I bought one and, as every smoker of standing in Madras does, I lit the first weed of my life on the small rope with the burning tip, which hung by the stall and served as the lighter. I coughed a little and inhaled (unlike the former president of the US of A who did not). Maybe life would have taken a different course if I hadn't. A trice later, I reeled. The nicotine was going to my head and making me dizzy. As the sensation of giddiness came on, so did the image of the macho guy in the Marlboro ads, and I was hooked for the next twenty years.

I staggered back and took my place in the queue, the cigarette between my fingers. Uncle J looked at me and said, "That's better, you don't have to do these things on the sly."

Sitting here, looking at the Indian Railways website, I wonder how life would have been, if back in 1966, we could have booked our tickets with the click of a mouse, instead of the eventful journeys to Madras Central to book tickets.

My wife after reading this let me in on this long-guarded secret. She used to study at Stella Maris College, and lived in the college hostel. Stella Maris College, Madras, is best known for the determined efforts of the nuns who run the college to ensure that their wards' moral fibre remains of a high order, and the equally determined efforts of their wards to negate the nuns' efforts. Accordingly, the inmates of the college residence could go out only during specified hours, and with appropriate chaperones.

The one exception was when they had to go to Madras Central to book their tickets for the end-of-term journey home. Invariably the girls would remain out the entire morning, on the pretext that they were at the station, booking their train tickets to go home. The nuns did not realise that there was a separate Ladies' queue and that it took all of ten minutes for a lady to book her ticket. My wife is thankful that she did not have

the facility of online booking, and could have unsupervised fun, not to mention breakfast at Woodlands, on the pretext that she was going to be out the whole morning to book her ticket.

I continued my surfing of the Indian Railways website. I saw that I could access railway timetables for all trains online. Reading timetables of the Indian Railways was a pre-requisite for any railway journey that I undertook between the ages of twelve and eighteen. Prior to the journey, I would have established a hierarchy of the stations en route based on the amount of time the train stopped at the station. By the time I was 17, I had mastered all the codes on the timetable, and knew the difference between VRR and NVRR (Vegetarian Refreshment Room and Non Vegetarian Refreshment Room). I also knew the different station codes, and the mysteries of why Dadar was DRJ and Olavakkot was OJJ. So I could not resist this ability now offered to me to surf the net and find out how long the Madras Mail stopped at Venkatanarasimharajuvariapeta, which is the railway station with the longest name in India and comes between Renigunta and Arakkonam.

But the world of high-tech timetables is different. First you need to know the Train Number. That you get by entering the first three letters of the start and destination city. My struggles to find the timetables for travel from Bombay to Madras were all in vain for the first twenty minutes. Reason? I was entering the socially inappropriate names of Bombay and Madras. When this epiphany struck, everything fell into place, and soon, I had the timetables of all the trains that ran between Mumbai and Chennai.

The Bombay/Madras Mail (9Dn, 10Up in days of yore) is the oldest train to run the route. In 1926, when my father lost his job with the New India newspaper, Dr Annie Besant paid his fare of Rs.10/- or so for him to travel to Bombay to find another job. The Madras/Bombay Mail had already been running for over twenty-five years then. Today the Mail pulls out of Chennai Central and Mumbai Chhatrapati Shivaji Terminus (earlier, Victoria Terminus or VT) every day at around 10.00 pm, and reaches the destination station around 5 am, a day after the next.

The Mail is like a runner whose legs have been shackled. The train is not allowed to go any faster, because it would then reach its destination at a much more ungodly hour. In fact, often the train is held up at the 'outer' near Perambur or Perambur Loco Works on the Madras end, because the platform to receive it is not ready at 4.45 am.

The Madras Mail used to be about the last train of standing to leave VT. After the Mail had left, you had only lowly Passengers and Fast Passengers leaving. The ticket checkers would wait till the train crossed Dadar and do their ticket checking, waking up the gentry who had already pulled down their sleeper berths and gone to sleep. By the time they had finished, the train would be drawing into Kalyan where the Central Railway used to attach a second electric locomotive to the train, to push it up the steep Bhor Ghat into the Deccan Plateau. Oftentimes, in the monsoons, there would be a sharp rain falling, and I would watch the mighty shapes of the hills of Khandala and Lonavla loom up, and the thunderous waterfall that the monsoon had just created. By the time you reached Poona it was past midnight.

In the old days, the electric locomotives of the Central Railway would give way at Poona to the loud klaxons of diesel locomotives of the South Central Railway. In the sixties, before the diesel locomotives came, the steam engines would take over.

One would generally fall asleep after Poona, waking up to the cold air of the morning as one pulled out of Sholapur. It is surprising how the early morning air, travelling in a train in India, is always cold, irrespective of the season of the year.

From Sholapur, onwards to the cement town of Wadi. Wadi was the first stop in non-Prohibition land,

Karnataka, and my worst memories of Wadi are drinking some country liquor at age eighteen and having an awfully upset stomach. At Wadi, the hawkers would invariably be offering whisky and beer, which we swallowed, irrespective of its quality or the time of day. Having alcohol in your system was sufficient justification.

By mid-day you were at Raichur, the longest stop on the Bombay/ Madras haul. The Mail stopped here for an hour, enough time for food to be served. You could order the South Indian Rice Meal or the North Indian Chappati Meal and for those of us who fancied the white man's ways, you could order a Western Meal in which you were served the world's greasiest cutlets. No Westerner would have the stomach to digest those cutlets, but we ate them fully convinced that this was how they lived in Cheltenham Green, in the Queen's own country. In the old days, when the Southern Railway took charge of your life at Raichur, ticket checkers would re-check tickets to ensure that no wily Bombayites were slipping by ticketless.

Once we pulled out of Raichur, the Madras Mail sleeper coaches would fall into a heavy slumber in the hot afternoon heat of the Deccan Plateau. Whatever you did, you could not escape that mind-numbing heat. I have spent several afternoons wistfully hoping for air-conditioning or the wherewithal to fly. You would be awoken from your slumber as the train rolled across the mighty Tungabhadra bridge, and into the peaceful whistle-stop station of Mantralayam Road blessed by the presence of Sri Raghavendra Swami and his ashram.

In time for evening tea, you were at Guntakal. Before the broad gauge train lines were extended south of Miraj, this was where everyone who wished to go to Bangalore changed trains. Guntakal station was always full of langur monkeys who would snatch your food if you were not watching. After Guntakal came Gooty, where

the evening meal was served. Then, on to Cuddapah, and around two in the morning, Renigunta, gateway to the temple city of Tirupati. One generally did not notice

16

the next major junction, Arakkonam, because you were asleep by then.

And then the train raced past Trivellore (now Tiruvallur), Avadi, Ambattur, Korattur, Villivakkam, Perambur Loco Works, Perambur Carriage Works and Perambur, not realising that going so fast did not help. It would always, always, have to wait at Basin Bridge at the 'outer' for the platform to clear. The whole experience was almost like having sex; the rush, the sudden climax and the languorous lull.

As I sat looking at the electronic timetable, I realised how much it has all changed. There is now a twenty-four train (Train No. 1062/ 1063) to and from Mumbai and Chennai. The high and mighty Raichur Junction where life changed from the white solar topis of the Central Railway to the green ties of the Southern Railway now merits only a two-minute whistle-stop. The longest that the train stops is at Pune, for a measly ten minutes. How do you buy your batata wadas in ten minutes and also fill water? But then, there's Bisleri and Aquafina now. There is air-conditioning, and of course, you can check the timetable on the net.

All this reminds me of an old joke. A man went up to the stationmaster at Vaniyambadi (or Katpadi or Guduvancheri) and said, "What is the use of your timetable if all your trains are running late?"

The stationmaster, without batting an eyelid replied, "If there was no timetable how would you know that the train was late?"

Tokyo Confidential

Anthony Koithra

It's between the sixth and seventh round of beers at Kaz's house that he mentions he does in fact have a vague idea where Daigoku district is. He pulls a map out of a corner of the immaculate Yokohama apartment he shares with his wife Maki and several teddy bears, and spreads it on the coffee table in front of the rest of the dinner party.

"It's kind of a big area, sort of an industrial kind of place. This parking lot of yours won't be easy to find."

It's close to midnight, and people are already leaving to catch the last train back to Tokyo. I've been blathering on half the evening about a parking lot somewhere around the Bay Bridge where illegal street racing is purported to occur on occasion. My blather is based on the worst kind of unsubstantiated rumour-hearsay, I-read-it-on-the-web-somewhere nonsense, but it eventually leads to a taxi headed in the general direction of the bridge.

Yoshi has come along to keep me out of trouble. Fortunately, because I have no idea where we're going, or what the taxi driver is saying – and he's saying a lot. From Yoshi's translation: the roads are too quiet tonight for it to be a race night, but we are going to drive around and see what's going on.

After going around in circles for a while, we come to a high-walled compound somewhere inside. The driver grins and stops. Clouds of exhaust smoke are rising from inside. The sound of engines, music and shouting is everywhere. A quick scout around reveals that all the gates are padlocked. We jump the walls and find ourselves waist-deep in souped-up cars and assorted automotive weirdness. It appears Daigoku is in session.

An hour's train ride away in Tokyo, the Nissan Skylines that race the central loop highway (known

18

locally as the Shutoku) have engines that sound like they belong on light aircraft. One night at Sei's place in Tokyo's Azabu-juban, we hear the familiar droning from the direction of the Shutoku and drive out to get a closer look. Parked under one section of the elevated highway, we wait to hear the engines again, as the racers pass by on the next lap. It's a perfect night-time street racing loop – wide lanes, minimal traffic, unconcerned policemen and a single toll payment that gets you as many laps on the giant irregular shaped circuit as your neon and chrome monster needs.

Each lap takes the Skylines about fifteen minutes or so according to Sei, so it's no surprise when we soon hear a series of roars from the highway above. Sei pays at the tollbooth and we roll out onto the Shutoku – cruising the circuit, waiting to be passed. Fifteen minutes pass, twenty, and then we see bright flashing lights up ahead of us, and what little traffic there is seems to have slowed to a crawl. We can see a tow truck and an ambulance now, which takes off, siren blaring as we get closer. A white Skyline is impaled on the back of a trailer truck, its front mangled and crumpled from the impact and its windshield and windows shattered. There's no sign of the driver – the ambulance lights fade into the distance. Policemen put up hazard signs and reflective warnings around the crash site. Rubbernecks, us included, pass by slowly, gawking.

This particular night in Daigoku however, there is no racing – just a whole lot of showing off. Crowds of people have gathered on either side of a central parade strip and the tricked-out cars are lining up to rumble slowly past the screaming groupies. As the cars get to the centre of the strip, people gather around them dancing wildly, beating drums, setting off fireworks and furiously waving flashlights and neon glow-sticks. It becomes apparent that the cars are expected to rev their engines as loudly as possible over and over again, and only once the crowd is satisfied with each car will they be allowed to pass. The sound of the engines mixes with the chanting of the crowd and the beating of the drums and it's all backed up by raging music from every direction.

19

Among the scores of vehicles in the parking lot are a number of gleaming metallic-gloss-painted vans, entirely filled with speakers. Literally. When the rear doors open up, all you can see is a wall of outward-facing speaker cones. The degree of music co-ordination between vans varies rather widely. Some are alone, playing music for what one guesses is a niche audience – several people squatting on the tarmac and smoking. In one corner, someone throws a very large stuffed rabbit in the air, over and over again. Other areas have several vans parked in a curve, backs open, their giant speaker arrays pointed at crowds dancing in the centre. The vans themselves are works of art – tall fins and spoilers loom high above them and intricate artwork adorns their side panels – but sound appears to be their primary purpose.

It all adds up to the sort of deafening background din that makes shouted concise conversation an absolute necessity. "The best thing about this place is the bitches!" yells Sean, a Navy aircraft technician and regular at Daigoku. Like the crowded streets of Tokyo's Shibuya and Harajuku districts, fashion in this place seems to have sprung straight off the pages of a comic book – wild coloured hair, gigantic tattoos, masks, string bikinis and clothes that would be classified as bondage gear in most places. A pickup truck with three girls dancing in the back rolls slowly past. As they wave and shout at the video camera, the truck speeds up and they all fall in a somewhat undignified heap on the floor of the truck, much to the amusement of everyone watching.

Apparently the camera could have got me in trouble – someone tells us that a television crew that had visited the site the week before had been rather badly beaten up. Yoshi explains that I'm just a clueless tourist and no threat to anyone. That seems to satisfy them.

Many hours later, back in Tokyo and stumbling through the streets of early morning Azabu, I start to wonder if perhaps some of these people trade in their greasy leathers for Vuitton during the week. Maybe I've even seen some of them around the office, but didn't recognise them for the pinstripes. Is all this fringe craziness the logical fallout of the rigid, ritualised work culture? A few equally pithy and pointless musings later, I eventually decide that in its current state, my mind is probably not up to this sort of intellectual heavy lifting, and attempt to concentrate instead on remembering how these traffic light/zebra crossing things work.

At another Tokyo pedestrian crossing several months and kilometres from that one, the traffic lights start talking to Manav.

"No, dude, seriously – the traffic lights are talking to me."

He's somewhat unnerved by the fact that they would choose to strike up a conversation with him, one-sided as it is, but more disturbed by the fact that he doesn't know what they're saying. Considering the primary purpose of a traffic light at a busy intersection, it's reasonable to assume that anything it has to say is pretty important. Hiro assures us that, yes, the lights do talk from time to time, but that we're not going to get run over either. So we press on fearlessly, armed with this information.

We're on our way back from Sushizanmai in Tsukijishijo, which serves what is apparently the best sushi you can get at 2 am on a Saturday. Although he was highly reluctant at first at the prospect of raw fish and rice, Manav walks back a true convert. It doesn't take too many pieces of extra-fatty Meguro to change most people's minds.

At a previous sushi evening at the same place, Colleen closes her eyes and enthuses, "It's better than sex!"

Yoshi, her boyfriend, nods and grins, "Sometimes, yeah."

Then the chef slices the heart out of a fish and places it on the counter-top, still beating, pulsing in and out. "They make good earrings," he says. As an encore, he pokes a freshly cut slice of tuna with a wooden skewer and it suddenly flaps wildly, up and down by itself on the wooden board. The chef shares his plans for the future and says that he intends to become either a movie star or a politician. Twenty minutes later, the tuna is still flapping.

Ramen is another great late night favourite, particularly when it's really cold outside. Walking through the sliding doors of a ramen shop, out of the freezing wind and into the spectacle-fogging, multi-flavoured steam, you navigate the narrow alleys between the long counter tables and settle on a barstool. In minutes, a bowl of thick noodles in boiling soup topped with slices of meat or vegetables, usually with an egg of indeterminate nature mixed in, is sitting in front of you.

"Slurping of noodles is perfectly normal and in fact expected in Japanese ramen restaurant," reads a rare English menu. Judging by the sounds around you, this seems highly accurate – and after a few second degree burns on the roof of your mouth, you discover that slurping ramen is not only a highly efficient noodle consumption technique, but it seems to enhance the flavour as well.

Practically every restaurant in Japan, whatever its theme or speciality cuisine, gives you a moist towelette before you start eating. In some places it is warm and steaming, in some places it's cold, and in some places it's lukewarm, presumably having been warm and steaming at some point previously. Here's a tip: there is a marked difference in the proper usage of these towelettes depending on who you are and the company you are in.

The first restaurant I went to in Tokyo was an expensive rooftop-city view-type place. I was with my boss at the time, a middle-aged Japanese businessman. When the towelette (warm and steaming) arrived, he wiped his hands with it and then his face. So I assumed that that was the customary practice, and did the same with mine. So far, so good.

The next day I have lunch with some people from the training program I am on, all of us in our early twenties. Towelettes arrive, "Arigato-gozymas," slight bow, smile, apply towelette to hands and face, fold neatly and place next to green tea.

Cue shocked looks from everyone at the table. Sharp intake of breath from the twins, Keiko and Tomoko.

Hiro shakes his head and says, "Uh, you're not supposed to wipe your face with it." He continues before I can protest. "If you do that when there are, like, girls at the table they will think you are, like, not cool."

The various disapproving looks from around the table indicate that pretty much everyone thinks that I am, like, not cool. After I apologise and explain that I was led astray by my towelette-usage role model and so on, it seems that I am somewhat forgiven.

"Only older guys do that," explains Utako helpfully.

Much later, I brought the towelette-etiquette issue up with my boss and asked him to explain the subtleties of the system. He rolled his eyes, shrugged and grinned. "Pffft. Women."

Speaking of food, in Japan there is porn right next to the sandwiches at the neighbourhood convenience store. It's on the same shelf as several teen fashion weeklies and a kids' magazine that presumably focuses on the lives of a group of purple elephants (but that may have been just that issue). These shelves are also where men of varying ages will stand after work, still in their suits, briefcases propped against their legs, reading, or at least perusing them very, very thoroughly. Grandfathers read black and white porno comics on the train, while their grandkids scramble all over the seats. It's a bit of a recurring theme – porn just seems more out in the open than in most other countries.

It takes some getting used to – as do many things in Japan.

"Stay around here long enough and you start to expect weirdness constantly," says Kim. "Oddness is just kind of a way of life."

Like the island of Miyajima. A twenty-minute boat ride from a dock in Hiroshima, it is encircled by a stony white beach and home to an ancient and probably very historic shrine. The most striking feature is a huge, dark orange structure in the water, a short distance out from the beach around the shrine, shaped sort of like a symmetric Kanji character – a kind of tall 'H' with a roof. Lamps and torches provide both lighting and atmosphere, making it all very exotic and oriental. The only odd part is that there seems to be almost no one around.

In the little town itself, there are a few old men sitting on the pavement. We wander further in and in the gathering dark, are surprised to find that the place seems populated almost entirely by children. Street after street of small children running around quietly. And deer. There are deer everywhere – in the streets, sleeping on the sidewalks, on the beach and park benches – everywhere.

It also becomes apparent that an odd wooden paddle-shaped instrument is somehow very important here. It's drawn on the walls, little paddles hang from the doorways, and hundreds of them line the souvenir shops. Eventually we come to a paddle the size of a large truck and covered in red and black writing. Sid suggests that perhaps this is why the world is in so much trouble – everyone's up a creek and all the paddles are in Miyajima.

A post-trip Google would eventually reveal that the paddles were, in fact, rice ladles and/or talismans, but right now we are quite perplexed by their proliferation and sheer incongruity. Overall, with the deer and children and everything, we eventually decide that this island in the twilight is on the wrong side of the line between charmingly quaint and mildly creepy and we make for the docks. It's not unpleasant or anything – just a little strange.

One unpleasant phenomenon you rarely need to deal with in Japan is cold toilet seats and the momentary flinch and shiver that becomes a nasty part of morning routines in any country with a real winter. But through the wonders of technology, that's a thing of the past - or it should be. It amazes me that Japanese toilets have not caught on in more countries. Heated seats are practically a given – most loos have them. But there are several other high-tech features that aren't quite as easy to appreciate or operate. The novice toileteer may be a little apprehensive when first confronted with the intimidating control panel built into the seat. Depending on the make and model, the icons that show what the various buttons and knobs do are either completely mystifying ("There is definitely NO part of me that looks like that!") or bordering on the obscene.

Personally, I prefer the obscene – because in a situation with as much inherent vulnerability as this, it's better to have as clear an idea as possible of what is about to happen before it does. Anyway, the toilet will take care of all your washing and drying needs, in as comprehensive a fashion as you are likely to need – variable nozzle strengths and spray-types, ranging from a gentle shower to high-powered jets, fully controlled by a conveniently located dial and set of push-buttons. Drying is handled in an equally professional manner, with adjustable temperatures and humidity levels.

Naturally, embracing technology so completely contributes to the creation and proliferation of another Tokyo staple – the amusing auto-loo anecdote. My personal favourite is the one about the gaijin (foreigner) who was used to the older model auto-loos (which have a red button to switch off the spray nozzle), and was horrified when, mid-wash, he realised that he couldn't find the off-button. Certain that he would be drenched if he got up, he eventually unlocked the stall door with one hand, hitched up his pants with the other and kicked the door open while leaping off the seat simultaneously. With a quiet click and a hiss, the loo switched itself off – automatically.

Gaijin stupidity is legendary. Stories of silly westerners and their crazy antics are an integral part of the conversation in any izakaya (little smoky after-work bars – great for atmosphere, just watch what you're eating). And in the same way, conversation in a group of gaijin inevitably turns to crazy Japanese customs and complaining about how weird everything is.

"It just always turns into such a bitchfest," says Gigi, who is half-Hawaiian, half-Japanese, and consequently has default membership in both camps.

The city does have a bit of an oil and water theme in some ways. Certain areas, like Ropponggi, are informally designated gaijin territory and foreigners can (and do) get up to pretty much anything they want without fear of upsetting the locals (well, any more than they do normally). The locals see gaijin as crude, arrogant, womanising drunks, and gaijin see the locals as inscrutable, narrow-minded, unfriendly drunks. There are enough stereotypes around to propagate both images, but as in any highly polarised environment, the reality is much less extreme on both sides. Except for the 'drunks' bit.

This country takes its booze very seriously indeed. On the way to work in the morning, it's not uncommon to see people, gaijin and locals alike, often in three-piece suits, passed out on the streets or in the subway stations, sleeping off the excesses of the previous night.

Commuting is a little surreal as a result. After stepping over the snoring (and occasionally somnambulating) inebriates, and stopping at Tully's for coffee ("Douburr-torru Raatte!" – figure that one out), I wait for the train in front of an ad that says, "They are the dinosaurs of your life." Once inside the train, the advertising continues. The subway tunnel walls have images placed at regular intervals, designed to use persistence-of-vision so that when viewed from a moving train, they give the impression of a single video display. The ad that's playing, however, appears to be advertising a soft drink with a woman and some power-tools. Also on the train are several businessmen with more black-and-white porno comics, and a little old lady wearing a T-shirt that says "Get it while it's HOT!"

26

Once in the office building itself, the security guards provide a final surreal touch to the commute. For the entire hour or so during which most people arrive at work, these guys bow repeatedly, up and down, up and down, bellowing "Gozymaaaas!" in deep baritones. It's short for "Ohayo Gozymas", which means "Good Morning". All very heady, especially early in the morning, low on sleep, hopped up on caffeine and with last night's last round still making my head throb.

My head is in a similar state when I first meet DJ Joysticka. It's a little after 1 am, and I'm waiting in line for a taxi back to my apartment, when the girl in front of me gets in a cab and tells the driver rather loudly to take her to Azabu-juban – which is the same area I'm going. So we split the cab and get to talking – it turns out she's a DJ and going to a club in Azabu, where a friend of hers is headlining that night. She has a pair of backstage passes, do I want to go?

The place is called Luners, and it looks like a bit of a hole in the wall from the outside, but the inside turns out to be rather big. Nondescript entrances are a symbol of exclusivity – like Spacelabyellow, also known as just Yellow – which for several months had no sign outside, just a small neon yellow square on the wall. Once it got really famous, even the square disappeared. Now, you'd have no idea there was a huge club behind those doors – no conventional publicity, and it's still packed solid most nights of the week.

As we walk in we see that Luners has a split personality: respectable bar and restaurant on ground level, drum and bass cavern underground. People crowd the dance floor, surging around the stage, where a tubby guy with long grey hair called DJ Nakata is scratching a mix heavy enough to make the rickety girders rattle. Green laser lights make interlocking mesh spirals above the throngs and smoke machines pour clouds. A projector is flashing manic visuals, onto a large screen behind the DJ and his turntables, vaguely synchronised with the music. The building was probably a factory or warehouse to begin with, and the industrial look is accentuated by large steam pipes and sheet metal on the walls. An out-of-place disco ball glitters uncomfortably in the darkness.

We're watching from an elevated platform one storey above the dancers, but one storey below ground level. It's dark and a little grimy, and it serves as the club's cramped backstage area, with a walkway that connects it to the stage itself. A couple is sitting on one of the sofas, discussing something very earnestly. A hookah sits on the floor behind them. Nakata finishes to whoops and cheers from the crowd, and a dreadlocked girl takes over and spins a set with a slightly softer edge. A scruffy guy with a laptop switches the video being projected to some abstract lava-lamp-type shapes.

"Good," he says, lighting a joint, "More hippy."

That seems to be the extent of his English, because his response to everything else is a smile and several nods.

Joysticka explains that she has DJ'd with him many times before. "Wakande. He is amazing." She also says she has played gigs in London, New York, Goa and other places, but her favourite was a 'hippie party' in Byron Bay, Australia. "Live in bush, making party. Very good." She makes the thumbs-up sign.

By now the couple on the sofa has decided to get to know each other better, and have moved on to a more non-verbal form of communication. More DJs have shown up, ready for their sets, including Joysticka's friend, DJ Yo*C (pronounced YoSee, or Yoshi – which is his real name). He's obviously well known, and makes the rounds, slapping backs and doing that hip-hop fist-bopping-handshake. Joysticka introduces me in a volley of high-speed Japanese. DJ Yo*C grins in recognition and nods.

"India. Cool."

I ask if this is a good crowd tonight. He grins again and shakes my hand. "Cool," he says again. Thumbs-up sign. After a quick discussion with the laptop guy, he takes the stage.

"Wakande. He is amazing," says Joysticka.

Yo*C's set is easily the most varied of the lot, and

sounds (at least to my highly untrained ear) the most technically accomplished. He's also the most energetic of the DJs that have performed so far, switching records every few minutes, spinning them in his fingers and pumping them in the air. Laptop guy has set up a series of looping animations of Yo*C's name in various colours and styles to play behind him as he scratches. As the main act of the night, his set lasts quite a bit longer than the others.

The couple on the sofa is now on the floor behind it, out of view. The dreadlocked girl looks bored to tears – DJ Nakata appears to be lecturing her on technique. Finally she says something sharp to him and stomps off upstairs. Stifled laughter from the other DJs sitting around. Nakata looks unconcerned, says something dismissive and lights up a pipe.

I leave somewhere in the middle of Yo*C's second set, as the place is beginning to wind down. It's 6 am and the crowd is thinning out. Goodbyes are said, contacts are exchanged and promises to keep in touch are made. I proceed to stagger back to my apartment, exhausted. Several months later, I heard that Luners underwent a change in management. It is now a well-known gay club called The Bird Tokyo.

I've also heard that there's a tanning salon somewhere in Shibuya called Black People. I've heard that the makeup guy from the Evil Dead movies opened a bar in Roppongi called Screaming Mad George's Paranoia Café, where the walls are covered in eyeballs and disembodied limbs. I've heard that there's a Japanese concept car called the Fuct Cube.

But those are other peoples' Tokyo stories – stuff I haven't checked out for myself yet. It's hard to cover all the places you want to see, when each of the little alleys along the way are just as interesting. And when everything is on fast forward all the time, it's easy to miss things as they whiz past you. That's why every time I leave, I'm thinking about when I'm coming back – and all the wonderful weirdness still waiting for me to find it.

Sunset on the Longest Beach

Nikhilesh Dholakia

"We used to ride motorcycles up and down the long, sandy beach at Cox's Bazaar," reminisced Ben. Now nearly eighty, Ben has vivid memories of the 'Indo-Burma-China' theatre of World War II.

Living across the street from us in Wakefield, Rhode Island, Ben and Juel have become good friends and neighbours. As we all grow old together, the interactions have become warmer and family like. Ever so often, Ben provides riveting and wistful accounts of his days as a young American soldier in Calcutta, Chittagong or Cox's Bazaar. He even remembers the name of the bar on Dharmatolla Street in Calcutta where the young American GIs would hang out during the War.

Ruby and I tried to visualise young GI Ben and a couple of his military colleagues, in their camouflage fatigues, barrelling down the packed long stretches of sand at Cox's Bazaar, chasing each other on old beat-up

Harley-Davidson bikes. Through Ben's accounts, the name 'Cox's Bazaar' was etched in our memory. And the guidebooks were unequivocal – 'It is the longest straight beach in the world!'

So when Ruby got a chance to do an assignment for USAID in Dhaka, she decided to 'do Bengal' like a tourist. After all, she traced her roots to both Bengals. Her father – in search of business opportunities – had migrated from what-was-then East Bengal and is now Bangladesh, to Calcutta, where Ruby was born and lived as a little girl.

While doing the USAID project in Dhaka, on most holidays and weekends, Ruby made trips to various towns of Bangladesh – Sylhet, Comilla, Noakhali, Rajshahi, Narayangunj and so on. She saved the more detailed sightseeing – Dhaka, Chittagong, and Cox's Bazaar – for the Christmas break when I could fly in to South Asia.

***

"Darn…. I forgot to pack a swimsuit," fumed Ruby, on the nine-hour ride from Dhaka to Cox's Bazaar, via the port city of Chittagong.

The lumbering jeep-behemoth with diplomatic plates had already rolled through the rickshaw-choked streets of Dhaka and even passed the outlying industrial suburbs. Through the gradually thinning thicket of humanity, we were beginning to catch glimpses of the fabled 'Shonar Bangla,' the golden Bengal. The verdant green fields, the banana plants, paddy farmers bent knee-deep in water, bays and backwater inlets with stretched fishnets reflecting the golden sun…. yes, one can still find images that hark back to the lyrical-poetic worlds of Rabindranath Tagore and Kazi Nuzrul Islam.

The January air was crisp, even through the industrial smog of the teeming port city of Chittagong. We made a stop for lunch at the field office of the USAID project in Chittagong and drove through a narrow but well-paved street lined with palatial bungalows, many with 'To Let' signs. Well-heeled émigré Bangladeshis had invested in swank properties. Since they lived abroad, many of these bungalows were available for rent. The project office was in one of these cosy, modern bungalows. The lower floor had offices while the upstairs rooms had been furnished to function as a guest-house. In the common area between the guest bedrooms lay a dining space.

Carmen, the office manager at Chittagong, was like a mother hen. Piping hot Chinese food was brought in from the local restaurant favoured by the project staff. Hovering around the dining table, Carmen insisted we sample all of the various spicy, Bengali-Chinese dishes arrayed on the dining table.

There was no time to linger after lunch. We were told – rather firmly – that the trip from Chittagong to Cox's Bazaar would take the better part of three hours and we must reach Cox's Bazaar in time to enjoy the setting sun over the Bay of Bengal.

Besides Ruby and me, the project vehicle – a Sports Utility Vehicle or SUV in American terms – was loaded with Tonda Gillespie, the project leader's wife and an old friend of ours; Momtaz Faruki Chowdhry, a senior project officer from Dhaka who had become Ruby's new best friend and professional confidant; Faria, Momtaz's loquacious eleven-year old daughter; and our indefatigable driver Nur Hawaldar who negotiated the crowds and culverts with equal ease.

With at least an hour to go before sunset, Nur pulled into Cox's Bazaar. The atmosphere was unmistakably beach-town: row upon row of ocean-facing hotels, guest-houses, and tourist lodges.

The brand new five-star hotel where we were booked was still a work in progress, with floor polishing machines and carpentry scaffoldings at various places. A huge wedding banquet was just getting underway. A serpentine row of cars and vans was disgorging wedding guests, who were being sprinkled with rose water and led up a flower-strewn stairwell to the banquet hall of the hotel. Momtaz decided to hop off the car, walk past the crawling wedding-related traffic, and go straight to the hotel reception.

"Only a 30% discount."

"What do you mean – I personally spoke to the manager who offered a 50% discount!"

After some more such sallies, Momtaz gave up – and settled for 30%. We needed to change and head to the beach before sunset. We got to our rooms to find they offered magnificent views of the beach.

We emerged, Tonda in pants, Momtaz sporting a floral salwaar kameez. Faria in Capris. I had pulled on a light ethnic shirt on top of shorts. Ruby wore pants that could be hitched up to the knees. We headed to the beach, a five-minute walk after crossing the road in front of the hotel.

There are beaches... and beaches... and there is the beach at Cox's Bazaar. Ruby had pretty much seen it all – topless tropical beaches of Bali and Tahiti, topless summer beaches of Scandinavia and the Adriatic Sea, G-string bikinis at Copa Cabana in Rio, the MTV generation strutting in high-fashion beachwear at South Beach in Miami.

At Cox's Bazaar, a mass of fully clothed humanity – except for some young men who dared to put on shorts – met the sea. Men had shirts and pants on, or shirts and lungis. Women wore salwaar kameezes or saris. There were a few ladies with more conservative headscarves, and even a sprinkling of burquas. There was not a single swimsuit to be seen, let alone a bikini! Islamic modesty proscribed beachwear – even the pants and salwaar hitched up by Ruby and Momtaz were a bit scandalous and invited stares. Goa, Bali, or Phuket it ain't!

"And you were lamenting leaving your swimsuit behind," I laughed.

Like any touristy beach, there were touts renting lounge chairs or clamshell-like cabanas. Many families, obviously the more affluent ones, had rented these items and created little family bastions amidst the bustling hordes on the beach. No one actually 'lounged' in the lounge chair – in fact, the lounge chair was employed as a bench where three or four people could sit, usually segregated by gender.

It was a weekend and it looked like half of Bangladesh was fording the waters at Cox's Bazaar. There were thousands of people on the beach, stretching all the way from where peanut and jhaal muri vendors plied their trade to about half a mile into the shallow waters.

Tonda decided to wander off on the sand, away from the water, where she was followed by a Pied Piper platoon of children, constantly peppering her with, "What nationality? American? Australian?"

We hired one of the young camera-toting men standing waist deep in water in green Fuji Film T-shirts. He knew all the tricks to shoot the sunset and the sunset watchers. "Hold each other's hands," he would say and he would shoot such that the low-slung orange orb of the sun would appear to lie on the clasped hands. "Stand facing each other," and he would shoot so that the radiant dying sun would be a bright spot profiling the two faces. Click, click, click... he must have shot the entire roll of 36 exposures. Two hours later, he delivered the processed photos to the hotel and collected payment. Talk about service – the beach-based businesses of the affluent West cannot compete with Cox's Bazaar photo service!

The warm water with gentle lapping waves was pleasant, but there was no point in continuing wading fully clothed waist deep in the sea. Once the sun had set in a spectacular burst of orange and purple, we headed back to the hotel, to warm showers and a change of clothes. By the time we re-emerged, it was dark and the string of beachfront hotels had their colourful lights turned on. We went shopping to the local market, looking for Burmese merchandise – woodcarvings, tart berry pickles, fabrics. The typical beach town in the United States is overloaded with shops peddling ocean-oriented souvenirs – T-shirts, beachwear, beads, and shells. There was not much of that in evidence here, but we saw one T-shirt with 'Cox's Bazaar' prominently on the front, and grabbed it.

"This is a beach town... there must be an

Oceanside restaurant where we could sit and listen to the crashing waves," suggested Ruby. We looked, we asked, we explored... the people said there probably is *one* such restaurant! Beachside grill owners of Izmir and Mykonos, you have nothing to fear from Cox's Bazaar competitors!

We finally found this one restaurant perched right on the edge of the beach, the last outpost before the straight beach turned into jagged coastline. Tonda had wisely called it quits after the shopping trip and returned to the hotel. Momtaz, Faria, Ruby and I sat at a table by the beachside, finally able to hear the gentle murmur of lapping waves. By now, it was really dark and the chill wind from the Bay of Bengal had picked up. We were freezing and tried to find any layer of extra fabric to ward off the wind! We found a few things in our luggage in the SUV and piled on extra layers. When the soup and the fried rice finally came, we gulped it down, paid the bill, and rushed to our SUV.

We bade each other good night at the hotel, after the wonderful evening savouring the sunset at the longest beach in the world.

***

It was the third week of January in Rhode Island, and the snow on the ground was six inches deep. Ben and Juel were all excited; they wanted to know all about my South Asia trip. I got to enjoy Juel's wonderful onion soup and perfectly poached salmon as I described my adventure, especially the visit to Cox's Bazaar. I showed them the pictures on the beach, with the setting sun framed creatively in clasped hands.

I pulled out the T-shirt with 'Cox's Bazaar' emblazoned in front, and presented it to Ben. He was thrilled – to get a memento from over sixty years ago and pulled it on soon after dinner. I imagined him in that T-shirt attempting to ride a motorcycle through the swirling sea of humanity at today's Cox's Bazaar – impossible! An era bygone, a world transformed, and yet the memories linger on.

Computers International

Preethi D'Sa

OK I confess. I'm a well-travelled computer geek. The single most important thing I look for in a city I'm travelling to is a proliferation of computer shops. My partner in crime is my Angrezi friend, who also doubles up as personal tourist guide and haggling artist par excellence. Most importantly, he possesses an MA in Computer Literature and therefore has an obsessive interest in computers to the extent that his family consists of a wife

he calls Dell and their two children, Apple and Mac – or so he maintains. It is no surprise therefore, that he has been the key to many a successful computer holiday in England, United Arab Emirates (UAE) and Singapore. When it comes to shopping for computers and accessories (no, not hair accessories), it's him I turn to and depend on.

Other than the hardware/software that I am purchasing, what is the most interesting thing about the whole international computer shopping experience? It is not the computer shops per se; they look the same no matter where I am. Marbled tiles or monotone carpets invariably embrace the floor. Software packs line the aisles: Microsoft products on one side and Linux operating system packs on the other.

What then, you may ask, is the most interesting aspect? It is of course the Indian salesman, who appears to be a constant in computer shops the world over. I may be standing on London's Tottenham Court Road, breezing through Singapore's Funan IT Centre, shuffling between Abu Dhabi's Zaf brothers and Dubai's Computer Street. There may be varying accents ranging from British to Singaporean all masking the underlying Indian inflection; a multitude of garbs varying from suit to lungi, polished shoes to chappals; different attitudes (or IT-tudes if you like) but they are all Indian.

Let me elaborate.

Starting point – London's Tottenham Court Road..

My first introduction to Tottenham Court Road was many years ago, when my love for computers was considerably less pronounced. Under the guise of sightseeing, my friend dragged me up and down the street for four hours while pointing out computer shops and cyber cafes.

"Why can't I be just like a normal tourist and take those hop-on buses and go see Buckingham Palace?" I argued.

"Because you are with me. And I am different. I like computer shops. I like London. So you get to see the computer shops in London." My friend deserves a slap. But I like him, so I shut up. So our mornings were spent around the computer shops, while our evenings revolved around having dinner in restaurants next to the computer shops.

Now, converted to geekdom, I am able to appreciate Tottenham Court Road's many computer goodies – better than expensive chocolate. Computer shops line up against each other like soldiers in an army – Gultronics, Computer Exchange, Micro-Anvika – I am spoilt for choice. Here is the place to bag some of the best deals, as long as I have a haggling tongue. But as I don't, I delegate the task of bargaining to my friend.

I am here to buy a 1 Gigabyte (GB) USB drive, which for the uninitiated, is a portable hard drive. I can plug it into any modern computer (my parents' ancient machine doesn't count) and it has now become a more important component of my handbag than a lipstick. My friend knows what I'm looking for, so I trot behind him into a lesser-known computer shop. He successfully translates my needs into computer jargon.

One would expect the young, smart, posh-looking, tie-wearing, spiky-haired Indian salesman avec l'accent Anglais, not to ask me irrelevant questions, right? Wrong.

"So, is your boyfriend going to pay for this, Ma'am?" he asks, pretending innocence.

"He's not my boyfriend," I bark at him. I wonder if he is trying to gauge if I am unattached. "And I'm paying. Not my friend."

I'm thankful that my friend has been oblivious to this conversation.

What is with the Indian mentality, I wonder? I'm seen with a man who is not my father, brother or relative, and it automatically means that the man is my boyfriend!

I want to tell the guy off, "You are British. You should know better than to ask me such a question." And then I remember the films 'Bend it like Beckham' and 'Bride and Prejudice'. When it comes to Indian culture and tradition, the BILB British Indian family equals the BAP traditional Indian family from Amritsar.

The salesman has now learnt that my friend is a manager in Abu Dhabi, UAE. He plunges into a sea of questions.

"Oh sir, if you know of any jobs in Abu Dhabi, can you tell me?"

'Sir', I mean my friend, stands tall like the Big Ben and says, "Of course. What kind of jobs?"

"Anything will do, sir. My family wants to get out of India, you know?"

I wonder secretly why they would want to work as

labourers in the UAE. Such jobs are not well paid. Moreover, they will be separated from their extended families for years till they become the typical Indian salesmen I'm acquainted with in the UAE.

I whisper to my friend as he is handing over his business card to the salesman. "I'm sure his whole family will land in Abu Dhabi on the next plane."

"Not to worry," my friend comforts me. "I'm there to protect you."

And speaking of Abu Dhabi...

If there is one thing I don't like about walking around in Abu Dhabi and Dubai, it has got to be the ogling that I get from the Asian salesmen. It does not matter if I'm naked or fully clad, if I'm obese or anorexic, if I'm bald or beautiful. I just cannot escape from the stares if I am out on my own. They probably think that I am selling *my* goods instead of the other way around.

My friend patronises a particular shop that he affectionately calls the Zaf Brothers. The shop is loaded with computer boxes standing one on top of another like gymnasts performing a balancing act.

"This computer shop has definitely gone upmarket," my friend says aloud, "and the salesman's English is more pucca."

"But they are still wearing chappals," I direct his gaze to a salesman whose T-shirt barely hides the big mound of his belly. Thankfully, there is no burning incense, as we are about to spend the next hour discussing the specifications of the computer that I want to buy.

I get the feeling that these guys will rip me off (in price terms if not in clothes terms) if I didn't know anything about computers. Thank heavens for my computer-obsessed friend and especially for his white skin. Not only will my computer needs be met but I get elevated to a new level of treatment in his company. Let me explain. Suppose I wear a sari and a big bindi and walk alongside an Englishman, I become the Maharani of Jodhpur. I am an Indian woman with power – that power being in the form of an Englishman. But if I wear the same garb and conquer the streets on my own, they think that I'm someone's servant.

I am tired so I sit on the staircase, but I have to keep on getting up to let people use the stairs. This constant movement rewards me with a headache. Unknown to me, the salesman has been eyeing my periodic movements. He immediately offers me a dusty stool to patronise.

"I'm thirsty," I mumble between parched lips.

My friend tells them, "She needs tanda paani." Yes, by now, he knows a smattering of Hindi, which can sometimes be very amusing to listen to.

Paani arrives from the food court next door. The bottle's seal is broken and I wonder if I should drink it. After all, I would never eat or drink in these small food courts for fear of getting a Delhi Belly right here in Abu Dhabi. However, I weigh the consequences of not drinking water and I quickly gulp it down. Glad to say, I'm still alive to tell the tale.

The Zaf brothers confirm that they can build a computer from scratch. "No problem for the Angrezi sahib. We just need some deposit, sir."

My friend is OK about giving them a deposit. "Here you go," he hands them a 100-dirham note.

The salesman is not OK with it. "Sir, I mean, a deposit of a 1000 dirhams will be better...sir." He stares like a hopeful puppy and is rewarded with a flash of another 900 dirhams.

My friend asks, "Can I have the computer tomorrow?"

I gasp. Isn't that too early for them to prepare it, I wonder?

The salesman grins, his teeth sticking out of his smile in agreement. "No problem, sir. For you, we do anything."

While we've had a relatively smooth experience with the Zaf brothers, it is not the same in another shop. My friend wants an ATI 9600 graphics card.

"Oh, but sir, we don't have that mowdel," replies the

salesman, his Keralite accent prominent.

"Ha," my friend bellows, "I'll go to your competitors, then!" And he pretends to stomp off, in the best imitation of an Indian housewife at the local bazaar. The salesman, scared of losing the little business that he gets, jumps up, runs to the next shop, grabs the graphics card, and sells it to my friend for an even cheaper price.

And he says, "Sir, we have the best beshnesh," his Keralite accent becoming more prominent by the minute.

My friend has got a look that says prove-that-you-have-the-best-business. "Does this wireless network card work under Linux?" He fingers the PCI card look-alike.

"But sir, no one ever asks such questions."

"Well, there's always a first time. Find out the answer!"

"If you go to that counter, you can find it out for yourself, sir."

"You're the salesman, not me! Call the manager."

The salesman now whimpers and I feel sorry for him. "If this angry sahib makes more fuss," his frown seems to say, "My manager will flog me."

His fear erupts into molten anger when he looks at me, as if it's my fault. By then, my friend and I have decided to leave the shop, as the manager himself seems to have hidden himself from the fury of the Angrezi sahib.

I can still feel the glaring eyes burning my back. "Why is one of *our* kind going around with him? And a computer freak at that!"

Dubai's version

Computer Street in Dubai is a typical back street. Narrow lanes wind their way to the bottom of the hill, lined on both sides with small shops bursting with electronics and many a chappal-clad aadmi.

The difference between Dubai's Computer Street (or Khalid bin Waleed Street) and Abu Dhabi's Zaffar Computers (the official name of the Zaf brothers) is that a typical Computer Street salesman thinks that he can take my friend for a ride. Or me for that matter.

41

In one shop, the leering eye of a salesman has clamped itself on my countenance. He tries to sneak in a conversation with me while his colleague has tied up my friend in an interesting debate on Windows.

"Can I help you madam?" He gazes at my breasts and I hastily try to adjust my T-shirt. He continues to gaze at me unfazed, from top to bottom.

"No. I'm with my friend." I stare at my friend's direction, but his back is towards me.

"Are you from India?"

"Yes...uh..."

"From Kerala?"

Ah, they think that all Indians are from Kerala. No? He looks hopeful that I will strike a conversation in Malayalam with him.

"Arre, bhai," I want to lie, "I live in England." What does it matter if I'm made in India, exported to Arabia, have frolicked in Far East Asia and am settled in England?

That doesn't stop him from trying to make more conversation. My friend, sensing that I'm in trouble, comes to my rescue. The salesman sees a six-foot shadow looming behind and he melts into the background. He reminds me of the hyenas of the Lion King fame, who want to attack Simba but run away when Mofasa, Simba's father, arrives on the scene.

Sometimes I feel sorry for these men. I try to rationalise that they must miss their family and when they see us Indian women, they think of their lovely wives and daughters. But then I realise that if they don't see their family, they should look forlorn, not lustful.

In Al Ain Computer Plaza, Bur Dubai, my friend starts his now familiar search of things high and low (meaning high-speed chips and low prices). One salesman there has managed to amaze my friend with his knowledge of alternative operating systems (OS).

"What OS does this USB drive work with?" My friend points to the 1 GB USB drive.

42

"All versions of Windows, sir."

"I don't use Windows." My friend winces.

"Well, then, it works with Mac(intosh), sir."

"I don't use Mac." The glare intensifies. "Does Linux ring a bell?"

"Oh, yes, sir! I use RedHat and Mandrake. And so far the USB drive seems to be compatible with RedHat."

My friend buys a lot of computer goodies from this shop. "One CD of each colour. And I don't mean ceedee, as in ladder," he adds, showing off his linguistic skills.

Upon exiting the shop, I start quizzing him. "Who's RedHat? And Mandrake? You don't mean the cartoon character Mandrake the Magician?"

"No, you dummy! These are versions of the Linux operating system. I think it is time to buy you some 'Linux for Dummies' books."

Singapore's Sim Lim

Everybody knows about the Singapore Sling, but I'm more interested in Singapore's Sim Lim. Sim Lim Square is a stark contrast to Singapore's other famous computer centre, the Funan IT Centre. While Funan IT Centre is modern and caters mostly to foreigners, the Sim Lim Square is reminiscent of a crowded Indian market. The escalator, loaded with people, loops upward into eternity. A distinct pungent smell permeates the air, not to mention the dank monsoon air tugging at my clothes. I intuitively clutch at my handbag for fear of losing it to an inconspicuous handbag snatcher.

But where Funan IT Centre beats Sim Lim Square in terms of modernity, Sim Lim Square offers competitive prices. As I wait in line with my friend to buy a load of batteries, I think ruefully that there is no anecdote of an Indian salesman to take home. But I should have known better.

"What's the bad news?" my friend questions the salesman.

"Bad news, sir?" The salesman stares blankly at my

friend and so do I.

"Money. How much does it cost? If it costs more than it is worth, then it is definitely bad news!"

"Ha ha ha, oh sir, I see what you mean," he smiles bashfully as he logs in the prices. He limps into more conversation. "Uh…sir, if you don't want the freebies that come with the batteries, may I have them?" A shy pause. "For my kids."

With that, my friend and I rip the plastic covers off the batteries (after paying of course) and hand the free toy cars to him. At least I know that a child is smiling somewhere in Singapore.

I'm an In-di-en, in-the-end

"You are fit to be a computer salesman," I say to my friend, after one of our many computer-shopping sprees. I try to imagine my friend in a lungi and an untucked shirt, his chappal-clad feet sticking out from beneath the lungi. I'll admit, it's a funny picture.

"Can't. They won't accept me," he answers.

"Why not?"

"Arre yaar, I am not Indian, no?"

Desi Down Under

Alex Joseph

My wife Mariam and I migrated to Australia over twenty-one years ago – one of the biggest milestones in our lives. Perhaps that's why most of the events relating to that period are indelibly stamped on our minds.

Initially, I was not keen on the idea. We were living in a beautiful little town called Batu in Indonesia. I was running a large textile mill with over two thousand employees, one of the biggest industries in East Java. The factory was running smoothly, we were making good profits, and my already substantial salary had just received a boost, courtesy of a grateful board of directors who were far away in Jakarta and who rarely interfered in the running of the plant. Why would I want to give up all that to go to Australia? The suggestion came from our best friends, the Sahais, who had been toying with the idea of migration for some time, and wanted us to join them in this venture.

I was most reluctant to give up my plum job to migrate. Mariam however was enthusiastic about the move, and the prospects it would bring for educating our children there. At the time our elder son was studying in India, and though he did come to Indonesia for the holidays, his absence was the one thing that was spoiling our idyllic interlude in 'paradise'!

Reluctantly, I came around to her point of view. Very soon, our younger son would have to be sent to India for his studies too. I too could not stay for long in Indonesia, as work permits were getting harder to get. Opportunities in India for professionals were not many in the early 1980s. Indira Gandhi was back in power and socialism was the order of the day, with salary restrictions and high taxation.

Many immigrant forms, interviews and formalities later, our passports were ready to be stamped. I went down to the office, only to find our usually cheerful Immigration Official (IO), looking serious and unsmiling. My heart sank, but the IO silently stamped all the passports, signed them, and gave them back to me. Then he said, "I have disobeyed orders, but I think it is alright to do so in your case."

He showed me a long telex that had come the previous day from Canberra. The new Minister of Immigration had ordered a review of all skilled migrant quotas, the category under which I was applying. Australia was going through its worst recession in decades and there was an outcry about the high levels of migration when locals were being thrown out of work. Several sub-categories had been reclassified downwards by at least one notch. I came under the sub-category of 'mechanical engineers'. It had gone from 'minor shortage' to 'surplus'! In such cases, the instructions were to withhold the visas till further advice. The Immigration Official had coolly disregarded the order, backdating the visas by two days, to make it seem as if they were issued

46

before the telex arrived! "Keep it a secret, won't you?" he said. "You are so qualified and experienced, you ought to have absolutely no problem in finding a job immediately." I felt reassured.

Mariam and I decided to leave the kids in India, bringing them over to Australia only once we were settled. So it was, that we found ourselves at Singapore airport on the evening of 26th August 1983, waiting to board a Qantas flight to Melbourne. Qantas being Australia's national airline, it gave intending migrants a very cheap one-way ticket to Australia, and a baggage allowance of 40Kg. We had actually gone well over 40Kg each, our total was nearly 120Kg! We had splurged on woollen clothes, shoes, utensils, and appliances, even a sewing machine, thinking (wrongly, as it turned out) that all this would be far cheaper in Singapore. The girl at the counter saw the total weight and spoke to somebody on the phone. A Qantas official walked over, looked at the migrant visas on our passports, smiled and waved us through. Another helpful soul!

We changed all our remaining money to colourful Australian currency, very different from the sober shades other countries favour for their notes. The 50-cent coin was the most attractive and elaborate coin I had ever seen – a large 12-sided piece, with a complete coat of arms.

I did not look at Mariam as I boarded because I had tears in my eyes. The enormity of what I had done hit me like a hammer. All sorts of premonitions of doom flooded my mind. One of the airhostesses asked me if I was a migrant going for the first time to Australia. When I asked her how she could make out, she said, "I saw you crying as you boarded. Migration is a big step to take, and you don't have to feel ashamed to be emotional about it. Just remember, very few migrants regret coming to Australia."

It was a slack time for the cabin crew, and she was free to talk, so we chatted for a while. She too was a migrant, but she had come as a small child with her parents from Italy. Her parents did not know a word of English when they arrived, but they had raised a family and all the kids had done well for themselves. I hoped I could do the same! When I went back to my seat, Mariam jokingly said that I was a fast worker; chatting up the first Australian woman I came across!

On landing in Melbourne, and before we were let off the plane, the cabin crew walked up and down the aisles spraying some sort of insect repellent to kill bugs that might have got in. This strange practice was stopped only a few years ago. At the airport, everybody seemed to be smiling – warm, heartfelt smiles. Though we had three trolleys with suitcases and other packages, there were no problems with Immigration or Customs. So far, so good, I thought.

My relatives, Tony and his father Peter Jacob, came to the airport to receive us. Peter was twenty years older than I was, so in true Indian fashion, Mariam and I called him 'Uncle'. He had retired as the Principal of a well-known school in Malaysia and, after migrating to Australia in his 50s, had started a new career in Melbourne as a Maths teacher.

As Tony drove us through the city and into the suburbs, we noted the absence of people. Melbourne, like other major Australian cities, is spread out over a large area, as land is relatively cheap. Uncle told us that all migrants were eligible for unemployment benefits (known as the 'dole'). Mariam and I had been quite willing to spend the savings we had accumulated over four years in Indonesia, to establish ourselves in Australia. Now it seemed we were eligible for some assistance! Remarkably, we were entitled for the full range of benefits from the moment we set foot in the country as migrants. In those days, the Australian government did not discriminate between citizens and those who had just arrived as permanent residents, when it came to social services. Over the years, the entitlement criteria have been tightened up a lot, but the benefits themselves have improved considerably.

 We both went and registered for the benefits within a few days. We were not supposed to get

anything for the kids because they were not physically present in Australia, but the rules were a bit vague. The official who dealt with us somehow interpreted the rules in our favour and we got benefits for the kids also.

Being on the dole had several other perks. We got a card that entitled us to very cheap doctor's consultations and prescription medicines, and half fares on public transport. Uncle Jacob had given us some very sage advice – not to be too proud to accept the dole and all its attendant benefits. Mariam and I fully agreed with him. We got about $350 a week, (as a couple with two dependant kids), till I was employed (The dole is discontinued if one spouse is employed). The dole was tax-free and it was more than enough to cover rent and utilities for our flat, and to allow us to eat the best food available. We even saved money on it! Of course, we did not buy a car as long as we were on the dole. But we did not need one, as we were in an inner city flat. We had good, cheap public transport at our disposal.

The first few weeks went in a daze. We opened a bank account to cash our precious dole cheques, which came in like clockwork. After three weeks in the motel, we moved to a comfortable, if somewhat cramped, flat. Some furniture and other items, which we had sent by sea from Jakarta, arrived. There was only one small matter to be attended to. I needed a job.

I had applied for a few jobs but no replies had arrived. When a month passed without a single reply, I started getting worried. One day, Uncle Jacob asked me casually how things were going on the job front. I told him about the lack of replies. He asked me what kind of jobs I had been applying for. I called out the details over the phone. All I heard in response was a thoughtful "mmmm...": the kind of noise adults make when they are forced to deal with a child who should know better.

After a few moments, Uncle said very gently, "Alex, these are not the kind of jobs you should be

trying to get as a new migrant with no record of achievement in this country. Now, look here, I need to come to town for something tomorrow evening. Will you and Mariam be at home? I want to discuss this job issue with you at length."

What kind of jobs had I applied for? The very first one (strange how one remembers unpleasant things!) was the post of Assistant General Manager, Maintenance, of the Tasmanian Railways. Tasmania was Australia's smallest state, an island to the south with a population of less than 5 lakhs, hardly 150 km of track and no passenger services. General management experience was all that was required, and the candidate needed to handle about 50 employees. I considered it a low-level job, but I thought it might be a good idea to cut my teeth on something easy. After all, I had successfully run a plant with over 2000 employees in Indonesia. All the other jobs were in a similar vein; executive positions with job titles that included the word 'manager' in it.

Uncle and Aunty Jacob arrived the next day. Mariam had planned to ask Uncle to stay on for dinner, now that Aunty was also there she decided to make it a nice social evening. Well it was social all right. And it was an evening. But it was not all that nice. For me at least.

After a few pleasantries, Uncle came to straight to the point. He knew that despite an engineering degree from IIT Madras, I had no hands-on experience as an engineer, having gone straight to IIM and then been employed in various managerial positions. Though I had started out in production management, I had never held a spanner or a screwdriver at work (in fact, since the second year of engineering, the only times I ever used such tools was while fiddling with my son's Meccano set!). So, though I was good at giving orders to engineers, I had never worked as an engineer myself!

"Alex, you may find it difficult to work as an engineer in an Australian company. May I suggest an option? There is a desperate shortage of Mathematics and

50

Science teachers in secondary schools. The government is taking qualified people like you and training them as teachers, while giving them a full salary, and then guaranteeing them employment in government schools. And during the one-year training, if you manage to get a good job in industry, you can leave. There is no bond. What do you have to lose by applying?" I was in too much shock to protest. He then pulled out a newspaper ad from his pocket. Uncle had planned it well!

Of course, I had realised that I could not get a job similar to the one I had in Indonesia, but to give up hopes of an executive position for the foreseeable future was hard to accept. Aunty Jacob tried to point out all the advantages of life in Australia... but I was in no mood to be consoled. Mariam and I spent nearly half the night talking about Uncle's suggestion. To become a bloody schoolteacher! I would be the laughing stock of my classmates in IIT and IIM! And what would my relatives think? Finally, with a very heavy heart, I decided to go ahead.

Everything went like clockwork. There was an interview a few weeks later, followed by a medical, and then I got an appointment letter. I was to report to a school on the southern fringe of Melbourne, on 31st January 1984. It was now late October 1983. I had a job in my hand. Lousy job, with a salary less than half of what I got in Indonesia, but a job nevertheless. We made arrangements to get the kids over from India. Their visas had expired, and we had to reapply. Fortunately, all went smoothly and they were scheduled to fly in by March 1984.

We turned our attention to what Mariam would do. She had never worked before and I had never intended for her to work in Australia. But we decided that a humble teacher's salary might not be enough, so Mariam would need to seek some kind of employment. She had a degree from Kerala University in Home Science, but it was not recognised in Australia. It was treated as equivalent to a High School pass! Fortunately, she got admission to a good secretarial institute located very near our home. Her course was due to begin on the same day that I started at school.

Despite having got the teaching job, I continued to make desperate attempts to get a job in industry. In all, I applied to 104 places! (I have kept copies of all the applications, Mariam thinks I have some psychological problem which compels me to keep records of these unpleasant things!) But I got only four face-to-face interviews. And not one firm offer!

Now that I had a job, I bought a car. In Indonesia, I had a brand-new Toyota Corona, with a driver who was at my disposal practically twenty-four hours a day. I often went about in a Mercedes meant for the exclusive use of VIP visitors like the directors. But, here I had to be satisfied with a second-hand Corolla, not even air-conditioned! What a comedown! But a car was a car, and it gave us tremendous mobility. In those days, it was easy for Indians to get Australian licences by just showing your Indian licence. Mariam had an Indian licence, even though she had hardly ever driven in India! So, after getting her Australian licence, she went for driving lessons to gain confidence! The driving instructor was quite amused; Mariam was the first student he had ever had who took lessons after getting the licence!

Though most of our friends were Malayalis we met through the Malayali Association, we got on very well with our neighbours – a microcosm of Australia. Most of them were from Eastern Europe. Our next-door neighbours were a young couple, Mustafa and Pirkko – she was Finnish and he was a Turkish Cypriot. They smoked pot and I worried that the smoke drifting across from their balcony would make us addicts. When we attended their son's second birthday party, we were the only non-hippies in the room. We made excuses and left once the special cigarettes were lit up. While we baby-sat their little fellow whenever they wanted, Pirkko taught Mariam the intricacies of Melbourne's public transport system and showed her the best places to shop and eat. Mustafa had a part-time job as a parking station attendant, but he gave it up because he felt it was a crime to work in the summer. It was so much better to lie on the beach! After all, when the dole was so good, why work?

Another couple with whom we got on very well lived in the next building – Brian was an Aussie in his late forties; Lois, barely twenty, was Malaysian Chinese. Lois had responded to a newspaper ad, which Brian's friend had jokingly put in a Kuala Lumpur newspaper. Brian got two sacks full of replies – Lois' letter was the first he opened, he chose her straightaway and threw away the rest! Brian was a colourful character – he had gone through two marriages and had children older than Lois. After our sons came, Brian referred to them affectionately as the 'little Pakis'. He took the boys and me on several trips, we engaged in 'manly' things like fishing and duck hunting. On one trip we visited one of Brian's friends - an inmate in a prison 300km to the east of Melbourne! Sadly, Brian died a few years ago, of a heart attack. Lois is bringing up their young son and daughter.

Soon, it was 31st January. Mariam was excited; she was looking forward to beginning studies. I was apprehensive, worried how I would cope.

The first day was OK. There were no kids, only staff. I was one of two trainee teachers. The other guy was a Sri Lankan, Jay Jaykumar, who was much younger than I was, but who was in a somewhat similar situation. He was an engineer with a good job in an Australian company, but he had been retrenched during the recession – he too was hoping to go back to industry when things improved.

Jay and I were made to feel welcome by the Principal, the Vice-Principals and the other staff. The staff warned us that as non-Australian teacher trainees, we were being deliberately sent to this particular school – it was one of the toughest in the whole state – we had to prove ourselves capable of handling the worst possible situations. We were told that if we could survive here, we would be able to survive in almost any other school in the state.

Jay and I had to be at the school only on Thursdays and Fridays. Monday to Wednesday, every week, was spent attending lectures at a teacher-training institute in the city, quite close to my flat. The training was to last one year, at the end of which I would be given a Diploma in Education, a kind of licence to teach in any Australian school.

We were taught practical stuff, like how to make lesson plans, what sort of records we needed to keep, the legal responsibilities of teachers and handling difficult students. We also learnt some theoretical stuff like Educational Psychology and so on. I found most of it very easy, even a bit boring. There were no exams, only assignments and term papers.

School was different. It was unadulterated hell for many weeks, till I developed coping mechanisms. As a trainee teacher, I was required to teach some classes, but all my teaching was supposed to be supervised. My supervisor, Ewan Cole was a senior teacher in the same school. He was theoretically expected to sit at the back and watch, and comment on my performance after the class. He was also expected to step in, if any of the children made it too difficult for me to proceed. In practice, it worked differently. Ewan simply did not have the time to sit at the back in every class and he made that plain to me. He said he would come about once in few weeks to check on me. The rest of the time, I was entirely on my own.

On the rare occasions when Ewan was in the room, my students were like mice. They never interrupted me with silly remarks, they sat in their seats, they asked pertinent questions and they worked as directed. Ewan had a fearsome reputation in the school for his quick temper and sharp tongue and it was obvious to me that my students were being cooperative because of Ewan's presence. But when he wasn't there, the kids gave me hell. They were lazy and boisterous and extremely difficult to control. They made fun of the way I looked, the way I talked, the way I walked, the way I dressed. It was not that they were racist. They would have given any new teacher a hard time.

But outside, in the yard and in the corridors, they were completely different individuals from the monsters who tormented me in the classroom. They greeted me cheerfully and chatted with me like old friends. Once I accepted this, I found it easier. Note: it still wasn't easy, but easier!

The other staff members were very supportive. All the classrooms had windows that ran the entire length of the room, so it was very easy for someone walking past in the corridor to see trouble brewing. On many an occasion, when other teachers found me in difficulty, they stepped in and helped me out by hauling the offenders off to another room or to a designated 'time-out' room, a place where recalcitrant students were sent to 'cool off'.

I needed to get good reports from two people to pass the course and get my Diploma in Education. One was Ewan. I was confident he would give me a good report; he liked me and he frequently said I would make a good teacher. But I was not too sure of the other person. He was a senior lecturer from the institute, an elderly guy who had occasionally passed what I considered to be vaguely racist remarks. He did not show any animosity towards me, nor was he friendly, just correct. He had made one visit to the school to see how I was doing, in the middle of the year, and had been critical of some of the things I did. Ewan was not there and the kids had been a bit difficult. The criticism was justified, but I feared that during his next (and final) visit in November, he might find some reason to fail me.

Ewan was not free on that final fateful day. In sheer desperation, I decided to appeal to the chief troublemakers in the class directly. I made them stay back one day after the lesson and explained that I would like them to be very nice when the man came. All went well, according to my plans. Then, just before the end of the period, one of the boys called out in a loud stage whisper, "Were we nice enough for him to pass you?" The whole class heard it and burst out laughing. I did not know what to say, but then I saw that the lecturer, sitting at the back, was grinning broadly. I passed.

When I got the teaching job, in late 1983, I had not told anybody in India. But I did inform everybody when I actually started work in early 1984. The reaction was exactly as I had feared. Both my father and my father-in-law were totally against the move. I still remember one letter in which my father asked quite plaintively, why I should 'lower' myself so much when I have such excellent qualifications. My father-in-law did not put it so strongly, but I could sense the disappointment in his letters. He and my mother-in-law had visited us in Indonesia and he would have seen me as the uncrowned king of Batu. I felt for them, but all I could say was that under the circumstances, teaching was not such a bad option.

As 1984 progressed, things calmed down and folks back in India became a little more inclined to accept what I had done. One helpful development was the fact that both our sons seemed very happy in Australia. Mariam and I had initiated a rule: both the boys had to write a letter each, every weekend, to their grandparents. This practice continued right through the 80s. Receiving happy letters from grandchildren went a long way towards reassuring both sets of grandparents that all was well.

Finally graduation day arrived at the teacher-training institute. We all got our Diploma in Education and an envelope giving details of our initial posting. I had been posted to Hamilton, a small country town about 300km to the west of Melbourne. It was a huge disappointment. There was little hope of Mariam ever getting a job in a small country town. We would be leaving our circle of friends, and there would be hardly any Indians over there. Even if we really liked the place, we would need to come back to Melbourne when it was time for the kids to go to university. After having moved so many times over the last few years, the prospect of moving again was too much to bear. And if I wanted to have any chance of going back into industry, I needed to be in a big city like Melbourne, not out in the boondocks!

I approached Ewan, and asked him if he could get me to stay on in the same school. I had endured many awful days at this school, but it was better than going to such a distant spot. Ewan took one look at the letter and asked me to follow him. He marched straight into the principal's office, explained what had happened and made a strong plea that the Principal use his influence to see that I got something in Melbourne. I did not know at the time that the Principal was also the President of the Principal's Association for the state. Equally important, he was very friendly with Ewan. They were golfing and fishing buddies. My problem was solved on the spot. The Principal simply phoned the General Manager of the Staffing Division and I was offered an alternate vacancy in a school just 3km away. I accepted immediately.

I started in my new school on 1st February 1985. I have been here ever since. It is completely different from my training school. This school's catchment area is a semi-rural district on the outskirts of Melbourne; the kids are better behaved, with typical middle class backgrounds and values. More importantly, I got to really love the job. I got used to the security, the relaxed atmosphere, the informality, and the total independence I had in the classroom. I have also got accustomed to the benefits; short working hours (school finishes at 2.45 pm and I am usually at home by 3.15 pm) and long holidays (a total of twelve weeks in a year).

Most of all, I have enjoyed the total absence of tensions and politics associated with a job in industry. By the end of 1985, I was so happy with the teaching job that I decided not to apply for any more jobs in industry. True, I sometimes miss the status and the glory of a high power job. But, in compensation, I have been able to spend time a lot of time with my kids.

As for money, well, teaching does not pay much. But it is more than adequate to enjoy a comfortable lifestyle, even if we had been forced to rely on one income.

By a coincidence, Mariam started full time employment on the same day I started in my new school. She got a job as a data entry operator in a bank. After eight months she got into the Australian, Taxation Office. She has been there ever since. In Indian terms, she is an ITO. Unlike in India, ITOs do not get goodies at Christmas or New Year. No whisky, no movie tickets, not even a fountain pen! But then, unlike Indian ITOs, tax officers are relatively well paid, so they can afford to buy their own whisky or movie tickets!

I could have retired with a reasonably comfortable lifetime pension when I reached fifty-five, which was three years ago. But by now, I have no intention of quitting. I am now one of the oldest teachers in the school, and I enjoy the 'elder statesman' status. I am now teaching children of students I taught in the mid-1980s! When I go out shopping or to the bank, I invariably bump into one or more of my ex-students (according to a rough calculation, I would have taught at least three thousand by now). It is always a pleasant experience, for even the worst rat-bag (Aussie slang for a 'bad' person) student, turns out to be a nice, normal human being when I meet him or her on the neutral ground of a shopping centre.

I suppose only time will tell whether the Australian venture was a true success or not. There have been no dramatic successes or failures. For most migrants, the experience has been similar to ours. Their lives have been ordinary and unexciting but peaceful and pleasant. From that point of view, I am really glad I came here. And I trust Mariam would fully agree.

Menagerie A Trois

Mathew Chandy

Two years of hard work as a trainee in a prestigious international law firm in London earned me a couple of months of unpaid leave to do some 'socially responsible work'. I immediately seized upon the opportunity to spend some time working with animals in South Africa – something I had been yearning to do for a long time.

I started off with a month at Seaview Game and Lion Park in Port Elizabeth close to the famous 'garden route' of South Africa. Seaview is famous for its programme for breeding lions, especially the rare and beautiful white lions. Then I moved to Riverside Wildlife Rehabilitation and Environmental Education Centre, located towards the North East of South Africa near the renowned Kruger National Park. Riverside specialises in rehabilitating vervet monkeys.

The following are extracts from a series of e-mails sent to friends and family during my magical two months amongst the strange but wonderful creatures at Seaview and Riverside.

***

Overlooking the coast and set amidst 120 hectares of bush and grassland that are dotted with zebra, wildebeest and buck, Seaview is a slice of heaven. Strategically placed outdoor tables afford magnificent views of sunsets, and on a lucky day, one can spot whales thrashing in the distant sea. Most activity centres around the large restaurant with its high ceilings and the kitchen where the volunteers and workers congregate to prepare meals for the cubs and ourselves. Calm silences are broken by the loud roars of the big lions at night, the regular chattering of the baboons, the piercing shrieks and the rustling of feathers as peacocks perform their mating dances to impress the dull, unattractive peahens.

I've just been introduced to the English couple who run Seaview. They live in a cute little cottage with nine lion cubs, two dogs and one caracal – which is not a round boat for those of you picturing a coracle, but an African Lynx. Tonight I know I'll go to sleep dreaming of tomorrow – Monday morning, my first day with the cubs. Never happened before – not in my twenty-two years as a student and professional!

***

Could shovelling shit ever be fun? Throw in three of the most adorable and cuddly ten-week-old lion cubs that require bottle-feeding three times a day and six older cubs that have just begun developing their hunting instincts and use you as target practice – and the shit-shovelling becomes fun.

The baby cubs yearn for us in the morning. They rush out to greet us; their magi bearing porridge made from milk, eggs, cream, vitamins and gelatine. They have voracious appetites and knock back the formulas like shots of tequila. They place their baby paws (with not-so-baby claws) on our knees and raise the softest brown eyes ever.

The babies are in Janice's backyard. In her front yard, the big boys are waiting for us – bigger and bolder, with claws like curved fishing hooks that need to be painfully extricated from your flesh, and teeth sharp as knives – paper knives anyway. They stalk us and snap at our feet if they sense or smell fear. The trick is to stand tall and speak firmly (never mind the quaking inside) and tell yourself that they're just playing. They are. They do nothing to you that they aren't doing to each other. They don't know that human beings are just overly sensitive creatures without thick skin!

Whitey, a gorgeous white cub, gets the lion's share of the attention. Lovely, royal and rare, his great temperament makes him liable to abuse from enthusiastic visitors. Being white, he is five times more valuable. Sophie, timid and ladylike, is the only female in the pack and true to the sexist stereotype.

The other four, they're mates. Bosom buddies and brothers. They wrestle, suck each other's ears, bite each other's tails and smother one another while sleeping. In a few weeks, they will be adolescents – too big and dangerous to have visitors. They have already developed a penchant for human appendages; appendages that aren't built for wrestling, sucking and biting, not by lions anyway.

When we have visitors, I'm with the cubs showing off like I own them. And even when there's no audience, I enjoy being with them, fooling around and just watching. At night I go to sleep with the warm and earthy smell of the cats on my skin. Sweet dreams are made of these.

***

There is something special about the commute to work when you have one dog, six baboons, one African bush pig and two big lions competing for your attention.

I'm one of the pack now – welcomed by the older cubs with a gentle slash on my back. But Whitey is my runaway favourite – truly regal with the most beautiful, soft, brown doe-eyes. Every now and then she ambles towards me, looking straight into my eyes. As I watch mesmerised, she places her paws on my shoulders and rubs her cheeks against mine. I keep referring to Whitey as a female, but she's not. I'm in denial. I ask myself – how could anyone so beautiful and wildly attractive be male?

Eddie, a boxer with boundless energy, spends hours trying to play with the cubs through the wire grating.

61

Today, he tried to make friends with Brutus and Caesar – one-year-old lions. They were initially amused by his overtures: frantic yelps and endless tail wagging. But just when he thought they were getting friendly, he let out a bark. The lions reacted strongly, pouncing against their enclosure and roaring loudly. It was perhaps the first time they had done that. They succeeded in scaring even themselves. Eddie was off in a flash – his tail between his legs – all two inches of it.

Julia, a giraffe raised at the park, often visits in the evenings. Silent and still, she stands by the pathway – just enjoying being home again. She looks harmless enough, but there's terrific strength in those deceptively slim legs. They can rotate 180 degrees and kick a lion's head off. I am not allowed to wander late at night, lest I frighten Julia or the lone wildebeest, a bachelor banished by the dominant male in the herd. Speaking of loners, a little buck follows Julia around everywhere. He lost all his friends, as he wasn't strong enough to jump the park fence like the others.

The other day, I was in the workshop, stripping a trailer to build a new body. The baboons, intelligent but messy at the best of times, have become too aggressive to be kept in the park. Jamie, the big, aggressive female baboon, adores Linton – one of my housemates. She reaches out and steals spectacles, cell phones, watches and bracelets to get his attention. She is hilarious as she tries on the stolen spectacles. Brenda on the other hand is shy. She puts out her hand to be stroked, but turns her head away coyly as we approach.

Though we have men who can dare lions in their dens, everybody is terrified of the baboons with their razor-sharp teeth, powerful jaws and very, very sharp brains. So there I toiled in the workshop, ripping through sheets of metal with an electric cutter, stripping the trailer bare so that Ashley, Seaview's manager and the hand that feeds the big lions, could build a new body to transport them to their rehabilitation centre. The cutter kicks like mad and I enjoy wielding its power.

62

Tomorrow the adult lions get fed – a weekly spectacle for the public. Gory carcasses are devoured in a frenzy of snarls and growls. Simulated reality. Not virtual.

Everyday we grow more attached to the strange creatures and human beings who inhabit Seaview. Sam, a fully-grown, mature, white human male, aged forty-five, was reduced to tears when he left yesterday.

***

I've moved on from Seaview and all my friends down there to Riverside, a much drier part of South Africa, although a tributary does flow through one corner of the park. It is much more self-contained than Seaview as it isn't a tourist attraction. We live in cute cottages with thatched roofs, listening to monkeys fighting and playing. On hot afternoons, I take a dip in the pool, often in the company of one or more of the many dogs that roam the park.

Last week I swam with a somewhat more formidable companion – Jessica – an 800-kilo hippo with canines the size of sickles that even crocodiles respect. Amongst all animals, hippos are apparently responsible for the maximum deaths in Africa. Bob, the owner of Riverside, has told us to be wary of the wild hippos that splash around in the tributary. But Jessica is tame. She is bottle-fed eight litres of milk a day and insists on sleeping on the bed with her owner. She loves human company and allows you to ride her, only to throw you off midstream. If you ask her sweetly (in Afrikaans) she even permits you to kiss her between her eyes.

At Riverside, we work with vervet monkeys – similar in size and shape to the monkeys that roam our streets in India, but with black faces and prominent, bright blue testicles. Childhood nightmares of monkeys (inspired by King Louie in Jungle Book) prove well founded. They are vicious, aggressive and unpredictable creatures. Grooming you one minute, scanning your skin for salt crystals and dead skin, they could bite you the next. They are pack animals – perpetually seeking to dominate their troop, humans and anything else. The ones we work with are those abandoned by humans who were terrorised in their own homes by these once cute and cuddly creatures.

The most challenging aspect of rehabilitating monkeys is integrating them into troops large enough to survive in the bush. This attempt inevitably leads to bloody battles to establish hierarchies and pecking orders. We interfere only in extreme situations, as when one female would endure the electric fence rather than submit to other stronger and meaner females.

The babies on the other hand are very special. They look like tiny, hairy, emaciated human babies with enormous ears and large expressive eyes.

***

I am a mother now. Surrogate. At the dinner table Tiger hopped off another volunteer's shoulder onto my plate of steak and mashed potatoes to announce her arrival. Ever since, she spends a good portion of each day (and night) attached to me. Quite literally – on my shoulder, around my neck, in my lap, in a jacket pocket or clinging to my ankle, always sucking her four little fingers. She even goes to the toilet with me and sits on my back in the pool. Occasionally, I get this warm feeling spreading across my back – I know I'm just being a sentimental fool sometimes, but more often than not, it's monkey pee. On Saturday, Tiger had diarrhoea and I wasn't amused. No, I think I am not ready to be a mother yet, but I'm learning.

There are other strange and lovely creatures around. Chicken, a tame eagle, likes to be scratched under her neck. Georgie, the mongoose, marks my legs every morning with some vile-smelling stuff. Victoria, a dog, looks and eats like a hippo. Bully, a loveable mastiff, watches over the monkey babies at night, licks and calms them down when human endurance and affection fail.

I've left a lot unsaid about this beautiful country and its many contradictions; the deep, deep divisions in its society and the irresistible South African rhythms, but I'll save that for another day...

French Whine

Aruna Nambiar

I had already travelled to that great city in my mind – trilled along
with Shammi Kapoor as he warbled, "An Ewening in Paaariis";
sashayed with Naomi Campbell on its catwalks; walked vicariously
through its streets with Billy Crystal and Debra Winger as they
Forgot Paris. I had drooled over Gerard Depardieu and Michel
Platini, and more recently Zidane and Sébastien Grosjean. Moreover,
I had just read the autobiographical account of Peter Mayle's first
year in France, in his delightful book, A Year in Provence: a veritable,
love feast that touched heavily on the beautiful French countryside,
the bounteous and delicious cuisine, the ambrosial offerings
from the vineyards, the boisterous marketplaces stuffed with

cheeses and baguettes, the adorably eccentric, but always hospitable natives.

Consequently, when Raghu, the Significant Other, told me that we would be spending a week in Paris I was thrilled. It was late December and Erlangen in Germany, where we were living, was quilted with snow and swathed in zero degree temperatures. Paris, I divined from the CNN weather forecasts, was almost Mediterranean in comparison at a quite respectable 6°C. I dreamt about sipping champagne on a pleasant summer afternoon and strolling down the Champs Elysées, sailing down the Seine under a blue, cloudless sky and catching a show at the Moulin Rouge.

It was something of a shock, therefore, to be confronted by the Charles De Gaulle Airport, undoubtedly the largest and ugliest airport of my acquaintance (I've seen more charming industrial warehouses), the moment we landed in Paris. It is certainly not what you want to sight after hitching a ride on a rickety old Saab 2000 that has pitched and rolled all the way from Nürnberg to Paris. Adding to my discomfort, just a couple of days earlier, the shoe-bomber, certainly the dumbest would-be-terrorist in history, had tried to set off a bomb in his shoe by waving his leg in the air and vainly trying to light a match, and behind me, two Americans loudly discussed the probability of another suicide attack – imminent they seemed to think.

The airport does improve on the inside I admit, helped somewhat by gleaming floors and a lot of glass, but largely due to the abundance of the super-chic. Perhaps it was because I had just arrived from Germany that my first and lasting impression of Paris was of a sense of style rarely seen outside an Armani catwalk or a Grace Kelly film.

In Erlangen, I had rarely seen a crumpled T-shirt or an aged jacket, and many a time I had felt discomfited in my scuffed sneakers; but comfort and cleanliness seemed to be the driving factor as far as dress code was concerned. And while you just *have* to slip into a pair of pumps at your local

Schuhmarkt to fully comprehend the definition of indulgence, it's unlikely you'll see Claudia Schiffer or Milla Jovovich sporting them on any red carpet. Sensible, that's what German fashion is.

Here, there were perfectly cut mini-skirts and huge earrings; injudicious stilettos and ineffectually small, but darling tote bags; immaculately painted faces and chic haircuts. Even the teenagers, who rightfully should have displayed some sartorial angst, sported perfectly creased trousers and soft shirts, pretty flowered chiffon dresses and exotic perfumes (not all at once, you understand). I don't think I saw a T-shirt anywhere and certainly there wasn't any sign of the body piercing and tattoos of their Deutsche counterparts.

I noticed with a sinking feeling, and a sucking in of the belly, that all the women were as petite as Russian gymnasts, and as streamlined as race cars – there wasn't a wide backside or a hint of cellulite to be seen. This, I was to find to my lasting mortification, seemed to be some kind of prerequisite to being a Parisian. Three days into our stay, after miles of flat bellies, tight bottoms and sleek legs, I finally espied a chubby cheek at Versailles – but when I sidled up to investigate, my eagerness was dampened by the sound of a Texan twang.

Even in Paris' numerous cafes and restaurants, I rarely saw the denizens actually partake. The Parisian mealtime ritual seemed to consist broadly of the air-kissing of companions followed by a generous dose of people-watching, almost continuous wine-swigging interspersed with gesticulating chatter, and a sporadic nibble on a breadstick or a slice of cheese. I waited hopefully to catch a French binge but never did spot a wading into a crepe or the massacre of a tarte tatin.

We almost missed our Hotel Printemps on the bustling Rue de Commerce; its entrance, for some reason, a well-guarded secret squeezed between two brightly-lit shops. In the absence of an elevator, we dragged our luggage up two flights of stairs and collapsed into the room, fighting cardiac arrest.

"Well, it's not the Ritz, but it isn't bad," Raghu gasped.

It wasn't. Smallish, but wrapped in warm yellow wallpaper, it sheltered a soft, comfortable bed, a writing table and a closet. Through the thin door, I could hear the Australian students in the next room discussing their holiday itinerary. The pipes gurgled and gushed with the ablutions of the tenants above in an unheated and frigid loo.

Yes, frigid. For all its impressive display of snow and plunging mercury, Erlangen had felt warmer than Paris did now. Parisian thermometers may have been showing a deceptive 6°C, but there was no arguing with the bite of the wind and the nagging drizzle, which trounced all efforts to bundle up in thermals and woollens. Nevertheless, determined to derive complete mileage for our precious foreign exchange, we plunged into an icy breeze to explore the neighbourhood.

It was then that I started having my first misgivings. The city wore a grey, forlorn coat. Piles of litter lined the back streets. Grime adorned the stately old buildings. The stench of urine wafted from dark corners. And cakes of excrement (canine, I supposed) waited to be stepped on. Subsequently I was to note that the Metro was filthy: graffiti scrawled on tiled walls, dirty station benches and the fetor of urine assaulting our senses. Beggars rummaged through overflowing garbage bins, and drunks called out lewdly from corners. Inside the train, there was none of the happy family chatter of the Deutsch Bahn. Hollow-eyed commuters sat squeezed together on dirty benches, looking vacantly ahead, as musicians played strangled tunes on accordions and harmonicas. And not the rosy cheeked, well-dressed street musicians of Germany, but grubby, sad-eyed men, who didn't even acknowledge a coin dropped into a cynical hat. The City of Love, indeed!

Trying to turn my mind to something more agreeable, I looked in at the restaurants en route and noticed first with approval, and then with growing dismay, that there were loads and loads of them, almost four to a street – but all exorbitant. Expensive little sidewalk cafes, with the chairs all turned towards the road, and the clientele languidly appreciating the world outside. Italian trattorias with white-aproned, hawk-nosed waiters and exorbitant prices. Mexican joints and Indian tandooris, creperies and salad bars – all exquisitely quaint and charming – and all obscenely high-priced.

"What the hell are we going to do for food?" I asked Raghu. "One meal in a restaurant is going to set us back a week's expenses."

"Must you always think of food?" was his irate reply. "We'll find something later."

After gaping at the Eiffel Tower (which I found, to my chagrin, looked nothing like it did in the movies, but more like a badly maintained, out-of-control transmission tower) and getting frozen by glacial gusts from the Seine, we walked around searching for something to eat within reach of our Third World budgets. It was I who discovered the Traiteur Asiatique, a tiny Chinese joint facing the elevated rail transit, and displaying a menu with rock-bottom prices.

"10 Francs for a Kung Pao Chicken!" I pointed excitedly. "This is too good to be true!"

Actually it was. Too good to be true that is – though we realised this only when the bill arrived. I did wonder why each dish was being weighed in front of us, and why we were being asked, in excruciating pidgin English interspersed with animated French and increasingly expansive gestures, how much quantity weighed to the nearest gram we wanted per dish. I put it down to some quaint French custom and sat down to enjoy my meal, only stopping to swoon once the bill arrived.

At the price quoted for two minuscule chicken dishes, a bowl of rice and a diet coke, I would have expected a headwaiter fawning on us and lilies-of-the-valley on the table.

Instead of bone china, we had food slopping out of plastic containers onto a carrom-board size, Formica-topped table. By way of ambience, we had the proprietor's entire family sitting at the adjoining table, with what looked like the next day's ingredients – some rather smelly clams and positively rank tiger prawns – lined up for inspection in front of them. Two brats shrieked and ran past our table, pummelling each other and almost upsetting my ginger chicken. Just as I started praying that they would kill each other, their Mama, attired in a chic, red silk dress, let loose a volley of Oriental babble, the gist of which was, "Shut up, delinquents!" The brats subsided and their shrieks were replaced by the constant chatter of Mama, Papa and unidentified male relatives discussing the next day's Carte du jour.

"What do you expect at this price?" Raghu had asked and I had smiled indulgently.

And now this. After initial swoon, urgent whispered discussion, tentative query to Papa Chef, patient explanation in pidgin English, animated and angry gesture on our part and unapologetic, nonchalant shrug from Papa Chef, it dawned on us that we had omitted to read the very small print on the window menu, which said, 'All prices quoted per 100 gram portions'. And, of course, each dish weighed in at a minimum of 500 grams each. The scoundrels! It should have been called the 'Traitors Asiatique'. We left, muttering darkly.

Back at the hotel reception, we asked the garçon for a jug of water. We had blithely drunk from the taps in German Zimmers, but the frigid, gurgling loo of the Hotel Printemps had not inspired confidence with respect to cleanliness. Mercifully, we had omitted to order mineral water or wine at the Oriental deli, which would have probably been measured to the millilitre in a laboratory beaker.

"Water?" asked the garçon, as though I had just requested a nugget of radioactive plutonium.

"Uh, yes. L'eau," I said, dredging up a crumb of school

70

French from memory.

"In the tap – yes?"

"No, no to drink," I glugged expressively.

"Wine?"

"Nicht, no, nein, I mean – not wine, water."

"Water?"

"Oui."

"To drink?"

"Yes."

"Wine?"

After a five-minute exchange on such intellectual lines, we were finally given a bottle of water, no doubt from the tap, and 1 caught him giving us a bemused look as we toiled up the stairs.

Getting breakfast the next day was no easier, and I was beginning to empathise with the cavemen of yesteryears who had to grab their spears and poisoned darts and stalk moving nutrition for miles, before they could sit down to a decent meal. After a very perfunctory bath in the Arctic Circle loo, we headed for the McDonald's at the end of the road, where we hoped to breakfast on the crepes that we had spotted on their window menu the day before. It was closed – for Christmas. As were the sidewalk cafes and bistros and patisseries. Just as I was beginning to think that we would be the only tourists in history to die of starvation in the middle of Europe, we discovered a Boulangerie, just opposite our hotel, stuffed with delectable muffins, croissants, pastries, chocolates – and an imbecilic salesgirl.

By pointing stubby fingers, we managed to buy six croissants avec beurre and some coffee, but despite pleas of "With milk", "Café au lait" and a "mit Milch", the last of which was greeted with a frosty stare (you will understand the frosty stare if you knew the very bloody history of the Franco-Germans), she plonked down two very black coffees on the counter.

For some reason, the German which had escaped me over

my stay in the Fatherland was now bubbling forth like a boiling kettle, and Raghu warned me that if I didn't stop, I would probably be lynched to death. We even considered mimicking the milking of a cow as a final desperate effort, but voted in favour of the preservation of dignity and returned to our hotel, where we asked the receptionist for a jug of milk. Apparently the garçon had spread the word about the strange Indians on the second floor, for he brought us an enormous jug of hot milk without batting an eyelid. We trudged up to our room where we stuffed ourselves with soft croissants and hot coffee before plunging out into the cold.

This seemed to be the consistent theme of our entire visit. The next day at McDonald's, Raghu begged for sugar while a pimply youth pretended he didn't understand English. We contemplated complaining to the manager, till we realised that the pimply youth *was* the manager. On a freezing morning at the Place de la Concorde, we battled the river breeze and forked out ten francs for a cup of chocolat, our palates tickled by visions of Juliette Binoche pouring out molten chocolate into delicate chinaware, only to be served milky drinking chocolate in a plastic cup, already lukewarm at the first sip.

Raghu, feeling extravagant on the last day, turned up his nose at my suggestion of yet another meal of croissants and fruit, and decided we should splurge on a French meal. Investigations revealed that bouillabaisse was fish soup and foie gras was goose liver paste, so we opted instead for a fashionable Italian trattoria more suited to our less carnivorous tastes. My pizza was the size of the cocktail snacks served back in India, and Raghu's exotic sounding pasta avec buerre was just that – a spoon of boiled macaroni with a dot of butter. The head waiter almost fainted when we refused to order the exorbitant wine, and huffily turned his attention to a family of Americans at the next table who were ordering course after course with the abandon of CEOs on expense accounts. The only decent meal we had that whole week was an enormous bucket of oleaginous chicken at a KFC at the base of the

72

Montmartre – and thank the Lord I did, for American excess in this city of strict food rationing.

Half-starved and miserably cold, we were nevertheless, having burnt up three months worth of foreign exchange savings in getting to Paris, determined to see everything, even when foul weather and sound reason cautioned us otherwise. We went to Versailles, stood in a drizzle for an hour to get entry tickets, tramped miserably through room after room of dripping ostentation, and squelched dejectedly through straggly gardens. We visited the Centre Pompidou, and while Raghu enthused about the unique and futuristic architecture, I recoiled from the facade adorned with not statues or sculptures, but a maze of staircases and pipes, ducts and escalators. We braved an icy wind and steady downpour to shiver in admiration at the Pantheon, which, even though cold and disconsolate, I could appreciate was the most splendid structure that I had ever set my eyes upon. We strolled down the Champs Élysées, marvelling at the wide avenues and sidewalks, a-sparkle with festive lights and the neon signs of designer boutiques. During the only break in the rain, we sailed down the Seine in a Bateau-Mouche past the grand old buildings and the stately ponts.

But, above all, we museum hopped and gallery gallivanted and culture soaked till we were all but steeped – not as a result, I hasten to add, of any artistic pretensions, but of a low cunning to keep as comfortable as possible. It didn't matter that the Sacré Coeur was arresting, or the psychedelic windmill at the Moulin Rouge memorable – all I could think was – let's go see the Louvre, at least it'll be heated.

On our last day, as we glowered at the pelting rain and ate croissants and oranges for lunch and croissants and a couple of bottles of Bordeaux (stolen from the Air France flight) for dinner, I sat down and thought about our week in Paris. It was evident in retrospect that I had been setting myself up for disappointment. I had anticipated escaping from the cold of

Germany, to a warm cocoon of Mediterranean sunshine, and instead I had got buckets of rain and the beginnings of pneumonia. I had counted on kindly old Maurice Chevalier uncles and cuddly Gerard Depardieu men, and had received imbecilic Boulangerie salesgirls and duplicitous Papa Orientals. I had fancied Gallic kisses of the hand and the hospitality and Epicurean largesse that Peter Mayle so confidently talks about, and had received frosty stares and minuscule meals. I had seen the Notre Dame and the Moulin Rouge, the Eiffel Tower and the Pompidou Centre, but I had also lost at least five kilos (so not a complete fiasco, after all) and had developed a rasping cough. I couldn't say that I was loath to leave.

To my horror, I found Raghu making plans to revisit Paris the next summer. Yes, it was eight months down the line, but the pangs of hunger still haunted the nights at times.

"You must be out of your mind!" I said. "There's no way I'm going back to Paris."

"Oh, come, come. Don't judge it by the last experience. You were miserable because of the bad weather – we must see Paris in the summer."

"I'm not coming."

So, of course, I found myself on a bus speeding towards Paris for a weekend trip. There's really nothing much to say about that weekend. The hotel we stayed in was a little swankier than the Hotel Printemps with a heated loo and a television, and a breakfast package. The breakfast was pretty good – lots of croissants and orange juice and coffee.

To our delight, we chanced upon an Indian restaurant called the Kannimara just around the corner, run by a friendly Muslim chap from Pondicherry, who was delighted to find that Raghu spoke a somewhat hesitant Tamil. The restaurant was decorated in the most awful hotchpotch of Indian accessories; the wallpaper improvised from jute mats and ethnic bed linen, the walls plastered with mock Tanjore paintings, calendar prints of waterfalls, collages of Bollywood film stars and cloth paintings depicting Mughal kings and Hindu folklore. The tables, set in such a way that even Kate Moss would have found it difficult to thread her way past them, were covered with shiny red-rose patterned satin tablecloths. Very unfortunate. The food, however, was authentic and just heavenly, and for the rest of the weekend we survived on Kannimara's largesse and the croissants and chocolate puff pastries from a bakery across the road, whose windows were adorned with breadrolls shaped like giant snails and monster tortoises.

To be fair, the whole Paris experience was much more pleasant this time. The weather was crisp and cool and the trees in the Luxembourg gardens were already radiant with the colours of an early autumn. The ubiquitous doggie-doo of December, though not completely obliterated, was scant, thanks to what looked like a massive 'death to doggie-doo' campaign. There were notices everywhere forbidding owners from bringing in their pets and I even saw a cleaning van spraying the streets with water. The Metro was filled with drunks as before, but the stench of urine had abated somewhat. The Tuileries garden was now packed with sun-lovers in green deck chairs all looking as though they were contemplating the meaning of life (I don't know how the French do this – an American in the same situation would look as though he was thinking about his next burger, an Englishman about whether his shorts were a bit improper, an Indian as though mentally converting the cost of that Moulin Rouge key chain). Unfortunately, the Eiffel Tower, this time adorned with green scaffolding cloth like a sash around its middle, looked even uglier than before.

After a couple of days of revisiting the sights and deciding that Paris wasn't that bad after all, it was time to board our bus back to Erlangen. We went down early, hoping to beat the breakfast crowd, but it turned out that besides our group, three busloads were scheduled to leave post-breakfast.

There was pandemonium in the dining hall. The moment

75

fresh croissants were placed on the buffet table they would disappear, crockery was scarce and cutlery never made an appearance. The maid, an enormous black woman, whose formidable bust and behind seemed to weigh down her already snail-like carriage (doing herself a little too well on leftover croissants, methinks), crawled along, reluctantly reloading the toast tray. Inside, the cleaning ladies were evidently having a good gossip and she was patently missing out on some good stuff; so one couldn't really blame her for rolling her eyes and sighing heavily every time we asked her for a refill. On the French service industry rating scale that, I was beginning to think, ranged from unprofessional on the one end to downright rude on the other, I imagine she would have been looked upon as a sort of ministering angel non pareil.

What's Cooking?

Raja Ramanathan

My daughter, Geetanjali, aka Geets, Geethu, Pappudi, Dumkutz, Miss Tingaley, Tingley Moon et al, age: twenty something, lives in a downtown Toronto apartment since the last year or so, having decided to move out of the parental home in her quest for identity. Little did she realise, when she moved out of 'the dinky little room that I've lived in since I was fourteen', that every weekend her entire family would travel down from the family home in suburban Oakville, Ontario to her downtown studio apartment, to savour the delights that Toronto city had to offer. Having finally come to terms with the fact that there was no way she could shrug off this family that she had been born into, she decided to make the best of it. So this weekend she asked me to teach her to make vendakkai sambar...

Now one would wonder why a young South Indian woman of normal intelligence would ask her father of all people, to teach her to make vendakkai sambar. South Indian paters, particularly those born earlier to circa 1970 or so, have been known for many accomplishments. These have included helping NASA build rockets to reach the moon. However, making vendakkai sambar has not been a skill that they have been known to be proficient in. In most cases, paters of this vintage have been known to enter the kitchen, only to find out when the food would be ready. So why did this young woman, not ordinarily known to be mentally deficient, ask her father to teach her to make vendakkai sambar?

And therein hangs a tale...

Soon after my wife Lakshmi and I tied the marital knot, her family retainer moved in with us and saved us from starvation since neither Lakshmi nor I could, at that time, make anything more than a cup of tea. He stayed with us while he passed on his skills to Lakshmi, and groomed her into the mould of the gourmet chef that he was.

We came to Canada in the 90s, and when Lakshmi's father passed away soon after, her mother came to live with us. Like all good mothers-in-law of South Indian men born before circa 1970, my mother-in-law thought it an affront to her culinary skills if her son-in-law so much as added a dash of salt to the food she had cooked with so much love.

Such would have been the course of my life, but for my mother-in-law's most unfortunate accident – she fell down in the house one evening and broke her hip. She was admitted to hospital, and my wife had to spend many hours in the hospital helping her recuperate from surgery following the accident.

As I sat through the first few of those evenings, my alternatives were: to get a catered meal from one of the many Indian or other catering establishments in and around Mississauga; live on pizza or other such food; or just watch the pounds slither off as I starved. Having been brought up for fifty plus years on good homemade South Indian food, my conditioning was far too deep to settle for such alternatives.

So, one morning, about a week after my mother-in-law's accident, I hesitantly asked my wife to give me the recipe to make rice and paruppu (plain, cooked toor dal).

78

The beloved one looked at me with bewilderment.

"You are going to cook?" she asked. It seemed to be more of a shock for her than her mother's accident.

She sat down and took a deep breath. "No, sweetheart, I will keep the rice and paruppu in the cooker and go. You just open it and eat it in the evening," she said, fully convinced that at fifty-three, no man could learn anything new, let alone cooking.

The life partner's response posed a challenge; a challenge to my ancestors who had always done things new and brave, including my mother who is reported to have sung at the start of the Quit India Movement, circa 1942 or thereabouts, a Bharathiyar song from within the confines of her home as an English policeman passed by. History has not recorded whether the policeman heard the song or whether he had any reaction to it, but it got my mother into trouble with her father who said she was bringing ruination on the family by doing such things. Being the son of such a brave and valiant mother, who did what was right and correct, the mind was set. I would cook.

"Sweetie, just tell me how to put the rice and paruppu..." I said. Having brought up two children and a husband, my wife knew when to give up reason and put her faith in God. She walked me through putting rice and paruppu in the pressure cooker with the detail and precision of a kindergarten teacher teaching her wards how to tie their shoelaces.

Still not convinced that a disaster would be averted, she made a last try, "I will come home a little early today and you can put the rice and paruppu in the cooker when I am around..."

No. My mind was made up. I would do so on my own.

That evening I came home and put together – with a meditative awareness that would have made a Zen teacher proud (if Zen teachers are allowed to feel proud) – the pressure cooker as instructed. I waited for the pressure to come through with the hissing sound, and then waited the mandatory seven minutes the beloved wife had asked me to. Once the seven minutes were over, I held the cooker under the cold water tap to reduce the pressure. I could hardly wait till the cooker cooled to inspect my maiden efforts. When I opened the pressure cooker, the rice and paruppu looked perfect. I took one grain of each and tasted them.

The feeling was similar to what Neil Armstrong would have experienced as he stepped on the moon for the first time.

"One small step for man, one giant leap for mankind..."

"One rice and paruppu for me, one giant stride towards freedom for the male species..."

I put a little margarine (in lieu of good, homemade ghee) on the rice and paruppu, and ate. My son walked in a few minutes later and was thrilled to see something other than pizza or Kentucky Fried Chicken on the table. Father and son ate together and the guru herself came by late at night and sampled my first efforts. She was not unimpressed. For thirty years she had never thought that her husband would amount to much. Now there seemed to be hope. Strange are the ways of God, she must have said to herself that night...

The next day, I produced a tomato rasam ("a watered down sambar", is how one school of thought describes a rasam – there are more charitable descriptions); then a full-fledged sambar and potato curry (sambar and potato curry is a great Sunday lunch favourite in several South Indian homes); followed by a porichha kozhambu. Describing a porichha kozhambu is difficult, suffice it to say that any kozhambu is a gravy-like preparation generally eaten mixed with rice, and that porichha means fried.

In three months, I had graduated to paruppu usli (cooking this is generally a milestone achievement, it is a mixture of cooked toor dal ground and mixed with vegetables to make a yummy dish) and morkuzhambu (nearest translation, kadi). By then I was showing off.

I became part of an internet group that exchanged recipes. My wife scrutinised these e-mails from the

Ashas, Shyamalas and Ranjinis with some concern, but was too happy with her new-found freedom from the kitchen to really object.

These days she reminds me in the morning to soak the kidney beans before we leave for work, so that I can make rajma when I return in the evening. She comes home in the evenings, goes up, changes, gets into bed, switches on the TV, and gets served in bed by 7.30 pm. When my daughter invites her friends for dosas, guess who makes them?

Now, could there be greater women's liberation?

Are you Indian, Tonto?

Mahendra Rathod

My nephew was four years old: that special age when kids learn to use words and match them with concepts. We lived in a different country and we would call him often just to hear his voice on the phone and enjoy the odd bits he sprang on us from time to time. One day as my wife, Naina, was talking to him he stopped her mid-sentence.

"Are you Indian?"

We laughed. I realised that 'Indian' was a new concept to him.

***

I grew up on a diet of comics like any normal boy. Even now, at this ripe middle age, I love comics. Sometimes strange looks are shot at me from my Business Class co-passengers on intercontinental flights when they see this suit-clad fellow with reading glasses on the bridge of his nose take out a stack of comics for the long flight!

Along with Superman and Batman, one of my favourite heroes was The Lone Ranger. For those who have not read the comic strip, the Lone Ranger was the gun-toting Robin Hood of the Wild West. He fought the bad guys and helped the needy. Tonto, his American-Indian sidekick (it is no longer correct to call them Red Indians – they are Native Indians or American Indians),

82

embodied the perfect invention of writers – in the mould of Dr Watson, Col Hastings and Robin. Tonto was the highlighter pen that emphasised the hero in case you missed the point. With his knowledge of hoof prints and smoke signals, Tonto often had to rescue the Lone Ranger – thus providing proof that the bitterest of enemies – the white man and the American aborigine – could have a perfectly respectful and symbiotic relationship.

Completing the trio was Silver, the Lone Ranger's super-intelligent and obedient horse who came to the rescue when both the Lone Ranger and Tonto were trapped. They fought many battles together and the good guys i.e. the Lone Ranger and Co always won.

The Lone Ranger's heroics in a dusty land evoked images of endless plains where the good guys could run away but the bad guys had nowhere to hide. The stories, like others of its genre, were set in the barren countryside of the Wild West. To an impressionable mind their heroes were icons of manliness and bravery. I am sure most young boys have vivid imaginations, but I suspect mine was hyperactive. I remember I would actually enter the story (somewhat like the 3-D movies you see with special glasses) and would smell the horses and taste the dust as they galloped away. The few scraggly plants, the rocky terrain, the cold nights all seemed part of a perfect world. I always dreamed of touching those rocks and shrubs some day, and waiting for the stagecoach to pull in at noon sharp, trailing dust.

***

Our holiday trip to USA took a long time to plan as we had no feel for distances and our desire to see 'everything to see' was too vague for any friends to help. Finally after some elimination, Naina and I finalised an itinerary. We had decided to see everything the leisurely way – this meant staying at each place a bit longer, and exploring it to a greater extent than what a packaged tour would allow.

83

The Grand Canyon was no exception. We flew in from Las Vegas to Flagstaff, the nearest point to the Grand Canyon that has an airport. Flagstaff is a beautiful town with a majestic landscape and a leisurely ambience; a quaint, welcoming American town with a distinctively cultured, almost Mediterranean flavour.

As soon as we landed we knew we had miscalculated. We had been told that September would be 'nice' weather. And Las Vegas had been nice weather. But in our breathless excitement we forgot that Flagstaff was at 7000 feet above sea level! The ride from the airport to the hotel chilled our bones to the marrow.

After we checked in, we asked the receptionist to guide us to some shops for warm clothing. While we were trying out the clothes, I saw small sparks fly as I rubbed fabric against fabric. Wow! The air at that height was so dry that it was creating static electricity.

We got back and went for a stroll. Lesson number one on American culture – no one goes for a stroll in US of A. They get in their cars and drive. Of course in big dense cities you find pedestrian crowds and in plazas people do saunter around – but Flagstaff at 8 pm was empty.

Lesson number 2, was delivered at breakfast the next day. It was huge! And for a reasonable price. Three people could have eaten my share! When I asked the waitress if I could have a one-third portion, she probably thought I was trying to save money and replied, "Leave what you don't want".

We made many friends during our travels in USA. Our fellow American tourists were all, without exception, friendly. They always made the first overture.

"Where yoll fraum?"

"India!" we answered.

There was a moment's incomprehension as they tried to recollect which state India was in – like Rome, Georgia or Rome, New York; or Paris, Missouri or Paris, Arkansas.

 Then the penny would drop. "Oh from Gandhi country?"

We reached the Grand Canyon by 9 am. When we reached the edge of the ravine and looked out I was physically stunned. It was like a moment I would experience if God suddenly appeared in person – I would be blinded by the dazzle, humbled, wanting to go down on my knees, and wishing the moment would last forever. As every Muslim is exhorted to go to Mecca at least once to achieve salvation; so I think must every human being visit the Grand Canyon at least once in their lives!

The scale and panorama of the Canyon is mind blowing – the word gargantuan is insufficient. The width multiplies the effect and the straight drop to the ravine 5,000 feet below makes you realise that it is a great carving job – the work of a master sculptor, none other than the Colorado River herself.

The straightness of the ravine adds to its majesty and what the camera cannot fully appreciate – the eyes and the brain can. The Canyon is a viewer's delight – miles of layered rocks shaded in burnt sienna, red, brown and orange stretch out into the surroundings. According to the brochures, the upper rocky layer is 300 million years old and the lowest layer is 500 million to a billion years. Considering that the earth's age is estimated at 4.5 billion years, this thing is really old! The Grand Canyon is devoid of any vegetation except at lower levels and this adds to the clean, picture-perfect magnificence.

Naina had just tried an American hair stylist who convinced her to try the newest of looks and we now have for posterity a picture of the two of us with the grandest and oldest of canyons in the background and the newest of haircuts against it.

At the canyon too we made several new friends as we had done during our travels around the rest of the country. After we had our fill of marvelling at the earth's open vein, we decided to explore the countryside. We went to make enquiries at a tourist office. As I stood waiting to ask questions, I saw a poster inviting us to visit Indian reservations near

Flagstaff. Reservations are specially allocated areas, probably where the tribes had originally settled, where the Native Americans make their homes. There are many tribes in USA and some more in Canada and Mexico. They have been the fodder for keen writers to create exciting adventures. As I was salivating, an American Indian walked in: in full regalia – feather headgear, tall boots with spurs and a buffalo skin jacket.

My mind was made up. It was a matter of minutes before I convinced Naina, booked a car, prepared to have early dinner and go to bed early. Next day was going to be a trip to memory land. I had not anticipated finding the Wild West so close at hand and old memories came flooding back.

***

The Lone Ranger wakes early before daybreak. Tonto-she is sleeping soundly, dreaming of a quiet day after the hectic schedule. TLR yawns, brushes, shaves and showers. He gently shakes Tonto-she to wake her up. She opens one eye and goes back to sleep. More insistent shaking. TS is up and sits on the bed for an eternity. TLR is making noises. TLR wears his gun belt and stuffs his pocket with wallet, car keys, binoculars, maps, mouth freshener, and little notebook. He wears his mid-calf-high suede boots. They match the red dust of Arizona. He looks in the mirror. Rakish hat, sunglasses – did TLR wear them? Tonto-she showers and is finally ready. They get into the car, unfold the map and take off in a cloud of dust. Hi-Yo, Silver!

***

The landscape as you leave Flagstaff quickly turns to the much-imagined western country of brown open scraggly countryside. Miles and miles of nothing, with hills in the background. The red-and-brown-layered rock formation that you see in the Grand Canyon stretches into the surrounding area. There is a theory that the Grand Canyon was under the sea many aeons ago. It did look as if the terrain had had a good bath.

We finally reached the Reservation site, the Navajo 'nation'. The American Indian tribes are dispersed around the US and the reservations are semi-autonomous states within a state, hence the name nation. The reservations are actual dwellings where the particular tribes live under their own traditional mores and convictions. They freely practice their beliefs, and social intercourse is as per tradition.

At the entrance to the reservation was a large tourist information centre. There were information kiosks and shops selling authentic tribal handicrafts and food. The Indians were dressed in their native costume and it was nice to see that the relentless influence of American TV and Hollywood had not dimmed their desire to be unique.

There were many visitors and all of them were first timers, as curious as we were. We learnt that the Navajo people have lived in their homeland for thousands of years. They believe in rituals and had a strong belief in spirits and how they influence their lives. Like many traditions from ancient civilisations that puzzle the west, the Navajo's beliefs are based on rituals and the obeisance to the unknown forces. It is these rituals – a de facto warding off technique – that act as a social binding tool that keeps the people together as a community with shared values and beliefs. The Navajo culture is ancient but they still speak and teach their children the Navajo language. I suppose other American Indian tribes would have similar profiles with some modifications based on the environment and topography.

As I heard the guide describe their respect for the elements, their desire to worship the fire, respect for parents, social strictness and so on, I was quite impressed that there seemed to be so many similarities between the Indian and the American Indian traditions. I started speculating (wildly) that when the continents were one conjoined landmass millions of years ago, and one could walk from India to America, some Indians perhaps did migrate and this was possibly the reason for the American Indian spirit-based belief system.

Many, if not most, American Indians do not live any longer in those mud and bamboo houses we used to see in movies, but they have adopted the modern timber and cement methods incorporating the key features of their old systems. For example, the 'hogan' used to be a Navajo home, made of mud and straw. Now it is made from timber and the hogan is used as a communal centre for ceremonies.

An American Indian guide showed us a typical hogan – a six-sided structure made from clay and wood with a sloping roof, with one room and a door. Again there are some similarities, with many threads of Vastu-shastra and Feng Shui. For instance, the door of the hogan must face the east to meet the rising sun. This way the whole family greets Father Sun. The south side represents tools of livelihood – like weaving etc. The west is associated with social relations. This is where the visitors sit. The north is for ceremonies. The cooking area is in the centre of the hogan.

There are two types of hogan: male and female. The male hogan is a kind of cleansing chamber. A spiritual pre-shower area. You enter it first and walk around in a clockwise direction. Then you wash your feet and enter the other 'female' hogan. The male hogan traps all evil spirits that might have got attached to you so that no harm can be carried to the main hogan where the wife and children live. The homes are very basic and at some places they don't have electricity and running water. But superficially at least, to the tourist eye, the Navajos looked happy.

We smoked a 'peace pipe' to cement world peace and doffed the colourful Navajo headgear that represents vigour and strength for the camera, before heading to the impressive artefacts showroom. Most of the craftwork revolved around beadwork, rugs and leather replicas.

We were fascinated by 'the dream catcher'; a piece shaped like a spider's web and woven from colourful threads, beads and metallic fibres in a hexagon-within-a-hexagon design. A dream catcher is hung outside the main door to filter out nightmares and only let good dreams go in. The American Indians believe that dreams are floating in space and the dream catcher catches the best dream and allows it to be hooked up with the dreamer. Wow! I could use twenty dream catchers! I hung around the shop for a long time, my strong impulse to buy one almost overriding my usual scepticism. Naina convinced me that it was not worth buying so I reluctantly let it go.

All along, I had wanted to ask one of the American Indians if he knew about India. While Naina dashed off to use the facilities, I looked around and found a nice young Navajo in traditional dress. After exchanging pleasantries, I sprang the question. I sat him down and asked him if he could guess where I was from. He couldn't. I said, "I am an Indian". He laughed out loud as if I was pulling his leg. He looked at me and laughed again. I said, "Honestly, I am the original Indian. There is a real India far away and the people are called Indians." He looked at me quizzically. He had never heard of India, nor did he know that the word Indian originated from a historic mistake. I had to tell him I did not belong to any American tribe and I had travelled thousands of miles to come here. Sadly for me, he was not wonder-struck with this knowledge. In fact, I don't think he believed me.

Finally by about 6 pm we drove off. It had been a fabulous day for me, though I wished that I had bought a dream catcher. Oh well, next time, I thought. But as we prepared to go to bed that night, Naina suddenly darted to the wardrobe and returned with a 12-inch, 32-pearl smile and handed me a package.

"This is for you, my incurable dreamer." Seeing my astonished look she continued, "I bought it when you were talking to that young Navajo man."

I opened the package. Inside was one of the most beautiful dream catchers I had ever seen.

Itching in Istanbul

Rahul Rao

Every holiday has its moments of epiphany. I would like to say mine came as I sunbathed on a gorgeous Mediterranean beach in Bodrum. But actually I was cowering in the cool, dark recesses of a seaside restaurant, trying desperately to position myself in the path of the room's only fan, and avoiding – much to the bemusement of waiters and guests alike – Bodrum's chief attraction: the sun.

"Would you like a table outside?" a waiter asks me, gesturing to an empty spot under a beach umbrella, from where I could have looked out west over the sparkling azure waters of the Aegean Sea and up and down Bodrum's charming, if somewhat overcrowded, seafront. I shake my head miserably, squeezing big globs of sunscreen onto my palms and rubbing them over my red, mottled, blistering and itchy forearms and thighs, wretchedly recalling the £45 diagnosis that a Turkish doctor had pronounced only hours before: "Sun is guilty."

But back to the epiphanies – actually there were two. One was that while the more assimilated NRIs and ABCDs in the West – AB veryCDs – are called coconuts (brown skin, white consciousness), I was turning out to be more like an egg: white on the outside, and somewhat messy inside.

After three years in Britain, where summer

90

is a few hours of apologetic sunshine peeking out of dense, unremitting cloud cover, my skin was going Caucasian.

Second epiphany: I am admiring the view – a beautiful indented coastline where two graceful sweeping curves meet at a promontory that juts out into the sea and holds aloft the 15th century Castle of St Peter built by the Crusader Knights of St John. As I watch, a woman take off her bikini top to reveal, well, two more graceful sweeping curves, I hear the unmistakable cry of a muezzin calling the faithful to prayer from a neighbouring mosque: "Allah, Hu Akbar!" he cries; "Welcome to Turkey," I think.

I am in Turkey with Oxford friends and flatmates: Bengali-Malayali Niharika, (very clever, rock-climbing, vegetarian); and Scots-Irish Sinead (i.e. Scottish when intellectual and Irish when inebriated), who projects the image of a brittle, tragic Hollywood star but is really warm and fuzzy deep down inside. We are here to visit our friend Elizabeth, Seattle-born refugee from Bushistan, who is attending a two-month language course at Istanbul's Bogazici University.

Everything I have read about Turkey so far abounds in clichés about the place being a bridge between Europe and Asia, a meeting point of civilisations. This is all slightly annoying for me. The guidebooks make it sound like West never met East anywhere else, making me want to say, "erm...colonialism?"

Nonetheless, there is something unique about Turkey: the cultural contrasts are starker, more abrupt, the pieces more jagged and their juxtapositions more unexpected than anywhere else I have been. Partly this has to do with its history, with the monumental change effected almost overnight in 1923 from decadent, crumbling Ottoman Empire to modern, secular Turkish republic, and more recently with the efforts of this 99.8% Muslim country to enter the European Union. All of this makes for some curious contrasts: where else, my guide book asks rhetorically, would you find that the chief imam's cübbe (ceremonial robe) had been redesigned by an openly gay fashion designer?

Istanbul exemplifies all of these contradictions, feeling very much like a mosaic of neighbourhoods from different parts of the world – and all within easy walking distance of one another.

Elizabeth has a large airy flat in Beyoglu, which will be home to us during our time in Istanbul. With its high ceilings, wooden floors, large windows and its location in the heart of one of Istanbul's most lively neighbourhoods, this is like one of those Parsi flats in Bombay that you could only hope to inherit, although it possesses a malfunctioning toilet, a shower behind a pile of bricks in a corner of the bedroom, curtain rails that fall off at the slightest tug and no magnificent rosewood furniture (we are all on student budgets).

But our location more than makes up for these trifling inconveniences. We live on what is possibly the noisiest side street in Beyoglu, our neighbours comprising a bookstore, several restaurants and bars, a nargile (hookah) café and a club that advertises itself as Latin/Afro-Caribbean. Its choice of music turns out to be somewhat more eclectic, featuring a generous nightly dose of Punjabi MC and Euro-cheese. The DJ also seems to have an unfortunate affinity for long sessions of techno-trance that begin as early as noon, reaching a bone-rattling climax at 4 am every morning.

On one occasion after a nocturnal ramble, Sinead, Elizabeth and I are locked out of the flat and unable to yell above the din to rouse the evidently sleeping Niharika inside. This requires us to enter the building on the opposite side of the street, batter down the door of the third-floor leftist outfit whose windows open onto our own, explain to its sleepy but surprisingly good-natured occupants in broken Turkish that we cannot enter our flat and that it is imperative that we wake up our friend, attempt to do so by bellowing "Ni-harika! Ni-harika!" into the night air, and finally in utter desperation throw objects including large old Turkish coins at the window. 'Harika' being the Turkish world for 'wonderful' and with money raining down in the street, one can only wonder at the impression we created.

The centrepiece of Beyoglu is its main pedestrian boulevard – Istiklal Caddesi – teeming with life at all hours of the day and night. There is a faded, crumbling elegance about Istiklal, with its neo-classical facades featuring intricate wrought iron balconies and other delightful embellishments. Even the local Starbucks has an impressive two-tier chandelier and beautiful black and white floor mosaics. Alternating with brash new storefronts flaunting the latest high-end brands are old churches (hidden from street view by elaborate brick and stone screens because of a restriction, in effect until the 19th century, that forbade non-Muslim religious buildings to appear on the city skyline); embassies and consulates in period buildings; restaurants, bars, cafes and sweet shops; bookstores and shops selling old maps and calligraphy; the old French Lycée and markets in colonnaded arcades.

But my most treasured find is undoubtedly the Markiz Pastahanesi. With its art nouveau interiors and ceramic tile panels depicting the four seasons, and quiet restrained jazz, it is hauntingly evocative of turn of the century Europe. And it sells the richest, thickest, most decadent chocolate cake I have ever sunk my teeth into.

Istiklal Caddesi slopes down sharply through what feels like an entire district of music shops and hardware stores, past the conical capped Galata Tower built by the Genoese in the 14th century, taking you finally to the water; the Golden Horn or Haliç, a channel that bisects the European side of Istanbul. At this point, I am tempted to say something dramatic like, "Crossing the Haliç is like going from Barcelona to Baghdad", but nothing in Istanbul is quite that cut and dry. All the bewilderingly diverse elements in this city bleed into each other like masalas in some complicated and slow-cooking curry.

Nevertheless, there is something dramatically different about the southern shore of the Haliç. After the recreational pace of Beyoglu, Eminönü feels like one of those long-exposure photographs where the lights make bright, streaky lines and even stationary objects look like they're moving at high speed.

93

Everybody is going from somewhere to somewhere else, with Eminönü itself serving as a vast transit lounge for the city. People scurry to and fro; hop on and off buses, ferries, cabs and trams; dart into subway tunnels, pausing only long enough to enjoy a quick doner kebab or corn on the cob.

Only the fishermen on Galata Bridge and the pigeon sellers around the Yeni Cami (New Mosque, circa 1598) are virtually motionless, their respective transactions across species boundaries seeming to require infinitely more patience and serenity than is in evidence around them. Pausing for a moment on the bridge, we are treated to a stunning view of what must be one of the world's most spectacular urban skylines: red roofs tumbling higgledy-piggledy down steep slopes towards the water, punctuated by moments of splendour and seriousness provided by a thicket of minarets pegging down some grand Ottoman mosque or palace, and all of this sliced up by the shimmering blue of the Haliç and the Bosphorous Straits meeting each other at right angles in a watery T-junction.

Walking uphill from Eminönü, we pass Sirkeci station, which served as the last stop in Europe for trains from the west, including the legendary Orient Express immortalised in Agatha Christie's famous mystery novel. I wander into its cool, dark waiting room –

...the sun drives me into cool dark spaces at every opportunity, although prior to the Bodrum diagnosis, I labour under the illusion that I am suffering from some sort of allergy and therefore take refuge in anti-histamine pills instead of sunscreen. "It's symmetrical!" I exclaim triumphantly, vaguely recalling my mother explaining to me that allergies were often symmetrical, but forgetting that sunburn is also symmetrical unless you are wearing something very haute couture and asymmetrical (which needless to say, I am not)...

– to admire its beautiful wooden wall panelling and circular porthole-like stained glass windows. The frontage, unfortunately, is marred by an extension in what any Indian would recognise as the PWD style of architecture.

But all this is quickly forgotten when, a short tram ride up the hill, we are deposited amidst the grandeur of Sultanahmet – the heart of Byzantine and Ottoman Istanbul. Here we visit Topkapi Palace, which hitherto has existed in my imagination only as a seedy restaurant on top of Bangalore's Utility Building. Built at a slight elevation on an outcrop of land surrounded by water on three sides, the real Topkapi was the home of the Ottoman sultans for over three centuries. I have been reading Orhan Pamuk's intricate and spellbinding My Name is Red, set in the workshops of the imperial miniaturists of 16th century Istanbul, and as I move deeper into the palace grounds through its labyrinthine network of courtyards and pavilions, I can almost see clutches of scheming artisans huddled together in the corridors, plotting away their next intellectual coup.

Sinead loses herself in the imperial harem, convinced that she would have thrived in its luxurious and devious environs. I am less sanguine about her prospects, finding it difficult to imagine her sharing her living quarters – not to mention the Sultan – with three hundred other concubines. On the other hand, I surmise, it might be precisely that need for exclusivity that would drive her to become a modern day Roxelana (wife of Süleyman the Magnificent); outmanoeuvre her fellow concubines, banish their progeny to the far corners of the empire (and perhaps eventually have them strangled), assassinate jealous court officials who oppose her rise to power and generally push, plot and poison her way up the palace pecking order. Yes, Sinead would have been fantastic.

Later, in the Grand Bazaar, she goes looking for harem pants. I'm not entirely sure what these are meant to be, but she is shown and urged to try on a variety of costumes that would have made a samba dancer in Rio blush. These (usually) lecherous offers are brushed off with a stiff 'no thank you', but one vender takes great exception. "I am a designer, not a salesman," he snaps, as if to say, "I seek to undress you for the greater glory of art." Sinead remains un-persuaded.

Other transactions are more amiable; Elizabeth buys gomleks (kurtas), Niharika wrangles out of one shopkeeper an exquisite turquoise bowl decorated with tulips (a recurring motif in 18th century Ottoman art), and I – rejecting the mass-produced ready-to-hang block prints being sold in a government bookshop – return to a tiny hole in the wall to purchase a piece of Arabic calligraphy of dubious pedigree and authenticity. What I am buying is almost less important than where I am buying it: the world's oldest shopping centre, a half-millennium old market, where the shops still pay their rent in gold.

Despite my passionate dislike for shopping, particularly on vacation, I could have wandered endlessly through the maze of interconnecting vaulted passageways that is the Grand Bazaar, marvelling at the smorgasbord of traditional handicrafts, everyday necessities and sheer junk on offer. Jewellery, leather goods, bath accessories, metal and coloured glass lamps, Turkish rugs, souvenirs, ceramics, tea sets, silks, nargiles, sweets and savouries, chess sets, furniture, prayer beads, icons, football T-shirts, miniatures, old coins, nuts, dates, raisins, dried fish, kitschy trinkets, heaps of spices, old silverware and belly-dancer costumes leap out at us, fighting with each other to demand our attention, answering needs we didn't even know we had.

One need that I am always acutely aware of is the imperative of periodic retreat into cool, dark spaces where I can attend to the blistering, copper-red parchment that my skin has become. It is this, as much as their architectural and religious significance that takes me into Sultanahmet's numerous mosques. While the others admire AyaSofya's marvellous dome adorned with black and gold Arabic calligraphy and its Byzantine mosaics, and revel retrospectively in its historical importance as world centre of Orthodox Christendom and then Islam, I am considerably more preoccupied with the increasingly cracked, mosaic-like appearance that my skin is taking on. While the devout line up to place a hand inside a cold, clammy hole in a pillar and pray for fertility, world peace and other

96

trifles, I wish fervently that my itching would cease. Someone remarks on the Sultanahmet mosque's six minarets (unprecedented at the time and necessitating the construction of a seventh minaret at Mecca so that it could retain its pre-eminence); I can only think, Red Riding Hood-like, "What big scratching posts!" When subaltern historians get around to publishing their urban-studies anthology ('The Leper's Jerusalem'?), let not be excluded this account of Istanbul through the eyes of an itching itinerant.

There is something about Ottoman mosques that makes them look rather like Sumo wrestlers. They sit low and squat on the ground, their multiple domes looking like so many rolls of fat cascading down on every side. The illusion is quickly dispelled inside by their cavernous unified spaces, surmounted by magnificent central domes; delicate and detailed in ethereal blue in the Sultanahmet mosque; richer, warmer colours in the Süleymaniye. Vast, circular wrought iron chandeliers, in size the diameter of the dome itself, hang low over the centre, casting a light that plays with the sunbeams refracted through stained glass windows, to give the entire place a sort of dappled brilliance.

Ottoman tombs are considerably less inspiring structures, particularly if one arrives expecting the drama of Mughal mausoleums. Here instead are cramped polygonal structures, packed with monstrous graves (the monstrosity of the grave being directly proportional to the importance of the deceased), with a ceramic-tile to wall-surface ratio so high as to create the impression of a bathroom. Government tourist board-like signs extol the virtues and eclipse the vices of each Sultan in bombastic language.

(The state, incidentally, is everywhere in the form of a picture of Atatürk, founder of the modern Turkish republic, who, hitherto has existed in my imagination only as my grandfather's much loved horse. The more I look at his stern but sometimes kindly, weathered face, the more he begins to look like my grandfather – until slowly but surely, I begin to see my grandfather everywhere: inspecting military parades, on banknotes, teaching children the modern Turkish alphabet, drinking coffee, making speeches, signing treaties.)

Determined to get off the tourist trail, Niharika and I venture into the Western districts of Fatih, Fener and Balat. Poorer and reputedly more conservative, these are fascinating areas of the city testifying to a not-so-distant past when Christians and Jews made up nearly 40% of its population.

Making our way through a warren of streets too narrow to show up on our map, we find ourselves in Balat – the old Jewish quarter.

The Ahrida synagogue is closed and there is little to indicate that this was once a Jewish area, barring the old woman with distinctly Semitic features who squints at us fiercely from a high window. But we stumble upon an Armenian Orthodox Church not five steps away, where incense burns in hanging brass lamps. The weekly mass is being conducted to the strains of chanting for the tiny congregation that remains. There is a sort of cheek-by-jowl cosmopolitanism to this place, so characteristic of imperial trading cities. Yet despite the unique history of the area that drew this extraordinary hotchpotch of people together, in its outward appearance I cannot help but think, "This could be Shivajinagar, or anywhere..." The same hardware stores and wholesale depots selling the same utensils and plastic buckets and ball bearings, the same shop fronts and signs and fonts. I am very much at home.

But home is where the heart is, to use a cheesy cliché, and if Samuel Huntington forced me to choose from the vague continental-civilisational identities on offer in his thoroughly over-cited Clash of Civilisations, I suppose I'd be Asian. Straddling as it does – however nominally – both Europe and Asia, Istanbul is about the only place on earth where I can test this simply by leaping from one continent to the other. We take a ferry from Eminönü, stopping at Arnavutköy (the 'Albanian Village', still on the European side), to admire its pretty waterfront of timber Ottoman mansions, then

98

pass under an enormous suspension bridge connecting the European and Asian landmasses, and finally disembark at Kadiköy on the Asian side.

I fall to my knees and kiss the earth, I text my mother, I sniff the air – but alas, I feel no organic connection with the elements. There is an incredible sameness about the Asian side – not one thing I could point to that was radically different. Elated that I have scored a point (admittedly cheap and academically un-rigorous) against Huntington, Niall Ferguson and all the coffee-table gatekeepers of Western identity, I vow to bring them to Istanbul to rub their faces in the confusing, disorienting identity melange that is Turkey.

Perhaps Turkey's Asianness would have become more apparent if I had looked hard enough over the next few days, when we managed to tear ourselves away from Istanbul to venture east into Anatolia. Our first stop, however, is Cappadocia, where nature is so distracting that I fail to make any significant observations about how people live.

Famed for its canyons and gorges, we spend hours tramping through valleys in which wind and water have relentlessly carved the volcanic landscape into unimaginably weird and fantastic shapes. I name them arbitrarily – but, I think, appropriately – as we go along: Lemon Meringue Ridge, Wigwam County, Ku Klux Klan Milliners, Fairy Chimney Land, and – most impressively – the Valley of the Giant Circumcised Penises (this last really cannot be called anything else). More intriguingly, local communities, seeking refuge from marauding hordes, dug entire subterranean towns in the soft rock – most of which, I discover to my discomfort, were built for very short people.

But imagine being able to spend all your life in a cool, dark place – ah, bliss! Surely you want to know how my skin is doing? Cappadocia is simply awful, skin-wise. If Istanbul is hot, Cappadocia is baking, the occasional scrub vegetation affording little shade and the lack of human habitation providing few opportunities for retreat. Nivea lotion, Aloe vera gel and (finally!) sunscreen are the soothers of the moment, but their repeated and alternating application is quite literally confusing the life out of my skin cells, which are undergoing a rapid inflammation-contraction-sudden death-and flake-off cycle in alarming numbers. I observe, worriedly, that I am beginning to look like a bronzed god.

Our most interesting encounter with a human being in Cappadocia is with the apparently charming and helpful man who rents us a car, which we use to explore rock-cut churches, monasteries and cities in the countryside around our base in Göreme. Our day is uneventful – which is to say I drive brilliantly, barring occasional tense moments when I am on the wrong side of the road (in my defence, I have never driven on the right before), or when I reach down for the gearshift with my left hand only to hit the driver's door, or when I try to start the car (unsuccessfully) with the key to the dickey, or when I am stopped by police for a breathalyser test. Having negotiated all hurdles successfully, it is not without a trace of smugness that I deliver the car back to the rental agency just in time (we think) for us to catch our bus to Bodrum.

Aforementioned Charming & Helpful clerk inspects the car, sticks his head under it, starts it again and then, listening to the engine, asks darkly and mysteriously, "Can you hear that?"

"Hear what?" The question has more to do with my complete ignorance about cars, than with any attempt to feign blamelessness – i.e. being dumb, rather than playing dumb. An argument ensues, the upshot of which is that we cannot leave till Mr Charming-n-Helpful has contacted his manager and asked him what to do with us since we have 'destroyed' his car. My defence comprises of the words 'wheel', 'axle', 'engine', 'tuning', 'old' and 'car' strung together in various permutations and combinations (language is not an issue as we both speak fluent English).

Located next door to the bus company and knowing

full well that our bus is just about to depart – and, therefore, that he has us by the metaphorical balls – Charming-n-Helpful delivers an ultimatum. "I will let you go if you pay me 200 million lire."

Normally this would sound like a ransom line out of a high-stakes mafia movie, but in Turkey – thanks to a severely devalued currency – this is actually quite reasonable, as extortion goes. Not one to be outwitted and even less willing to reject a movie role, I threaten to call the American Embassy. No one stops to ponder what exactly a US diplomatic representative could and would do for us – it is enough that we have been able to summon all the wrath and majesty of the world's only superpower – but C&H roars in furious impotence, "Get out of Turkey and never come back!"

We flee to Bodrum, as planned. The only things of consequence that happen here are: (a) the epiphanies and (b) the diagnosis. Beautiful as the landscape is, Bodrum is synonymous with boredom, and bursting with beet-red boorish Brits, baking on the beach in bikini-briefs. Not a pretty sight.

Our penultimate stop is Ephesus, which all the guidebooks inform us is the largest and best-preserved ancient city around the Mediterranean. This is certainly true, with the ruins rivalling those of the Forum in Rome in extent and intactness. Now I am no archaeologist, but sometimes 'preservation' seems to imply putting together whatever is lying around, however mismatched, with large quantities of cement. Happily, this cannot be said of the superbly restored façade of the Celsus Library which – with the perfect symmetry of its massive Corinthian columns and triangular pediments – does not fail to impress even the most sunburnt. I want to go home, but having bought sunscreen of the appropriate strength, am somewhat relieved that the healing process has begun.

We spend the night in the neighbouring town of Selçuk, where we are the guests of a warmly welcoming and highly knowledgeable gentleman who talks us to exhaustion, threatens to deny us a single moment of privacy ("You want pizza?

101

I take you; You want kebab? I take you"), and is something of a control freak ("How many spoons of sugar would you like in your coffee day-after-tomorrow?"). Niharika is deputed to communicate with him on our behalf, as the rest of us – exploding into spluttering laughter at each new question or piece of information that he volunteers – lack the forbearance that this seems to require. She does so admirably, using the patient voice that is usually reserved for a lovable but slightly demented child. Nevertheless, she too invariably splutters and with much tee-hee-ing and haw-haw-ing, we manage to extricate ourselves from the overwhelming hospitality of our garrulous host.

No journey to Turkey is complete without a trip to a Turkish bath or hamam, and on returning to Istanbul – since my skin was on the mend – I decide that a visit is in order. Much more than just baths, hamams are integral to Turkish social life in a number of ways – many are closely linked to mosques; in patriarchal Ottoman society they were rare autonomous spaces for women, and they continue to be favoured places for such things as arranging marriages.

My hamam, it turned out, was a front for rather more amorous activities – and not ones that your parents or family elders arranged for you.

"Massage? Ma-ssage?" the front-of-house man asked puzzled, playing with the word as if it were a strange, unfamiliar concept that I ought to be pursuing elsewhere. "No massage," he said finally, waving me through a door into a large, square, tiled room in which men in various stages of undress poured water suggestively over their bodies.

All my politically progressive instincts militate against my adding to five hundred years of writing about the decadent 'Orient', but it was very clear to me at this moment that East was East and East was hot and West was coming East to get it. And some men were women (and quite possibly, some women men), for did not Virginia Woolf choose Constantinople (as Istanbul was then called) as the location for her androgynous Orlando's pivotal change from man to woman? *Of course* literature and postcolonial studies were uppermost in my mind.

Two weeks have sped by and I am on a plane bound for London. I am sad to leave, but for once I relish the prospect of returning to the coldest and darkest place in the world. Finally, I think, an end to dermatological misery. Istanbul will, however, continue to haunt me for many a night. Unknown to me at the time, even as I step onto Air France flight 2391, I am infested with body lice. I am a walking zoo. How? Bed sheets? Bus seats? Hamam? Haram? Who knows? I am still itching as I write this.

Face Value

John Mathew

I am an Indian but I have lived for so long in these parts that my facial features have evolved in to that of an Arab – an Egyptian to be precise. The immigration officer at the Abu Dhabi airport suspects that I am an Indian masquerading as an Egyptian, while his counterpart in Mumbai assumes I am an Egyptian impersonating an Indian.

I suffer from another handicap, this one of my own making – I am also a compulsive advisor. Some say one should seek J's guidance, and then proceed to do the exact opposite! Others come to me for advice because I look more intelligent than I really am. I just cannot resist the urge to give advice, or lend a helping hand, whether the other party needs it or not! My friends say, "You ask J what time it is, and he will tell you how to make a watch!"

My Arabic looks, combined with my desire to be

104

helpful can be a deadly cocktail, as I have found out the hard way several times.

I used to live in Bahrain in the late seventies where I frequented a grocery store – they call it a cold store there – which my cousin used to run in the rented premises of a residential building. When asked what connection I had with the shop, I would just say that it belonged to my brother, in order to spare the questioner a long explanation. I had no inkling that most people took in my Middle Eastern appearance and my statement that the shop belonged to my brother and concluded that I was the landlord's brother.

Now the Bahraini landlord – let's call him LL – was a very civilised and reasonable gentleman, who used to work for a bank, where my employer maintained an account. The tenants used to come to me with their problems and sometimes their monthly rent even, and I would dutifully pass them on to LL when I met him at the bank. The arrangement was working perfectly. A resident with a leaky roof or some such other hassle even got his rent reduced through my efforts. This last event must have assured even, the most sceptical among the leaseholders of my fraternal ties as well as influence with LL, for they started treating me more deferentially ever since.

With hindsight I realise that I was the only one who did not know that I was the Building Owner's Brother!

One of the occupants of the building was a Kannadiga named Ramesh, with whom I would converse in Kannada. I explained that I picked up Kannada in Bangalore where I was educated. Coincidentally, numerous Bahrainis were completing their higher studies in Bangalore those days. Little did I know that Ramesh was quite pleased to find an Arab soul mate who spoke his language.

That summer, Ramesh had a problem with his air conditioning. The exhaust of the air conditioning unit was blocked by the compound wall and the hot air expelled from his home was coming right back in through the ventilators. The

A/C technician suggested two solutions; he could either construct an exhaust outlet from Ramesh's house all the way to the roof of the building, or Ramesh could opt for the cheaper alternative i.e. knock down the offending compound wall. Naturally my friend preferred the second option.

And then he made the fatal error of seeking my advice!

Initially I did wonder why he had chosen to ask me, of all people, but then my vanity got the better of me. I convinced myself that it was only natural for Ramesh to lean on me, his most trusted and wise counsellor, in his hour of perplexity. It never occurred to me at that time, that what the fellow really wanted was the green signal to demolish the wall, and not my halfpenny advice.

I asked myself, what does it matter to me if he knocked down the wall? Pat came the answer; he could go ahead and dynamite the whole building for all I cared! So in my best imitation of Clark Gable I theatrically curled my lips and quivered my moustache and declared, "Frankly my dear, I don't give a damn!"

Ramesh seemed to be a firm believer in the hoary maxim 'Shubhasia Sheekhram' – the earlier the better. The very next Friday he brought in a bunch of Pathans who gave full vent to all their pent up frustrations on the offending section of the compound wall. Obviously my friend's neighbours were also in a similar predicament and they too went on to utilise the services of the wrecking crew. Overnight, the building acquired landmark status by virtue of being the only one on the entire island that was bereft of any kind of defence against the prying eyes of passers-by as well as the excremental habits of the local canine population.

To characterise LL's state of mind as incensed would be an understatement! The tenants of course denied any responsibility for what happened. They had after all obtained prior permission, albeit verbal, from LL's own brother! The rest, as they say, is history. Suffice it to say that it is only in Hindi films that long lost brothers sing and dance for joy when they eventually meet.

I wish I could report that I stopped meddling in others' problems after this humiliating incidence. No way! I am a prime example of the saying 'History repeats itself for those who do not learn from it the first time.'

The scene shifts to Abu Dhabi. Time: Twenty years later. One night, older but not much wiser, yours truly was driving back from the Water and Electricity Club after a strenuous game of badminton. Coincidentally some sort of a social event that was underway in the WE club also got over at the same time and a huge crowd was waiting at the gates for taxis.

A distinguished looking man waved to me, obviously requesting a ride in to town. But when, being my usual helpful self, I stopped the car, it was not just the gentleman who got in but also three plump, overdressed matrons – the type that we would instinctively address as "Mama" – each of whom had at least four children of varying girth in tow. Somehow they all managed to pile into the car.

Some five minutes into the journey my passengers realised that even though I resembled their compatriots in looks, I could not speak a word of their language; neither could any of them speak English. Somehow they managed to convey to me that they lived in a place called Imzan.

"Imzan? Where on earth is Imzan?"

Somewhere in the Tourist Club Area, apparently. I started driving around TCA in search of the elusive Imzan.

By now the car was beginning to get a little stuffy. The fat kid sitting next to me was holding his nose: he wanted to swap seats with one of his siblings at the back because I smelled. Of course I smelled – after two hours of badminton what do you expect? Chanel No 5?

That was the last straw for one of the Mamas, who decided to take over the navigation of the car from my incompetent hands. She started directing me at the traffic lights: a left turn here, right turn there, U turn at the next junction and so on.

I focused on driving as per the instructions being bawled out.

Suddenly the entire crowd chorused, "Hada Imzan! Hada Imzan"!

Their joy at rediscovering "Imzan" was akin to that of shipwrecked sailors espying land on the horizon. And Imzan? Well, it turned out to be the Emsons Departmental Store on Electra Road.

By way of adieu, the matronly figure who was directing the proceedings informed me in a stern voice, while pointing at the department store's neon sign – "Hada imzan, OK? Mafi mukh in the – no brains?"

I am yet to figure out how she was able to accurately assess my cerebral capabilities in such a short span of time, while my current employer who has kept me on his payroll for over two decades is yet to discover the truth that I don't have much of mukh!

My Middle Eastern looks, combined with my penchant for getting entangled in someone else's mess can acquire a disastrous dimension when members of the fairer sex are involved.

Once our church choir was taking part in a musical programme in Dubai. The lead soprano, a rather pretty one, had a genuine problem; her husband was not willing to let her travel with the troupe. The chap was suspicious of the admiration his wife has been garnering, particularly that of the male members of the choir, due to her vocal prowess as well as her physical beauty. Finally the gentleman relented because our priest managed to assure him that his wife would be delivered back to his home and hearth, virtue unsullied, before the stroke of ten that night.

As can be expected of any Indian event, the musical programme started late and it was well past 10 pm when it got over. The lady was naturally upset because the journey back by bus to Abu Dhabi would take another two hours.

It was then that I offered to drive her and a couple of others who needed to return home in a hurry in my car, a Nissan Patrol SUV with black glass. By the time we reached Abu Dhabi – around midnight – the girl was already in tears at

108

the terrifying thought of facing her husband. She lived near Salaam Street, in a building that also housed a very popular Arabic Restaurant, and was the last one to be dropped off. Our heroine alighted from the car still sobbing.

Imagine the scene, a wailing sari-clad girl stepping out alone from a darkened SUV driven by an Arab. People were staring at me. I knew what they were thinking and could not really blame them for their wild assumptions.

As luck would have it, there was a police car parked in front of the 'Shawarma' sandwich kiosk. The cops who had noted the unusual tableau stopped me immediately and demanded an explanation as to why the girl was crying. I told them quite truthfully that it was because she was terrified of her husband who might beat her for staying out so late.

"Of course, her husband, like any self-respecting member of the male species, will give her a sound thrashing for running around with a fellow like you, but that is going to happen only after she gets home. But pray, tell us why she is weeping now?" they demanded.

Before I could put my foot in my mouth, thereby absolutely convincing the officers that I was a sex offender / serial killer on the prowl, the girl's husband, who was waiting in the lobby for her arrival, stepped forward. His assurances in broken Arabic that he was in fact the girl's unfortunate husband and that there was nothing seriously amiss seemed to pacify the cops. With a stern look at me that seemed to say, "OK wise guy, you got off lightly this time but you better watch your step", the guardians of the law allowed me to go. And to the aggrieved gentleman they gave a final piece of advice.

"You husband, be careful," a deprecating gesture at me, "Hada Minni Minni! This guy is a tricky character."

Yes, maybe I should change my meddling ways, but I wish people would stop taking me at face value.

In Search of Penguins

M R Shetty

As a teenager, I once sat on the sands of Marina Beach in Madras, looking out into the vast ocean and wondering what it would be like to sail through blue seas to foreign lands. I have travelled widely since then, for work and leisure, and my annual holiday has become not only a pleasant distraction from the world of medicine, but something I look forward to with great anticipation. By the early 1990s, my wanderlust had taken me to all the continents but one – Antarctica.

It was more than just wanderlust that had me planning a trip to the seventh continent. When I first photographed wildlife in Africa, I sent one of the better photographs to family and friends as a Christmas card, to an appreciative response. Ever since, it has become something of a tradition. Every Christmas, friends, family and fellow doctors receive a Christmas card from me with notes from my latest trip and a photograph of one of the distinctive species of the land. I had begun to form an idea in my mind that it would be wonderful if one of my Christmas cards could carry a photograph of a penguin.

Consequently, I put my name down for a trip to Antarctica. Years came and went. Work and personal commitments made me postpone the trip time and again, but finally in November 1993, I was ready to sail. Here is a journal of what was one of the most memorable voyages of my life:

Thursday, 18ᵗʰ November 1993

I fly in from Santiago to Punta Arenas, considered to be the southernmost city in the world, though smaller towns and settlements do exist further south. As we land, I can see the ocean and the magnificent Chilean fjords running along the coast.

The largest city on the Straits of Magellan, Punta Arenas was once one of the most important Chilean harbours, used by ships preparing to cross from the Pacific to the Atlantic Ocean either through the narrow Straits of Magellan or around Cape Horn. After its completion in 1914, most commercial ships ply through the Panama Canal, but Punta Arenas is still a starting point for many scientists and explorers on Antarctic expeditions.

We gather at the quayside in the evening – about a hundred of us. I recognise some people who had been on the same flight with me from Santiago. There are groups of scientists, couples and single adventurers, and even a smattering of octogenarians. Boats take us to the enormous Columbus Caravelle (equipped to plough through ice floes), which will sail from South America to Antarctica. The sea is already rough, the ship pitching and rolling, and I am glad that in addition to my Gore-Tex pants, mittens, gloves, hiking boots, balaclava, waterproof parka and compass, I have also not omitted to pack my motion sickness pills.

In the evening, we all gather in the ship's auditorium where we are to be primed for our Antarctic journey by a scientist on board. Having already read up in preparation for my trip, I know I am about to embark on a journey of a lifetime.

Over five million square miles in area, Antarctica is 50% larger than the United States of America. Today an

island continent by itself, it was once part of a southern supercontinent called Gondwanaland that included Australia, India, Africa, and South America. The supercontinent began to break up about 160 million years ago when Africa separated and drifted northwards. Over the next 150 million years, landmasses separated and drifted, creating changes in the geography and climate of the world till it attained its current geographic configuration about ten million years ago.

After splitting from Gondwana, Antarctica drifted to its present position and the climate became colder. Today half its landmass is covered in ice. In fact, 90% of the world's ice is in Antarctica. Environmentalists say that chlorofluorocarbons, some of it present in our refrigerators, are greatly depleting the ozone layer resulting in global warming and the ultimate melting of the polar icecaps. Perhaps one day, the only ice left on earth may be the ice cubes in our refrigerators! The melting of the ice caps could be disastrous; the sea level could rise by as much as hundred metres and more than half of mankind would be submerged and homeless.

It is the world's harshest climate; even at the height of summer temperatures rarely go beyond 10°C and wind speeds can touch as much as 120 mph. The lowest temperature recorded here was a numbing -89.6°C in July 1983. Nevertheless, it is home to a great variety of wildlife.

When the ice melts in summer it releases tons of algae, the bottom of the food chain, which serves as food for billions of Antarctic krill, the shrimp-like plankton that in turn feed an estimated 65 million penguins, 35 million seals and 126 types of fish and whales. It is however, a very fragile environment; the ship's scientist cautions us not to trample over the moss and lichen that grows here, as it takes years for these feeble flora to recover.

We are going to be visiting the continent at a very interesting time: the penguins are currently laying eggs! We will however have to be careful; we are not to disturb the penguins in

112

any way. Only half of all newborn penguins live to adulthood, and by our presence we should not hinder their progress in any way.

Our orientation ends with a summary of the precautions to be taken. Dark glasses are to be worn at all times to shield us from the glare of the ice and the ultraviolet rays from the sun. Not a fossil or rock is to be touched, not a scrap of litter to be thrown overboard. "Use only established trails," the scientist warns, for of course the ice is fluid and treacherous, its superficial layers moving faster than the lower ones, much like a deck of cards being spread.

Friday, November 19th, 1993

At 8.00 am we make our first stop at the Seno Augustino glacier, one of the Chilean fjords. We board the small boats called zodiacs – the inflatable landing craft popularised by none other than Jacques Cousteau himself. They are said to be unsinkable, but certainly not any less dangerous, for they can flip over at high speeds and you can topple into the water, which, at sub-zero temperatures, will kill you in about three minutes.

The zodiac deposits us on the shore, where we wade through water plants and scramble up the rocks for a closer look at the glacier – a harsh mountain of jagged black rock patched with ice.

Being our first expedition, it's a good opportunity to get to know some of the other passengers. I find there are a handful of other doctors on the trip, a group of young scientists and an elderly schoolteacher who keeps me entertained with his dry wit. It is cold but not uncomfortably so, I've seen worse winters in Chicago, but of course it is the height of summer in the antipodes.

Saturday, November 20th 1993

We stop at Cape Horn, where the landmass of South America tapers off into a sharp scorpion's tail, to the point at which the Pacific and Atlantic Oceans meet. Cape Horn is notorious amongst sailors as one of the most treacherous points of navigation in the world, and stories abound of ships that have sunk and sailors that have drowned here.

113

Cape Horn is a sharp cliff that falls down to the shore. There are wooden steps on the cliff-side but as we climb I find that even the steps are slushy with wet mud, and slippery. Somehow I clamber up. At the peak there is a small cabin where we proudly get our postcards stamped as a memoir of our efforts. From the top, I see Chilean coast guard boats dotting the sea and our ship looks tiny against the expanse of water. On the way down, my fears are realised as I slip. I think I have torn a muscle – the pain is excruciating. My fellow passengers carry me back to the ship where I retire to my cabin.

At lunch, I get talking with a young lad from England. I have noticed him from the start – with his crumpled clothes and unshaven face, he stands out from the rest of the group. He tells me he is unemployed and I wonder how he has managed to get together the money for this trip, which is not inexpensive. He says he's been saving up for a year, literally putting aside a few pounds a day to fulfil what has been a long-held dream. The previous year he travelled to Greenland, also on a shoestring budget. He will be penniless at the end of our voyage but he doesn't care – a true adventurer, I muse.

Suddenly, as we sit talking, our plates, along with the plates of a hundred other passengers, fly across the room and crash against the wall. Our ship, a 7500 tonne monster, has been thrown up in the air like a paper boat. The seas are rough and I realise we are in the Drake Passage – the 400 mile long body of water between Cape Horn and Antarctica that is reputed to have the worst sea weather in the world. It is nevertheless the shortest crossing from Antarctica to any other landmass, so the obvious route for us.

There is pandemonium in the dining hall. I join the horde of passengers who are hurrying to their rooms and find that I have to hold on to walls and doors for support as the ship pitches and rolls. I wonder if I should stop at the toilets instead and give in to the nausea that is threatening to overcome me. Somehow I

114

make it to my cabin, where I fall into the bed and close my eyes to make the room stop heaving.

Sunday, November 21ˢᵗ 1993

I spent the whole evening in my cabin. The worst is over – I wake up to calm seas today. We are getting closer to our destination! We navigated the Antarctic conversions today – the point where warm and cold waters meet, creating a wall of fog. When we finally emerge it is 8.30 pm and we can see King George Island, the first of the islands off the shore of Antarctica.

Monday, November 22ⁿᵈ 1993

I wake at 4.00 am – it doesn't seem so early, for the sun has already risen half an hour ago. We are anchored at King George Island, one of the volcanic islands in the Admiralty Bay, which are home to whales, seals and Chinstrap penguins. It was first discovered in 1819. In 1820, cartographer Edward Bransfield charted these islands and on his return, described the abundance of wildlife in the area. This unfortunately resulted in carnage – over the next four years 320,000 seal skins and countless tons of elephant seal oil were plundered from these waters.

At 8.00 am, we board the zodiacs and are taken ashore. The islands are home to rocky mountains carpeted with colourful moss and lichen and strewn with patches of ice. A couple of sea lions frolic near the sea – falling into each other like a couple of football players. For the first time, I see what I've come in search of – penguins! Scores of them look inquiringly at us from the rookeries on the mountainside – plump Chinstraps, little Adelies and the Gentoos with the disti nguished white stripe across their heads. I am in photographic heaven, as I click furiously.

There's a Polish station on the island that researches the marine biology of the newly de-glaciated areas of Admiralty Bay. The scientists are thrilled to see us – they have not seen a soul for ten months! The poor folks get to talk to their families just once a week, over the radio. Surprisingly even in this remote place one can buy T-shirts and souvenirs!

Tuesday, November 23rd 1993

We hover near Cuverville Island, a landscape of mountains and glaciers framing a calm, cold sea. Blocks of pristine white ice float in dramatic blue-green water. I imagine I am as close as you can get to heaven on earth. We circle the beautiful islands in the zodiac, marvelling at the penguins visible in the thousands, guarding the shore like tin soldiers. We stop to watch as they step from stone to stone, remarkably human-like, their flippers extended like outstretched arms for balance. Some of them even slip and fall, like we are prone to do. But there's nothing human-like when they plunge into the water – they are effortless swimmers who dive and flit as they fish. I am certain that this year's Christmas card is going to be spectacular.

Late in the evening, we visit Danco Islands. The sun is just setting, lighting up icebergs that are as big as cathedrals. I see more penguins and their arch enemies, the white Sheathbill birds who steal penguin eggs.

The cabin of the British Antarctic Survey is empty so we move on to Neko Harbour. It is colder and it appears there is snow and ice everywhere. There is an Argentinean base camp here, but that too is empty. The trip is not wasted though – as the clock strikes ten we witness a rare and amazing sight. A huge wall of ice calves away from a glacier and plunges into the water with an enormous splash.

Suddenly I realise that we have touched the seventh continent – Neko Harbour is on the continent of Antarctica – not an offshore island like King George or Cuverville. For a moment, I harbour the thought of trekking to the South Pole, which one can do from here – but the moment we step on shore my foot sinks into waist-deep snow and gets stuck. I have to be pulled out by fellow passengers. I know now it would be near impossible to climb the huge mountain which stands between us and the southernmost point of the earth.

Wednesday, November 24th

At 5.50 am the ship drops anchor at Paradise Bay. An Argentine station on shore stocks stored food in case

116

anybody gets stranded in these parts. In 1921, we are told, two English explorers John Cope and Thomas Bagshaw got stranded at Paradise Bay, and survived for months on penguin and seal meat, till they were rescued in January 1922.

In the evening we touch Port Lockroy, but find that the penguins have already laid their eggs, so we are not permitted to go ashore in case we disturb them.

Thursday, November 25th, 1993

Thanksgiving Day. I wake up at 4.30 am to find we are in high seas, which are very rough. I am glad to reach Deception Island at 7.30 am. Deception Island is a horseshoe shaped caldera where water has filled the crater of a volcano. The volcano erupted last in 1970, leaving in its wake hot springs, fumaroles and steaming beaches covered with black ash – in the harsh cold of the Antarctic, the name Deception Island seems apt.

A hurricane envelops the caldera while we are there. The wind howls and the waves rise to forty feet. I go to the bridge to find the Russian Captain Balashov looking worried. He speaks just a smattering of English so he doesn't say much, but anxiety looks the same in any language. We are fortunate to be in the caldera and not in the open seas. Our trip to Hope Bay has to be cancelled, but we are treated to a turkey dinner in the land of the penguins.

Friday, November 26th 1993

The hurricane rages on. We move on to Half Moon Island and watch penguins, but there is no hope of making it to Hope Bay.

Saturday November 27th 1993

The sea is so rough that everybody is reaching for their motion sickness tablets. I am glad that we are heading home.

Sunday, November 28th 1993

We reach the Straits of Magellan – and the sea is finally calm. Tomorrow I will be back on land. I have sailed farther south than ever before, weathered the eye of an Antarctic storm, waded through waist-deep snow, witnessed a glacier

117

fragment, watched as penguins fished and seals played and birds hovered over the ice. Few things will surpass this experience, and if I had to strain a muscle, get stuck in snow and endure a few days of acute nausea in the process, so be it. I sit in my cabin thinking of my trip and in a rare moment of lyricism I scribble:

> *To see the rising of a different sun,*
> *Winds that whistle you off your feet,*
> *Waves that gobble ships, mice and men,*
> *Cathedral-like icebergs of spectral blue,*
> *Instant mountains from oceans dark,*
> *Where petrels wheel in perpetual flight,*
> *And penguins play like flightless angels,*
> *To be captured by both tranquillity and fear,*
> *Is to experience Antarctica.*

Athens Again

Anthony Koithra

Luton airport is a hole. It is a tiny, unpleasant, godforsaken collection of airstrips a couple of hours north of London that exists largely because several budget airlines operate their ageing fleets out of it. These are the sort of airlines that take World War II aircraft, give them a fresh coat of white paint and a logo, use recycled pub carpeting as upholstery and provide zip-loc bags as oxygen masks. They will, however, fly you across Europe for approximately $12, which makes excellent economic sense to the budget traveller. And having just started working a couple of months earlier, I was very much a budget traveller, although that term is usually used with reference to individuals actually in possession of a budget of some sort.

A little background is perhaps, in order. A colleague and I, both of us recently graduated and even more recently hired, had just finished a two month stint in London, and had five precious days of leave before we returned to Singapore, regular work and what, we felt sure, would be the end of our natural lives. A whirlwind European tour seemed like the logical way to spend our time, and it had got off to a good start – fortuitous timing had placed the last day of Oktoberfest, the first day of our leave and my birthday in perfect alignment. All roads pointed to Munich and thoroughly inadvisable amounts of beer.

As it turned out, the cheapest overall airfare solution was to be obtained by flying to each city in and out of London. Manav, my colleague, planned to follow up the debauchery in Munich with more debauchery in Amsterdam. I intended to hit Athens for a day, before we both flew into Barcelona to round off the trip.

When I was very young, my father worked in Athens for a time. We lived in a duplex apartment, above a family that owned the building. The Demestikas were incredibly friendly and kind people, often keeping my mum company while Papa was away, and providing me with playmates – Sotos (my age) and Marika (slightly older). I didn't speak much Greek and they didn't speak much English, but with the kind of communication skills that kids under four specialise in, the three of us became fast friends.

Watching over us more often than not was their grandmother, Yaya. I have no actual memories of all this – its an idyllic pastiche in my head, re-created from a pile of childhood photographs and several fondly retold stories I've heard from my parents – so going to meet these people twenty years later felt a little strange, but was intriguing nonetheless.

Which brings us back to Luton airport. All the London-Athens flights I could find on EasyJet and Go! originated at Luton, which is why, on that rainy English afternoon, I found myself trudging through its erratic

120

automatic doors. Visions of Teutonic beauties and a truly memorable all-day Munich piss-up were still fresh in my mind from the day before, and Luton, with its soggy carpets and day-old coffee was a considerable comedown.

For the sort of reasons only a rookie traveller can make sense of, I had arrived without an actual ticket to Athens – just the knowledge that there were two flights every 24 hours – one of which had already left. After complications with the internet-only booking, and uncertainties brought about by the vagaries of online banking and my inability to keep track of simple numbers, I had a ticket, and three hours to kill before the flight.

Outside the airport I could see only miles of rainy highway in each direction, so I wandered into the bookshop seeking an appropriate source of departure lounge amusement – and eventually settled on a Stephen Fry paperback, whose plotline sounded suspiciously like a story idea I had had about a year before. Like many people, I take a sort of perverse pleasure in discovering that someone else with the same idea actually did something with it and made some money. This is because later on, I can sit around and complain about my ideas being ripped off.

As I settled down, noting that the seat smelt of equal parts fart and vinegar, I saw that the two seats next to my window seat were empty, so I put my pack in the centre – allowing me easy access to the offending Fry book and my sketchpad. Minutes later, an exceedingly large man with his hair messed into an enormous, radial, unintentional afro walked up to my row and eyed my pack, and then me, with a quizzically raised eyebrow. I raised an eyebrow in response. He sniffed, sat down and proceeded to snore the entire flight away, takeoff and landing included.

The deeper I got into the book, the more it bothered me, because the story was eerily similar to my aforementioned idea. A scientist devises a technique of sending a small object back through time, and decides to

121

drop a newly developed, extremely strong male contraceptive pill into the drinking water of the village where Hitler was born, thereby rendering Hitler's father sterile and preventing the Holocaust. My version had a bomb and a more generic dictatorial figure, but the similarity, and the fact that Fry's method was way more imaginative combined with the gloom of Luton and the olfactory smorgasbord, put me in a decidedly foul mood.

When we landed in Athens, it was about five in the morning and the sky was frothing into an awesome cloud-soaked dawn. The new international airport, while in possession of a singularly unpronounceable name ('Eleftheriolos Vassilives' or something), is all sharp white lines and curved reflections – sleek, refined and downright cool. It was a little early to go waking people up, and the airport is about an hour away from the city, in a place called Spata (no, not Sparta, if that's what you're thinking), so I explored for a bit and discovered several things.

Number one, authentic Greek coffee tastes like strongly caffeinated gravel – but in a good way. Two, the lady who runs the airport internet place has some serious issues: she let me in at 5.40, then chased me out at 5.50 and told me to come back at six o'clock. When I asked why, she waved her arms around and peered at me threateningly over her bifocals. Three, a lot of the communication in Greece takes place through the frantic waving of arms. I was waving and miming as a sort of language substitute – but the people I was speaking to incorporated waving as a natural part of their speech patterns.

This continued in the taxi on the way in to Athens – the amount of time the driver spent with both hands clear off the steering wheel would have been disconcerting if his rapid-fire patter hadn't been so engrossing. In a fascinating hybrid language that consisted of more than just English and Greek (I'm certain he said 'hacienda' at one point), he complained about everything from the weather to his decrepit taxi's transmission. As a moped swerved across three lanes and cut him off, he cursed and swore and ranted about how all the construction and concrete was making the city messier than ever. Looking around it was hard not to agree with him. This was just before the 2004 Olympics and the entire city seemed like it was being pulled up by its roots and being cleaned and reconstructed. Building crews and earthmovers were everywhere, elevating Athens' notoriously pulse-quickening traffic to truly epic cardiac-arrest levels. Several screeches, near misses and burst blood vessels later, we arrived at the house.

It's a distinctly odd feeling to be standing next to a house that you've been told you've spent many happy hours in, but to not have the slightest recollection of it. A bit like expecting a wave of nostalgia that doesn't show up. The house looked exactly like the photographs, except for a huge, old, dusty black Mercedes hibernating in the driveway.

Suddenly there was a commotion from behind the car, a loud exclamation, and a gigantic man with even more gigantic glasses grabbed my hand and, laughing uproariously, attempted to dislocate my shoulder. Again, from the photographs – this was definitely Dimitri Uncle.

I was led up the stairs and into a noisy, carpeted living room filled with people, where I tried to quickly match names to faces. The elderly lady in the black dress and shocked expression had to be Yaya. The serious, bespectacled young man in the polo tee and loafers had to be Sotos. The tall blonde stunner in the summer dress must be Marika. And the kindly looking lady in the back had to be Katerina Aunty.

I was just about done with the identification process when they all started talking at once. Before I knew it, I was on the sofa, hot coffee and biscuits in my hands and surrounded by talking faces. Sotos' English was flawless, with just the slightest trace of an accent. Everyone else kept a constant stream of questions going – except Yaya, who was still staring at me with disbelief, clearly trying to reconcile the noisy little Indian kid she used to know with the goateed, pony-tailed freak of nature who sat before her today.

After an intensive, marathon catch-up session, both sides were more or less up to speed on what had unfolded over the last twenty years.

Marika, amazingly, was now a long-jumper on the Greek Olympic team and in the final phases of training for the coming Games. She had also recently won a local beauty pageant and had her picture in all the papers. As Sotos told me this, Katerina Aunty dropped a pile of newspaper clippings in my lap – all different angles of her daughter's megawatt smile. Marika herself seemed a bit put off by all the fuss and said something Greek and sharp, tossing her hair in annoyance. But the family was clearly too proud of their resident Olympic beauty queen to let her modesty get in the way.

Sotos was finishing up at University and planning to work as a diplomat in the Foreign Service or the UN. He speaks six languages fluently, said Dimitri Uncle, beaming and thumping him on the back till his eyes bulged out. Sotos spoke in quiet, confident cadences, translating for Yaya when necessary and conveying the kind of quiet intensity you'd expect from a future international dignitary. At the same time he was dealing with the prospect of having to sign up in the Army as per the Greek conscription laws, once his University days were over, but it was clear his parents were far more worried about it than he was.

As for Katerina Aunty and Dimitri Uncle, they had just finished building their dream island home on one of the smaller isles – the exact location of which escaped me. They had pictures of a beautiful stone house on a grassy hill, the walls punctuated by vines and wildflowers, all of it overlooking a deep blue expanse of water.

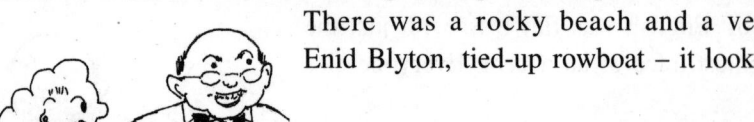 There was a rocky beach and a very Enid Blyton, tied-up rowboat – it looked

absolutely wonderful. I was made to understand that I was expected to visit them there with my friends, as soon as possible – and chided for only being able to stay such a short time in Athens.

Soon after, Marika said she had to leave for training, promising to be back for lunch. Sotos decided that if I was in Athens for less than twelve hours I ought to see at least some of the city, so we drove out to the Acropolis hill. The city is built on, around and under several low to medium sized hills – from above it looks like an irregular off-white blocky urban sprawl spread over an undulating surface. Here and there, pockets of steel, glass and global branding interrupt the Mediterranean palette and sepia-infused atmosphere. Some structures are clearly from another era – from the ruins of ancient auditoriums to cemeteries and cracked stone walkways.

The Parthenon itself was in the middle of a somewhat controversial 'reconstruction', and several earnest-looking architect types were peering at huge marble blocks trying to figure out where in the structure they went. Other groups were up on scaffoldings, painstakingly cleaning the yellowing, weatherworn stone surfaces – scrubbing the enormous columns and buffing the cracking walls. Sotos explained that one school of thought apparently disapproved of all this interference with the site – claiming that the dirt and grime and disorder were part of its long, distinguished history. The opposing view was that if left alone, the structure would be damaged beyond repair by the elements and the influence of the city surrounding it.

We eventually ended up in a little outdoor café in Placa – a warren of little cobbled streets directly below the Acropolis hill, full of tiny shops and bistros. This was apparently the old Turkish quarter of Athens – although now several boutiques and upscale shops populated sections of it. Sotos' buddy Pericles joined us after a while. After ascertaining that he wasn't pulling my leg, I came to terms with the fact that in modern Greece, people really do still use cool names like Pericles and Archimedes. A spirited discussion on kung fu films developed –

125

both Sotos and Pericles being fans of the genre – covering the profusion of Hong Kong style wirework in modern Hollywood films, Jackie Chan's alleged womanising ways, and how the Matrix series' martial arts sequences are derided by connoisseurs as silly and overwrought.

Lunch was a lavish affair – the whole family and more were at the little restaurant when we got there. It was a very homey sort of place, awash in afternoon sun, and run by friends of the Demestikas. The light stone and mortar building was clearly a regular haunt, since everyone seemed to know everyone else. I was introduced to a number of people, including Marika's coach and others that I can no longer remember.

What I do remember are the smells wafting out of the kitchen and filling the dining room with a heady mixture of meat, cheese and spice aromas. All manner of highly authentic Greek food made its way onto our table and was methodically and steadily disposed off. Everyone commented vociferously on the quality of each dish, rating it critically in comparison to the offerings of competing establishments, and occasional squabbles broke out as disagreements arose over relative rankings.

The rest of the day passed pleasantly enough, and fortunately there wasn't much activity after lunch – I needed time to recover. After collapsing gratefully into armchairs on the Demestikas' balcony, Sotos, Marika and I continued to catch up over coffee. The pageant, the Olympics, girlfriends, boyfriends, schools and universities were all discussed at length. They also sternly interrogated me as to why I was rushing off to Barcelona so quickly. I mumbled something about the street parties up and down the Ramblas side streets but was quickly interrupted.

"Huh! The Athens street parties are much better – you should stay – we will show you. Really," said Marika, clearly unimpressed by

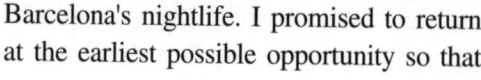 Barcelona's nightlife. I promised to return at the earliest possible opportunity so that

I could evaluate both and come to a fair and honest judgement.

Dimitri Uncle disappeared somewhere and returned bearing gifts, including a painting of a sailboat for my father and a Greek music CD for me, featuring Xaris Alexiou (although I didn't know what her name was then, since the cover was written in Greek script). Dimitri Uncle assured me I would love it and told me that she was very talented indeed, though from the looks on Sotos and Marika's faces it was apparent that this was a matter of opinion.

All too soon, my few hours in Athens were up and it was time to go. After several teary goodbyes and bear hugs, I left the house and Sotos drove me to the airport, stopping along the way to pick up his girlfriend. The last few days' lack of sleep and the after effects of lunch were conspiring to make me very, very drowsy and I just about made it on board the plane before passing out, much like the Afro-guy on the flight in. As I drifted off I remember thinking that while I had no recollection of them from twenty years ago, if there was any family I'd like to meet all over again, it would most certainly have to be the Demestikas.

Jamila, My Love

Deepa Ravi

"Camels! Camels!" I squealed like a little girl.

"Where...where...? Hey, stop the car, I have to take pictures!" screamed Sonia, our self-proclaimed photographer, as she battled with me for window space.

"C'mon guys, it's only a camel," said my husband from the drivers' seat, acting annoyingly grown up.

"If you don't stop the car NOW..." we threatened in chorus.

Minutes later we had tumbled out of the car and were taking pictures of the startled camel. He decided that we were too wild for him and stomped off towards the desert.

"Spoilsport!" we yelled after him and grumpily got back into the car, where my husband was giving us that 'I-told-you-so' look. But any words he intended to say were

128

silenced by our glares. We proceeded towards our pre-arranged meeting point with Ahmed.

When we reached the spot Ahmed was already waiting there, looking radiant in his traditional white kandura.

"Marhaba!" He smiled a welcome as we trooped out of our car. "If you will shift to my four-wheel drive, we can be on our way." He gestured to his battered pick-up. At the back, sat a haughty camel. She chewed ruminatively, and gave us all the once-over, much like those gum-chewing teenagers with oodles of attitude that one sees around these days.

"We travel in that?" I asked, sure that I had misunderstood.

"Yes...yes...that is a very good vehicle. Toyota. No broblem," he assured us in his Arabic-accented English.

"But what about that – thi... I mean the camel at the back? She will get off I hope," my husband sputtered, aghast.

"Jamila? No sir she will give no broblem. I have to take her to the gamp you see, for gamel rides tomorrow morning," Ahmed chirped nonchalantly, as though it was the most normal thing in the world to travel with a camel.

As we walked towards the vehicle, Jamila grunted and turned her face away.

"My! My! Miss Universe prefers to travel alone!" Sonia giggled.

To our further dismay, bundled on the back seat of the pickup was a big heap of vegetables. "Also for the gamp. If I keep it near Jamila, she will eat it," Ahmed explained, grinning sheepishly.

We ladies opted to sit at the back with the vegetables. We had a heated debate over whether the guys or the bags travel with Jamila. Finally Sonia settled it. "What if she pees on our bags?" she asked.

"Oh yeah? And what if she pees on us?" asked Babu, her husband.

"Well...you can bathe, can't you...?" I explained.

So the bags sat on the privileged front seat with Ahmed, and the guys cringed in a corner at the back as far away from Miss Universe as possible.

We were on our way! We were heading for a camp

in the Wahaiba Sands, the sandy desert in the heart of the Sultanate of Oman. We had driven down from the capital city, Muscat, to our rendezvous at a town called Sur. Now as Ahmed accelerated, the town receded into a speck of dirt on the horizon. Ahead we could see the outline of dunes and Sonia and I kept up an excited chatter. The men were quiet – we sniggered that they must be too busy gazing into Jamila's eyes!

Suddenly, Ahmed turned into a dirt track and there we were. Stretching ahead of us was miles and miles of silky sand. Ahmed steered the vehicle expertly on the sand, much to our admiration. Inspired, Ahmed accelerated, pausing only to put on a raunchy Arabic number on his rickety music system. Our entreaties to shut off the cacophony were smothered by the zealous Arab singer.

We gave up after a while and concentrated on the scenery. It was like being in a deep sea, except that instead of miles of water, all I could see was myriad shades of lovely brown. As we drove deeper into the desert, we lost all sense of direction and time.

Finally our camp came into view. Ten tents were arranged in a large circle. In the centre, a bonfire was ready to be lit up. Makeshift toilets stood a little distance away from the tents.

"This looks cosy!" I yelled to Sonia above the music. She nodded, looking equally thrilled. As soon as Ahmed stopped the vehicle we jumped out to inspect the camp.

"Wasn't that super?" I asked the guys.

"Excuse me...but next time *you* ride with Miss Universe here!" my irate husband burst out, "I was so tense. All through the journey she kept trying to sniff my backside. I had to keep wriggling out of the way. It was a good thing she was on a tight leash and could not get up or move."

We suppressed our giggles. But good humour was soon restored as we were escorted to the reception area (also a tent) and served khajur (dates) and kahwa (aromatic Arabic black coffee). This is the traditional Arab way of welcoming guests – we did indeed feel welcome and revived.

We dumped our bags in our cosy tent, which was lined with colourful sheep wool blankets to keep out the cold. We grabbed sand skis from the reception, from right under the nose of a small crowd of children who were looking wistfully at them, and set off into the desert. It was a challenge to climb the dune – the harder we stepped, the lower we sank into the sand. After struggling for over fifteen minutes, we were right where we started! At last we got the hang of it, and huffed and puffed our way to the top of the dune. For almost an hour we frolicked in the sand, gliding down, climbing up, gliding down, climbing up. Finally, exhausted, we handed over the skis to the sulking kids. "You should try it. It's great fun!" we advised, as they glared at us.

At sunset, we climbed to the tallest dune and sat breathless, drinking in the exquisite scenery. As the sun became an orange ball and the sand took on the hues of the setting sun, the whole place seemed to be glowing gold. A serene silence set in and we all watched spellbound as the sun made a spectacular exit.

We realised suddenly that it was very dark and very cold.

"Time to head back, guys," I declared shivering. In our enthusiasm to watch the sunset, we had not carried any woollies with us. Everyone got up slowly, reluctant to let go of the magical moment. By the time we got down, it was totally dark.

"Hey, which direction is the camp?" asked Sonia.

"I don't see any lights," I said, looking around, confused.

"Let's head back the way we came," said Babu wisely.

"Yes, but which way did we come? I'm totally disoriented!" My husband scratched his head, perplexed.

After some debate, we agreed to proceed in one direction, presumably that which would lead us to the camp. Our teeth were chattering as we struggled through the cold sand, which seemed intent on swallowing our feet.

"I don't know if this is the right direction, guys. You should have listened to me and walked the other way," I said.

A loud grunt was the sole response.

"Why are you grunting like a camel?" I asked, irritably.

"Run for your lives! It's Miss Universe! She's coming for us!" screamed my husband as he whizzed past us.

Startled we all turned... indeed there was a camel grunting and running towards us.

"How do you know its her? It could be another camel," asked Sonia irrelevantly.

"I would know her anywhere! She has the same demented look. In fact, look, she's headed straight for me...help!" My husband took off in panic.

Sure enough, Jamila was trying to bypass us and get around to him! The poor chap was running faster than he had ever run in his life. We started running too. If the situation hadn't been so serious it would have been seriously funny. Camel chasing man and all of us chasing the camel chasing the man!

My husband ran up a dune and we all puffed our way up as fast as possible. Much to our relief we saw the lights from our camp right below the dune.

"The dune was blocking our view. We have not wandered off too far," my husband shouted, relieved, and hurried down the slope. Jamila loped after him – but to our surprise she did not outrun him or harm him in any way – as she easily could have. We ran, slithered, slipped and rolled our way back to the camp and rushed to our tent.

"Oh there you are!" exclaimed Ahmed. "I was worried. Ah...I see that Jamila found you!" He smiled fondly at the animal. Ahmed led her away and we all heaved a collective sigh of relief.

We flopped down on the cosy carpets and there was silence while we caught our breath. Then I started giggling. Sonia joined in and Babu followed. We laughed so much that tears rolled down our eyes.

"She's in love with you!" we teased my husband. He refused to join in the laughter.

"Now I have real competition! There's another woman in your life!" I bellowed with laughter.

"Ya... ya... laugh all you want. You wouldn't be so

132

happy if she was trying to sniff *your* backside!"

Later, we stepped out by the bonfire, its flames warm and soothing.

"Hey make a wish! Shooting stars!" Sonia whispered. Sure enough, the night sky was blanketed with stars, some blazing a trail in the dark. We sat there by the dying fire, bundled in woollies, sipping hot soup and gazing at the stars. Finally, when the fire burnt out and it became too cold to stay outdoors, we reluctantly went back into our tent.

We woke up to a cold, crisp, mist-covered morning. Visibility was almost zero. We took a little walk around the camp, shivering in the cold, and watched as the golden glow of the sun chased away the mist and bathed the desert in glorious light. The exercise made us hungry and we ate a hearty breakfast of eggs and toast provided at the camp.

It was time then to go for our dune rides. This is what the guys had been waiting for! They climbed into the four-wheel drive like excited little children. The drive was absolutely mind-blowing. Ahmed skilfully drove the car perpendicular to the ground to the top of steep dunes and then brought it gliding down the sheer drop. We skidded around in the sand, drove on two wheels, careened off the top of the dunes – it was an incredible roller coaster ride.

And then, it was time for the camel rides.

My husband tried to sneak off to the tent. But we insisted that he ride.

"What's the point of coming to the desert and not riding a camel?" I asked.

Very grudgingly he agreed. "But I refuse to ride on Miss Universe," was his stipulation.

There were only two camels. Babu and Sonia took the first round and came back contented, albeit with sore legs. Then it was our turn.

I sat on Jamila while my husband rode on another camel. My husband waved goodbye as his guide steered his camel in another direction. Ahmed was guiding Jamila forward. But as my husband's camel went in the opposite direction Jamila stopped. She refused all entreaties from Ahmed to move forward. Suddenly she turned and started following the other camel. Startled, Ahmed managed to hold on to her reins. I was terrified – but Jamila was calm and sure-footed, so I tried to calm down too. As my husband's camel came into view, Jamila got excited. She quickened her steps and was soon right behind them. My husband, unaware of the peril, was gazing happily all around him. Finally, the grunts from behind made him turn and he let out an audible gasp.

"What is she doing here?" he exclaimed, almost falling off his camel.

Jamila edged closer as the other trainer tried to make his camel move faster. We decided to cut short our nerve-wracking ride. We headed back to the camp with Jamila staying stubbornly close on the heels of the other camel. At last, the camp came into view and we hastily dismounted and moved as far away from the camels as possible. Ahmed took a strip of cloth from his pocket and covered a scornful-looking Jamila's mouth, all the while scolding her in Arabic.

We left the scene and went to collect our bags for departure. Ten minutes later we were settled inside Ahmed's vehicle – minus Jamila this time...

As we bade goodbye to Ahmed, my husband asked him about Jamila's strange behaviour.

"Oh that... don't be angry sir. She is little excited on seeing you. When she like someone she like to bite his...umm...uhh...you know..." he stuttered uncomfortably.

"All she wanted was to give you a kiss...ummm...you know where..." I teased my husband as we drove back to Muscat.

"A teeny-weeny love bite..." Sonia joined in.

"Alright make me the butt of your jokes," said my husband, realising a little too late, as the car filled with the sounds of raucous laugher, that he had made the wrong choice of words.

Ennui in Erlangen

Aruna Nambiar

I remember the time a cold wave hit Mumbai. Mumbaikars, covered improbably in sweaters and shawls, formed little knots at coffee machines and in commuter trains, and mulled over the ravages of the cold – coughs, stuffy noses and raging fevers. For the first time in decades, fans and air conditioners lay unused, and blankets and hot water bottles took their place. The temperature had plummeted to a dizzying low of 16°C!

Even in Bangalore where I now live, single digit temperatures are as rare as orderly traffic. Of course, there are places in North India, the Himalayas for

135

example or even a Rajasthani desert night, which could rival a European winter and even teach it a thing or two, but they are places prudent people largely avoid and rarely experience. European winters, however, are omnipresent and inescapable, and for me, a tropical baby if there ever was one, I found my first winter in Germany singularly depressing.

By early November, the weather gods, awakening to the fact that winter was approaching and all these blue skies and sunny days were not the order of the day, sent down some of the foulest weather I had ever seen. The mornings dawned grey and gloomy, and clouds hung over the sleepy Bavarian town of Erlangen like a shroud. Parsimonious drizzles pattered down on the sidewalks. Gusts of wind dove past mufflers and gloves, and hungrily nibbled at exposed ears and noses. The colours of autumn were fast fading and leaves, shrivelled up with cold, fell in torrents from semi-clad trees.

My usual recreational activities – travelling and shopping – were beginning to take on the difficulty of Himalayan treks. Somehow, beautiful old buildings and pristine blue lakes don't thrill as much when there's a frigid draught dancing wildly down your clothes. And shopping was just an exercise in futility; hubby and I would pile on layer after layer of clothing, dart into the nearest shop to get out of the cold, fretfully peel off sweaters, jackets, gloves and mufflers in the furnace that was the heated interior, proceed to hang around browsing as long as we could without exciting suspicion and/or hostility, only to once again pull on sweaters, jackets, gloves and mufflers for the sprint to the next tropically heated establishment. Not fun, as you can imagine. As a result, travelling became non-existent, shopping rare and most of the winter was whiled away eating, sleeping and watching television.

To get cable television in Germany, you have to take out a great big wad of cash, buy a great big dish antenna and hook it up on your roof or in your balcony. We had a slight problem. We didn't have a great big wad of cash. Assuming that we did, our television could not accommodate more than thirteen channels. Yes, in this age of GPRS phones and biometrics, our house was equipped with a TV which had just thirteen channels, and whose screen was so small, that Raghu, aforementioned hubby, used his latest toy, a set of military binoculars, to watch the ball during tennis matches!

Of these thirteen channels, one was devoted to the only English channel – CNN, two were for sports and two for music – MTV and a Deutsche equivalent that played mind-addling trance and techno music almost incessantly. There were a handful of national and state channels, packed with news programmes, documentaries and the odd bout of German pop music. Last but not the least, were a clutch of private channels which would broadcast a range of entertaining and educational chat shows, dubbed American serials, agony aunt programmes and German soaps.

My initial instinct was to flip through the tried and tested American serials, but watching Jennifer Aniston repartee with Mathew Perry in a guttural German tone was a little more than I could bear, so I quickly graduated to a kaleidoscope of increasingly sordid German chat shows.

My first experience of a German chat show was one that featured a thinner, younger and infinitely more irritating version of Oprah Winfrey (and there goes my chances of being Author of the Month or whatever on her book club!). When I happened upon her, German Oprah, dressed in clogs that went out with the Spice Girls and a denim dress that held her not-quite-super-toned body in a loving clinch, was barking questions rapidly at uniformly unattractive and singly belligerent guests.

In retrospect, while said guests shouldn't have been unleashed on unsuspecting viewers without a face-lift or two and several coats of make up, I couldn't really blame them for being belligerent. The chat show producers, you see, had secretly videotaped them in various acts of indiscretion – here a lady cheating on her husband, there a man getting serviced by a prostitute. While the guests blustered with understandable indignation, GO as I was fondly beginning to think of her, harangued them with glee. Were there no privacy laws in this country, I wondered, and looked apprehensively around the room for miniature spycams.

On another chat show, a pretty young presenter stopped people on the streets of Munich, and requested them to drop their pants (or skirts or shorts) and display their underwear for the camera, which they did with compliant alacrity. I noticed that those who bulged and rippled in all directions were the ones who chose the skimpiest underclothing – thongs and sheer bras.

No, I am not pouncing on the one odd program to unfairly denounce German television. Much as I tried to prove otherwise, this seemed representative of Deutsche talk show content. On one, a man boasted about his prowess in the bedroom. On another, skimpily clad teens auditioned to become go-go girls at a nightclub while the spiky haired anchor looked on lasciviously. On a third...

"Why are you watching such rubbish?" Raghu asked, when he caught me at it.

"I'm trying to learn German," I retorted righteously. "This is the best way to pick up the language."

Nevertheless, I switched to watching news programmes – and was rewarded with even more interesting distractions. The news, you see, was never restricted to a dull round up of the day's events, but was liberally spiced with many general interest stories. Such as the interview with the topless model dressed in her work clothes. Or the chat with the blind man, who could tell your future from reading, or rather feeling, the lines on your behind, demonstration included. Actual stories I promise you, not on some seedy late-night spot, but on prime time television – wholesome entertainment for the entire family.

The late-night spots (which I watched only for the purpose of information and research, I maintain) ranged from soft porn flicks to educational documentaries, on topics such as a day in the life of a nudist family, or the shooting of a hard porn film where essentials were occasionally, and rather whimsically, blurred. And if you think I was getting any kind of thrill out of this, let me ask you this – have you ever watched a fifty year old woman in the buff eating breakfast while her equally bare, and aged, husband pours coffee? Yes, *you* try keeping your dinner down.

All this was quite a change for me. In India, a one-second peck in a Bollywood film incites mob fury and warrants reams of editorial pages. Here, on yet another show, men were being stopped on the street and invited to look at, and feel up, three topless girls to guess which of them had had silicone implants.

In all fairness though, there were some good shows. Most channels aired quiz programmes including German versions of Who Wants to be a Millionaire? and The Weakest Link. In an interesting programme called Kochduell, which I hasten to add means Cooking Competition, four chefs vied for top honours by cooking up gourmet meals with eclectic ingredients like say, a banana and a side of beef. There were documentaries and travel shows, which would have no doubt been more compelling, had I a better grasp of the language.

But above all, the most invaluable television programmes were the weather forecasts, available daily on almost every channel. In India, the weather is rarely an issue, being sunny for most of the year, and raining only in designated monsoon months. The forecasts therefore are perfunctory affairs, with a roundup of the maximum and minimum temperatures during the day and either a wildly inaccurate or a prudently non-committal prediction for the next. In Germany however, we were slaves to the vagaries of the weather – after all, if you were to set out in your shorts on a sunny morning and the wind suddenly started blowing, you could expect to return a human icicle. To my initial scepticism, followed by amazement, awe and finally, naked reverence, I found that German weather forecasts were detailed and highly accurate; if they said it was going to snow heavily in the middle of summer, you'd better dust off those winter clothes and snowshoes.

***

About the time Raghu discovered my predilection for German television, he came home with a piece of paper whose virulent pink hue was strangely reminiscent of Indian Railway timetables and digestive tablets.

"This looks interesting. Why don't you join?" he asked.

I looked at the sheet. A sketch of the Taj Mahal filled up half the page. Below was an exhortation to join a Frauengruppe.

"You want me to join a women's group?" I yelped.

"Why not? Aren't you bored sitting at home?"

"Not *that* bored."

I knew, though only from hearsay, what Indian associations abroad were like - and women's groups in particular. A gaggle of totally incompatible women and screaming kids, if any, would turn up at a hall once a month, each laden with their contribution to the meeting – samosas, vadas or some such thing, that had been painstakingly made after ransacking the supermarkets for Indian ingredients easily available in India, but often unheard of outside. They would proceed to sit on the edges of uncomfortable chairs and explore the boundaries of polite conversation, which would last the whole of five and a half minutes. They would pick at each other's homemade concoctions, choke a bit, then look up and compliment the manufacturer with bright, insincere smiles. After wiping their oily fingers, they would sit around grinning foolishly at each other, and wondering if they had already asked the person next to them where they stayed and how long they had been married. Occasionally, a fight would break out among the kids, providing a welcome distraction. About one hour into this charade, the first few brave ladies would start sidling out, remarking what a wonderful time they had had, thus signalling the end of an excruciating afternoon.

Raghu rolled his eyes when I propounded this theory. "Oh, please! Don't be so unsociable."

I had to admit that I was being rather misanthropic, but I had my reasons. Even in India I hadn't been the most gregarious of souls, but here I had become positively reclusive. When you've spent your whole life in a place, studied, worked, lived in the neighbourhood for aeons, you've had the time and liberty to choose your friends. Over the years, you discern the quirks and foibles of your associates and chums, and feel free, wherever possible, to sort the wheat from the chaff. But when you're thrown into the company of a handful of people, with whom the only things you have in common are the places of origin and current residence, as was the case in Erlangen, that freedom is severely restricted.

Here, the Indian ladies could broadly be classified into two categories. The first were what I've always thought of as desi Martha Stewart wannabes (pre-incarceration, of course); women who, having been in Germany for a while, took it upon themselves to guide and train the second category – viz. novices such as myself. They were generous with their advice – everything from where to buy groceries to how to protect the Indian ethos would meet with their wise counsel. They were unstinting with their help – they would rush to your side with homemade food when you were laid up in bed in your worst clothes or press on you loud Hindi movie DVDs that they had bought for an arm and a leg on an expedition to Nürnberg or Munich. They were excellent housewives, travelling miles to get just the right ingredient for that chicken curry and organising group embroidery sessions at home. They were everything I wasn't, and not wanting to be reminded of my inadequacies, I declined their – at first frequent, and gradually diminishing – invitations.

The novices and I exchanged notes on everything from our first feeble attempts to learn German to the best bargains available, from kitchen disasters to aches and pains brought on by housework. But one by one, they too were sucked into

141

the whirl of mutual visits and household activities (a fate I, being equipped with much inertia and little remorse, managed to avoid), till finally they transformed into desi Martha Stewarts themselves.

The circle of life, you could say.

***

Despite the diversions on television, with the sudden suspension of weekend trips and raids on the pre-Christmas sales, the days dragged interminably, so finally I resigned myself to taking up what I had been avoiding so long – viz. the study of German.

In preparation for my sojourn in the Fatherland, I had spent a couple of months mugging up German from a traveller's phrase book and by the time I boarded the flight for Frankfurt, I had begun to spout Guten Tags and Auf Wiederseh'ns with some expertise – or so I imagined. I was a bit shocked to discover therefore, that I couldn't understand a word of the German announcements on the Bangalore-Frankfurt Lufthansa flight.

On our first day in Erlangen, Raghu gallantly took me around to the local shop to explain the layout for future trips. I noticed with apprehension that everything from the Wasser to the Kaffee, and the Fisch to the Bier, and several unfathomable products in between, were labelled in German.

The next day, apparently taken in by my boasts of being something of a linguist, Raghu foisted a formidable grocery list on me.

"Just go around the corner and pick it up," he said, and I nodded intelligently.

A quick perusal revealed that the list included such exotica as detergents and window cleaners, which for the life of me, I couldn't begin to translate. My trusty phrase book, you see, had trained me well to talk about the weather, or to ask for directions in case I got lost and even covered the rudiments of how to flirt with a dark stranger in a hotel bar, but had left me rather ill-equipped on the grocery shopping front. It was a traveller's phrase book, after all, not a resident's phrase book. Travellers don't go around shopping for window cleaners, they just call up room service and say "Kellner, bitte reinen Sie mein Zimmer – Waiter, clean my room please." Or something to that effect.

I decided to take out the garbage instead. As I was struggling with the garbage bin lids, which didn't just lift up, like the average bin does, but had to be hoisted and jerked back, the forces working at an exact angle for the lid to slide open – a prodigy of a garbage bin, you could say – somebody startled me with a "Guten Morgen!" A man in an immaculate suit topped with a fluorescent orange jacket was grinning at me, while loading a garbage truck with plastic-gloved hands.

Back home in India, garbage men neither greet ladies, nor sport immaculate suits. I looked at him and try as I did, I couldn't remember what the appropriate response to the greeting was. I felt the colour rising to my cheeks and my ears burning in embarrassment, as I opened and closed my mouth a couple of times, and finally stuttered "Hello". I gave up the unequal struggle with the lids and abandoning my garbage by the side of the bin, I beat a quick retreat.

"Tschüs! Bye!" I heard him call. I accelerated around the corner and up the stairs, and only when I was back in the house with the door firmly shut behind me did it come back to me that the appropriate answer to the greeting was – you guessed it – a reciprocal "Guten Morgen".

Shaken, I spent the rest of the day indoors terrified to move out in case of repeated humiliation. Raghu had bread for dinner that night, and the night after, and after, till finally on the fourth evening he turned up laden with groceries and sporting a long-suffering frown. The garbage lay piled up for a couple of days until, unable to ignore the insistent fragrance from under the sink, I scurried out to the backyard, miraculously opened the bin, trashed the bag, scrambled back home and shut the door, thankful that I had not bumped into any German-speaking soul.

On another tentative foray outside, I was accosted by a cleaning lady. "Guten Morgen," she said, and prepared this time, I replied, beaming, "Guten Morgen."

Encouraged, she threw down her vacuum cleaner, abandoned her mop, detergent and assorted brushes, and settled in for a chat. I answered her barrage of incomprehensible questions with increasingly expansive and desperate shrugs, her response to which was to repeat them in louder and more pained tones, in the manner of a schoolteacher addressing the class dunce. Finally, I turned tail and ran, leaving behind a very puzzled cleaning lady who, no doubt, would go home and tell all her friends of the strange Indian woman she had met.

I cracked under the strain a few days later. Here I was, walking down the street, with my head down and eyes averted, minding my own business, when a car screeched to a halt beside me. A man jumped out, and pointing to a map and letting loose a volley of German, asked me for directions! Me, the only brown face in ten square miles, sporting a look of pure bewilderment and wearing clothes that were no doubt la mode back home but looked definitely out of place here. I gave him a filthy look, and hurried on, not even bothering to embark on my elaborate routine of shrugs and stutters.

I finally gleaned the movements of everyone in the building, by watching out of the window and listening by the door for the comings and goings of cleaners, garbage collectors, newspaper boys and neighbours. The garbage truck and the cleaners came and went in the morning, kids came home from school around lunchtime, families went out for walks and playtime in the late afternoon, and people came home from work from early evening onwards. I figured that if I dashed out of the house between 2 and 3 pm, skulked down by-lanes and avoided eye contact, I could safely spend the rest of my days in Erlangen without a single attempt at speaking German.

But ennui is a powerful motivator, making one do things one really shouldn't. So six months later, as the mercury dipped and the wind howled, and the rain hammered against the windowpanes, I toiled over German vocabulary and pronunciation, and bled, sweated and wept over grammar.

For English speakers, German is really quite a simple language if you ignore the grammar. English, everyone will tell you, is a cousin of German, and the similarities are evident. For one thing the alphabet is the same, but for a few ö's and ü's here and there (those dots above the vowels are called umlauts by the way). German pronunciation is a breeze if you remember to pucker your lips for the umlauts, silence your j's, pronounce z as ts, and s as z, v as f, w as v, and pretend to clear your throat for the "Ach"s.

The vocabulary is startlingly similar to English at times, and almost hilariously logical as one progresses. To give you an idea, the German words for to send, to bring, to sink are senden, bringen, sinken. Taking it a step further, the German words for to rain, to snow, to help, the sun and apple are respectively regen, schneen, helfen, Der Sonne, Apfel – you see the connection?

Once you master the basic vocabulary, all you do is break up the big words and work out what they mean literally and you'll pretty much be able to guess their meaning. For instance, punktlich literally translates to point-like and means punctual. Fertigmachen or ready-make means to prepare. Mitkommen, or with-come, translates to accompany. And, my personal favourite, Magersucht, or stomach craze, means anorexia. Easy, hmm?

German grammar on the other hand, is torturous, incomprehensible and insurmountable. If you are willing to believe the probably inaccurate words of a very confused beginner, here's a summary of what you can expect.

Just for starters, every noun in the language is classified, very randomly I may add, as masculine, feminine or neuter. I could never understand why Fräulein was neuter while

145

Frau was feminine or why Deutschland was masculine and Turkeii was feminine.

Next, articles. When attaching articles to nouns, you have to keep in mind the gender, number and usage of the noun. Articles attached to masculine nouns are different from those attached to feminine nouns; singular articles differ from plural articles and even within the same sex group, articles show a mercurial nature depending on whether the noun is used as an object, a subject, a possessive object or an indirect object. And these are just the definite and indefinite articles – *twenty-eight* distinct permutations for the English equivalent of 'the' and 'a'!

Moving on, pronouns. One look at the relevant pages will reveal that you will have to wrestle with not just personal pronouns, but relative, indefinite, intensive, reflexive, demonstrative and interrogative ones too, each with their own unique permutations and combinations. Skipping relevant pages hastily...

...turn to next lesson – adjectives. If you want to say 'the good man' there are four ways to do it depending on the usage of the noun. Four ways to say 'a good man.' Four ways to say 'a good woman' and another four ways to say 'the good woman'! And when you think you're over the worst, there are the infamous strong and weak verbs, constructed without a dot of logic and changing with tense and person.

Final stop, a couple of stiff drinks later: sentence construction. I've never figured it out (perhaps it was the stiff drinks) but tell me, what can you say about a language where your sentences read so, and I quote from my notes:

John was by the pretty young Priscilla in decisive way very quickly chosen.

He has his mother work help.

She had the painter paint see.

Convert to the belief that if you don't succeed the first time, be smart enough to give up, I threw in the towel. Thereafter, whenever I worked up the courage to speak

German, I constructed my sentences in the most logical English way. I'm sure I amused many an Erlangener, but I must say they were smashing about it.

That is what surprised me the most about Germany. There's this perception of Germans as an unfriendly, uni-lingual lot and while they are uni-lingual – in thought and action if not in actual prowess – I've rarely come across the unfriendly types. Of course, most of them expect that you learn their language if you plan to make their country your residence – fair enough, surely? Try speaking German in France or England! Some of the older Germans are even a little surprised to learn that there *are* other languages in the world, but most of them are thrilled to see a foreigner attempt to speak German, and will warm to you instantly if you try – no matter how badly you abuse their mother tongue. Ah, a wonderful country, after all...

Baba Lepwalle

Mahendra Rathod

"You must go to Baba Lepwalle," said Rajwade, "he's a miracle worker. He cured my back pain! And both Shirish and Nikhil, who work for me, had incurable knee problems. Two months of lep and they were cured. " Seeing me hesitate, he added, "Try it. I too was a reluctant first timer."

Against the backdrop of our own despairing search for a remedy, we were powerless to refuse. I have always had my difficulties accepting strange cures, but Naina, my wife, is an evolved soul who looks at everything with a fair amount of openness. I am learning to be open, so I said, "Yes, let's try the lep." I had read that some lep mixtures, herbal pastes that act as poultices, have the power to draw out 'poison' – the things that cause pain.

Naina and I had arrived in India in early August to spend a month with family, complete some necessary chores and generally soak up India. This 'soaking up'

148

was a recent phenomenon; age seemed to have introduced a strange virus into our systems: homesickness. It sneaked up insidiously as the decreasing returns of joy and engagement from material comforts started to become evident.

Two days after landing in Mumbai, Naina's ankles and feet became mysteriously swollen. We thought – flight-related, it will go away – and treated it with the usual home remedies. When, after four days, the ache showed no sign of abating and in fact worsened, we became worried. A visit to the family doctor brought reassurances but no cure. This was followed up by visits to experts. Each new expert wanted X-rays, ultrasound scans, Doppler scans and so on, in the confidence that the test would somehow give a Eureka kind of diagnosis endorsing his expertise. No such luck. We were tossed from expert to expert and our anxiety and frustration grew exponentially. One month went by; by then, Naina was limping severely.

We decided nevertheless, to make our usual trip to Pune – a place we had decided to make our home after we returned to India. Pune was ideal by our calculations; we both were fluent in Marathi, the language of Pune; we liked the easy laidback mindset of the Puneite and the many activities on offer in the city. It was also a place where I could indulge my great passion – golf. Our Pune trips were routine by now – to visit our mothers who lived alone and to clean up and check our vacant apartment. It was our brief reconnect with something 'homely' and a time to ponder the big question: 'Is it time for us to come back to India?' We always convinced ourselves that a few more years outside India was fine. We needed India; but we needed comfort more.

September that year was gorgeous – cool, cloudy and inviting – so we decided to stay longer than usual in Pune. Our itinerary was a perfected routine: have the apartment cleaned, check it for any leakages, enjoy the cool peace of Pune, meet the Ravals – our lovely neighbours, who would

149

entreat us to return to India ("How long are you going to make money?" was the refrain), and finally wind up and return to Mumbai.

I had been meaning to meet up with old friends – each trip I made a new resolution for the next trip – but had been too busy to make any moves. I justified it by thinking: our trips are too short. This year, with time available, I decided to search for some of my old college friends, if I could locate them after thirty odd years. After many false attempts and running into some irate false calls, I managed to locate a dear old classmate: Rajwade, who I hadn't met in the thirty years since graduating. I had known he had done well in the private sector and had gone on to become a successful entrepreneur. When I called him up he was thrilled to hear from me and we agreed to meet in the evening after his noon siesta.

Rajwade turned up that afternoon, wearing open-toed sandals and chewing gutka. Chewing tobacco had become something of a rage in India. Time has a dual character. Real time ages you, gives you double chins and makes you bald. Memory time has a strange compressible character; everything seems like yesterday, near enough to relive it vividly. It took me a fraction of a minute for this image to catch up with my memory of him, but when that was done he was the same except for a balding pate and a handlebar moustache. His appearance was a bit of a surprise because subconsciously I had put him down as a suit-boot fellow.

Rajwade wanted to show off his own chemical company. We drove in his Maruti, Rajwade holding the wheel with one hand while the other hand took care of the cigarette dangling from his lips, his insistent mobile phone and the changing of gears. I looked for a seat belt – there was none. I held tightly on to the armrest.

Rajwade was quite oblivious of several near misses.

"Pune traffic is like this only," he said indicating that he was a skilled driver, which he probably was.

We reached his office, a two-storey building in an outlying part of Pune. It was his mini factory and warehouse as well. "My main factory is on the Pune-Bangalore road," he said, "we'll go there tomorrow." I could see he had achieved quite a lot in thirty years. More importantly, he seemed contented.

We climbed the stairs to enter his office. It had a steel desk and a chair in one corner and a huge photo of Swami Samarth, a revered saint, along one wall.

"My guru and protector," Rajwade said. He took some oil from a bottle and lit the lamps near the image. He lit some agarbatti, recited a small prayer and paid homage. Then he put vibhuti on his forehead and came and sat cross-legged on the chair, across from me. "Swami helped me spiritually, when, some years ago, I was in deep trouble in my business," he explained.

He called his assistant and asked him to fetch a cigarette and get us two cups of piping hot tea. He invited us for dinner, but preoccupied with Naina's pain, I thought I had better decline. I explained Naina's problem and our worries and helplessness. He listened attentively, stared at me for an embarrassingly long while and then asked, "Are you willing to try an unorthodox method?"

"Sure, I'll try anything," I answered with not much hope of an acceptable unorthodoxy.

That's when he told me about the Baba and his Lep treatment. It had worked so well that he had never had the problem again, touch wood.

"Touch wood," I intoned.

I called up Naina and we agreed we would give it a try. We were there for a short stay, and Baba's treatment normally took three to four weeks at the minimum, but we were told that even one or two leps had worked at times. We set out for Narayanpur, the Baba's village, the next Thursday, with Nikhil and Shirish who planned to pray at the beautiful Lord Datta's temple there, as they did every week.

"How far?" I asked, dreading the answer, since long road journeys in India gave me the jitters.

"Not far," Rajwade answered, "just two hours drive."

I knew from experience that the average Indian's time estimate was always optimistic. We finally set off at 2 pm instead of noon as planned. Rajwade stayed back to make room for us in the back seat. As I am 5' 9" and Naina is 5' 7", both Nikhil and Shirish kindly offered to pull up their seats. It meant Shirish had his knees against the glove compartment and poor Nikhil had the steering against his chest but we accepted the generosity rather selfishly.

The road out from the centre of Pune is quite busy, but we were completely unprepared for the highway. It was bursting at the seams, with heavy trucks competing ferociously with daredevil car drivers, overtaking each other with a timing precisely calibrated with merely a nanosecond to spare, to avoid head-on collision and certain death. Nikhil was no exception. We swerved from side to side and braked hard every hundred yards as we tried to squeeze back into our lane between two trucks whose drivers, reflected in the side mirror, were laughing gleefully at us amateurs, I could swear.

Naina was unruffled, taking in the unfolding landscape as we left Pune and headed south. After half an hour's mad driving there was a semblance of order on the road. I commented on the width and the quality of the road. "This is the grand plan of Vajpayee," said Nikhil, turning 180 degrees to look us in the eye. My heart missed a beat as I saw two trucks fighting to overtake each other on the opposite side.

"Nikhil, look out!" I cried, trying to control my fear.

"No problem. Relax," was his nonchalant reply.

After about an hour's driving we turned off the highway and started climbing a steep hill. After the heavy rains that year, the hills were lush and green and thin wisps of clouds were floating across the peaks like the agarbatti smoke I had seen wafting across Swami Samarth's image in Rajwade's office. The sudden absence of humanity and its appendages was such a contrast from the highway, and the silence so

152

all-pervasive that it was as though the ubiquitous public loudspeaker had been turned off in the middle of the night.

We continued to climb, with Nikhil and Shirish taking turns to tell us stories about several temples in the area and their unique histories. Of late we had become interested in old temples with their rich heritage and folklore. "Narayanpur used to have a Lord Shiva temple, which was very old and famous, and had wonderful powers," said Nikhil doing his 180-degree neck turn. We were travelling, no slower, on a small, winding, semi-tar road with wicked bends and a drop of several hundred feet on one side. "This temple is wonderful, it seems to reach out and talk to you," continued Shirish. I decided to direct all my questions henceforth to him – that way Nikhil could keep his eyes on the road.

"How do people manage a living in such a remote place?" Naina asked.

"Well they farm and keep some for themselves and sell the rest."

"Don't they want to come to Pune and work?" said Naina.

"Why? They are very happy where they are." I wondered if I could live in such remote and lonely places.

We climbed some more and reached a peak. "We will now descend for a while and then climb again," said Nikhil, not turning around as if he had sensed my fear. "There...... you can see the temple," he said pointing to a temple dome with a spire in the distance.

"Baba sits there on Thursday, taking care of those who come to him," said Shirish. "We are in good time".

"The Shiva temple has been here for two hundred years and it had wonderful powers, but recently, some ten or fifteen years ago, there was a discovery of a swayambhu murti of Lord Datta and a decision was made to build a new temple to house that murti," he continued.

Swayambhu murti, I learned, is an idol that according to mythology, appears on its own –

that is, it is discovered during excavation or a mudslide or tilling the land. This is considered an auspicious sign that the deity wants to be discovered and wants to make a home there. The new temple had drawn away the traditional local worshippers and the Shiva temple wasn't as busy anymore.

We kept climbing and the scenery became almost unbearably beautiful for a desert dweller like me. Not a single hut or village along the way. We did meet a few cars and some heavy motorcycles, the preferred option of the farmer, as they are more fuel efficient and manoeuvrable on the goat-track type of roads.

Finally, we reached the village of Narayanpur; a small collection of mud houses and shops and two temples – a typical farming and temple town. The shops were all selling offerings to Gods and blaring cassettes of prayers and bhajans, no doubt in the notion that the devotees needed cajoling to buy. And of course there were eateries, now mandatory everywhere in India. To eat out is de rigueur.

"Baba sits until late, so he should be here," said Nikhil as he parked in front of the Shiva temple. We got out, cracking every joint. The temple was about ten feet below road level with stone steps that looked as if they had been in use for hundreds of years – even granite can be worn out by centuries of rubbing by the soles of naked feet. The temple stood at the back of a long courtyard. A few sadhus sat silently under large peepul trees. Who, I wondered, had the brainwave of building a temple in this remote a place? It did look serenely beautiful with the setting sun as a backdrop. For us it was our temple of hope.

We sat at a bench near the entrance, removing our Reeboks. Nikhil came out of the temple "Baba has gone off as there were not many people today."

"What do we do?" I asked.

"Not to worry, we will go to his house. He also treats there."

We drove ten minutes up a hill to Baba's place. The village was a cluster of four

154

houses, made of mud and cow dung. Smoke rose from the chimneys as the women prepared dinner. A flimsy pole provided support to a power cable, and another pole supported telephone wires.

Already there were three cars and several people waiting outside Baba's house. A group had come all the way from Andhra Pradesh, many hundreds of miles away, which surprised me. We nodded to each other, each one enveloped in a mixture of hope and despair. Twenty minutes later, a group of breathless kids ran up to us and announced that Baba was coming. He arrived in a few minutes with a small entourage in tow. His stocky frame was dressed in a white pyjama and shirt and a Nehru cap – the typical attire of rural Maharashtra. He appeared quite homely and did not display any air of self-importance.

He moved us all to a larger house at the back, where we waited on the chairs outside as Baba started his consultations one by one. A naked light bulb swaying in the wind relieved the engulfing darkness. A few specks of light could be seen in the direction of Narayanpur. The rest was dark hilly farmland.

I was impressed to find that a healer with divine powers was venerated as a healer, not as divine. No one touched his feet. I was told he grew his own herbs and the secret was in what he picked and how he mixed them. And importantly, he could transmit healing energy through his hands.

When it was Naina's turn we were called inside. A huge steel bed occupied half the small room. Kids played on the bed. We could hear women talking and laughing in the kitchen next door whilst they cooked. I sat on the one chair. Baba sat on the ground with a pot of poultice and some waxy cream. He asked Naina to sit on a small stool. He examined her ankle. He held it with his large hands and closed his eyes. After a while he opened them and started applying the lep with a spatula. When the ankle and foot was all covered with the poultice, he applied the brown waxy material to the edges. "To hold the cotton," he told me, perhaps sensing lots of questions hanging in the air. Finally, he covered the paste with swathes of thin cotton roll. "To allow it to breathe," he said.

Seeing the simplicity of it all, Naina asked me whether she should tell him about the knee as well which was also aching. Why not, I said. We were all shooed out of the room and he called up his wife to help Naina remove her salwar. Naina came out ten minutes later with instructions not to bathe for a day to allow the paste to set. We had told Baba that we could not come again as we were visitors. He said one visit would not work, but no harm trying.

We thanked the Baba. I asked him how much I owed him. "Nothing at all, I do it because it is God's will. I am just a conduit," he said, "Faith does the healing." I had struggled all my life to include faith in my belief system. But rational thought is a strong sceptic, a barrier to unbridled acceptance of faith. Baba bade us goodbye and asked Nikhil to be careful on the road back. Nikhil and Shirish were still perky but we were tired. Naina dozed off as soon as we were back on level ground and hit the main road. I was kept awake because Nikhil was driving even faster with less traffic on the road and the desire to reach home quickly.

The next day Naina felt miraculously well. We were astounded. Thinking it was a placebo effect, we decided to wait and see. But Naina was feeling even better the second day. There was something to it after all, I thought. We stayed for a week and took three more leps. By the time we returned to Dubai, Naina was ecstatic. She did have pain but it was manageable. She could walk freely.

We had eight months of heavenly relief. But alas, it did not last. The pain was back slowly and she was soon back to square one. Rajwade had said we needed to stay for three months to cure such a big problem. But we did not have three months. We had to manage with a partial cure.

It is now precisely two years since we saw the Baba. The pain is still there though managed by strong medicines. If we had three months, we would go again and try what had worked for half a year.

Taxi!

Sarita Mandanna

Where would I be without cabs? Probably stuck haplessly at home, wondering how to get from Point A to Point B. Maybe I exaggerate, but there is no denying the fact that as someone who has yet to – officially – learn to drive, cabs are an integral part of my existence.

Why only cabs? The beginning of this long love affair can be traced back to a wild auto-rickshaw ride one wintry evening in Delhi. Spanish class had ended, there was some mix-up with the car, and I found myself stranded and shivering near Bhartiya Vidya Bhavan. I flagged down a solitary auto, and as we bumped along towards South Avenue, the rickshawwalla, a young Benarasi, started chatting. He had run away from home, he confided. Life was so much more exciting here than in sleepy old Benares. What a city Dilli was, you never knew what lay around the next corner! Did he miss his family, I asked. He fell silent, then abruptly turned around to look at me, grinning widely.

"Would you like to go faster?" Partly alarmed at his no-eyes-required-on-the-road-ahead policy, partly guilty at reminding him of family left behind, and mostly because I am a speed-junkie idiot,

"Yes," I replied.

Benarasi gripped the auto's handles, honked its little horn and took off. We shot past Curzon Road and up Mansingh Marg, whizzed past India Gate and screamed up Rajpath, the rickshaw straining at its joints. I clung to the backseat for dear life, shaken, rattled and rolled, but laughing nevertheless, caught up in the sheer optimism of it all, traffic cops be damned. Somewhere in the back of my mind, as the Benarasi jumped red lights in gay abandon, and squealed towards Rashtrapati Bhavan, I did realise dimly that I could die.

Nothing untoward happened however – fortune does favour fools – and I reached safely home. The Benarasi and I both laughing out loud, exhilarated by the wind in our hair, the sheer good fortune of not a single bus running us over, Horn OK Please.

Blithely avoiding driving school, I traded rickshaws for taxis in Bombay. I would step gingerly into them, manoeuvring broken door handles and lopsided windows, and we would sometimes chat, the drivers and I.

There was the Allahabadi who grumbled that people here could not speak Hindi. Why did they call potatoes batata? Didn't they know it was aloo? And really, what was with the kothmir? Dhania, it was dhania! There was the sweaty, disgruntled driver who wanted to know if my office had A/C? It did? Did I know, he snapped, that his skin was really coloured as light as mine? That sitting by the hot engine day after day had scorched it black?

There was the elderly gentleman in a neatly pressed shirt and trousers. When I complimented him on his spotless cab, he smiled gently. "What is work," he asked, "if you don't take pride in it?" He had gone to the Gulf many years ago, to make a living driving the Government taxis there. It had been good money, he had sent his sons to engineering college, and got two daughters married. He had retired last year and returned to Bombay, but life at home was terribly dull. So he had started working again, doing what he knew best: driving a taxi. His

158

children were embarrassed. What was the need, they asked, didn't they have enough money now? But why should he feel discomfited? "Imaandaari ki rozi hain, kisi ka jeb to nahin kaata." It was an honest living, and one he was thankful for. No, he would drive as long as he was able.

In Dubai, there were glimpses of the other side of his story. There was the burly Pathan who sang a raw, haunting song in Pushtu as he drove his taxi. He talked dreamily of the beautiful bride waiting for him in their mountain village. Her name, he said, meant a 'waterfall of flowers'. There was the Pakistani who had the most exquisite piece of embroidery dangling from his mirror. When I complimented him on it, he said shyly that his wife had given it to him when he went home last year. "She told me that she made every stitch taking my name. That as long as I hang it in my taxi, I will have good luck."

There were Keralites and Sri Lankans, all with similar stories of chasing the Gulf Dream, of parents, wives and children left behind. Each dreaming of returning home, of striking it rich at the lottery, of making enough money to send children to schools, to build new roofs, to buy a TV.

And then there was the Pathan who was horrified I was not married as yet, at the ripe old age of twenty-one. What were my parents thinking, Ya'Allah, sending me to work? No fiancé even, not a betrothal in sight? Shaking his head, he refused to take the fare from me.

"Sister," he said sorrowfully, "Sister, I simply cannot."

Gradually, these mini-conversations have become a habit. Years have passed. I have lived in four different countries. I still do not drive. It must be karmic coincidence then, for me to end up in New York, a city so unabashedly immersed in cab culture.

They come here from the subcontinent and the Middle East, from Latin America and Ethiopia, driving cabs for a living, forming the backbone of this City. They

159

drive like the City herself might, impatient and unapologetic. Ferrying ulcerous Wall Streeters and ladies-that-lunch, couples on first dates and grandparents in their Sunday best, tony Upper East Siders and multi-tattooed teens, a dizzying mélange of passengers up, down and across this town.

Ignoring the all-important rule of any dyed-in-the-wool New Yorker – Do *Not* Initiate Eye Contact – I strike up conversations. "Where are you from?" I ask. There was the Punjabi from Pathankot. Did I know where that was, he asked hesitantly, and was thrilled when I told him that not only did I know the place, but that I had actually been to his town. For the remainder of the ride, we waxed nostalgic about Pathankot's chhole bature; spicy chhole in peepal-leaf cups and crisp, chewy bature, with just the right tang of buttermilk.

There was the elderly Pakistani who told me about his mother. As a child, he never understood why his mother cried so much. He would look on impatiently as she and her cronies huddled together on charpoys, talking and weeping over endless cups of tea. Much later she told him her story. Her village had been massacred during the Partition. The villagers, seeing the approaching mob, had hastily banded the children together and hidden them in the fields. The children had run blindly through field after field, holding hands and completely losing their bearings. When they were finally discovered, they found themselves in a strange village, on the other side of the border, irrevocably far from home. They made new lives for themselves here, married the local men, took on new names and a new religion. The women would gather together from time to time, and remember old festivals, people long dead, a village forgotten. "My friends are my only link to my childhood," his mother had mourned. "When we die, our memories are gone, entire lives lost forever."

I sat silent in his cab, watching the lights and sounds of the East Village flash by, couples walking hand in hand, laughter spilling onto the sidewalks. "She died

160

last month," he told me, "still dreaming of the guava trees of her childhood."

There was the young Sardarji who took me up the wrong avenue when I was in a hurry – and in peak traffic too. "No, no, Sixth Avenue!" I exclaimed, but it was too late. Rookie cab drivers! I was reaching irritably into my wallet when he stopped me. He would not take any money he said, I was from his country and like a sister. Now, this happens often enough with desi cab drivers, and one accepts the gesture but insists on paying the fare – a convenient solution that leaves both driver and passenger happy. No matter what I said this time however, the cab driver merely shook his head. There was no way he could accept money from a sister. I made it in good time for my meeting, ashamed at my earlier impatience, strangely touched and smiling.

There was the gentleman who single-handedly ensured I made it to my sister's wedding. I was late leaving work, it was rush hour and the highway to JFK was backed up. Close to tears and clutching my pounding head, I begged the cabbie to go faster. "What time is your flight?" he asked and looked thunderstruck when I replied. Without another word, he swung off the highway and into Astoria. Greek restaurants, white-doored houses and grandmothers walking little girls flashed by in a whirl of Popsicle colours. We whizzed up and down back streets, wove in and out of traffic and made it to the terminal in the very nick of time. He brushed off the extra tip. "You are fortunate you found me," he said. "It was your kismat. I live here, near the airport and know these alleys like the back of my hand."

Then there are the crazies. Like the cab I hailed one evening, after a friend's birthday celebrations that had carried on fairly late. I was gazing quietly out of the window when the cabbie demanded to know if I had completely forgotten my culture.

"Excuse me?" I said startled. Yes, yes, I had heard right, he barked. That was the problem with all these desi girls; they came here, to phoren, and forgot

161

their culture. Roaming around at night without any shame, I was a disgrace! I laughed it off at first – prudent policy in NY – but when he kept burbling on, I snapped at him to mind his own business. "Just drive and get me home," I told him, "you are older, like an Uncle, and I do not want to get into an argument with you."

We drove on in festering silence. When we reached my apartment, he turned around for one final salvo and I braced myself.

"You can say anything you like," he said bitterly, "but do I look so old that you had to call me Uncle?"

There have been Ethiopians who told me how similar their culture was to ours – "We respect old people, yes?" Latinos astonished that I was not Puerto Rican, Egyptians telling me how much they loved Amitabh Bachhan in their country and asking me if I would marry them. No? Was I sure? What about the next life then? There were the second-generation desi cabbies, nattily dressed and making clubbing plans on their cell phones for when their shifts end. There were academics and high-school drop-outs, sailor-mouths and opera lovers, new arrivals still talking of returning 'home' and long-timers with wives, children, brothers and parents all gradually brought over to this new country.

And then there was the cabbie who was convinced that I am Sridevi.

"Don't you remember me Madam?" he asked. "Last year, from the New Jersey show, I was your car driver?" I looked blankly at him. "Madam," he continued, grinning happily, "You are Sridevi Madam, no?"

"No!" I exclaimed. I mean, the lady is undoubtedly lovely, but given the significant difference in our ages, this was not exactly a compliment.

"You can tell me, madam," he urged, "I know it is sometimes difficult with fans and all, but I was your driver Madam. You are Sridevi Madam?"

"I am not, I am not, I am not!" I cried.

162

Looking hurt, he subsided. I looked pointedly out of the window for the rest of the ride, resolutely ignoring him even as he tried to catch my eye. As I was handing over the fare, he turned around once more. "Madam," he whispered conspiratorially, "you are Sridevi Madam, no?"

So it goes, day after day, our paths crossing randomly for ten or fifteen or thirty minutes. When we talk, it is of politics and movies and food, of places left behind and faces that are missed. It is an immigrant glue that binds us together, however loosely, and I peep fleetingly over their shoulders. Open a cab door and step briefly into someone else's life, wonder at other roads travelled.

And now, in a bizarre instance of life having come full circle, there is a brand new mode of transport in the City. Cycle rickshaws have taken a recent bow, thumbing an eco-friendly nose at honking cabs and over-heated subways. I stare bemused as one swings past me, a blond, soccer-legged rickshawalla pulling two perfectly coiffed matrons carrying crocodile handbags. In a flash, I am transported across continents, back to the cycle rickshaws of Delhi University. To rickety, smoke-spewing autos, a wintry evening, and one exuberant Benarasi. I wonder where he is. I gaze at the disappearing lights on the rickshaw as it passes down the block, and send up a silent prayer. Wherever he may be, I hope he is happy, his spirit still stubbornly free.

On Top of the World

M R Shetty

After my unforgettable voyage to Antarctica in 1993, it seemed not just obvious, but inevitable to plan a trip to the Arctic. While I had visited Antarctica with the main aim of photographing penguins, this time my goal was more geographic. I wanted to visit the North Pole.

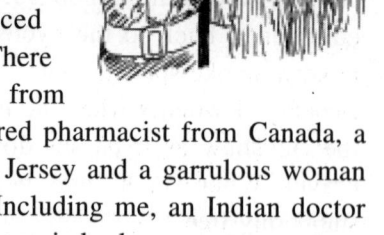

I joined a team of like-minded explorers in Edmonton, Canada on the 27th of April 2000. In the evening, our team of Arctic explorers met for the first time. Our team leader, a smart young man who had set up a Seattle-based adventure-travel company, introduced himself and the rest of our group. There were just seven of us: a neurologist from Italy, a German businessman, a retired pharmacist from Canada, a well-travelled accountant from New Jersey and a garrulous woman with her nervous husband in tow. Including me, an Indian doctor living in Chicago, it was a diverse group indeed.

Our team leader ran us through the itinerary and the precautions to be taken for the trip. We were to tour the northernmost bits of Canada at first, stopping at little settlements on the way to experience how the locals, or the Inuit, lived. We would make a detour to Greenland to take in some of its breathtaking scenery before flying back to Canada. Finally we would attempt to touch the North Pole. We were all excited at the prospect; I had even got a flag made which proclaimed 'North Pole!' for that fateful moment.

The next day we flew to Resolute Bay on Cornwallis

164

Island, a former World War II base with a local population of just two hundred! It was evening by the time we reached, but we had hours of Arctic sunlight ahead of us, so soon after we dropped our luggage at the local inn, we piled into a van and were taken out to survey the island. The village was small and neat, with a church and healthcare centre, and the little huts of the Inuit made of whalebones that dotted the snow-covered landscape.

The next day, we all climbed into a Twin Otter, a twenty-seater airplane fitted with skis, and flew to Ellesmere Island in dreadful weather, foggy and dark. Sitting right behind the cockpit, I watched worriedly as the pilot and co-pilot concentrated on the controls. When we finally landed, the airplane humming like a buzzing beehive, we all clapped in relief.

Ellesmere Island, Canada's northernmost community was formed in 1953, when two families from Quebec and one from Pond Inlet settled here. A tiny village, it rests on a narrow beach at the foot of the two thousand feet high Griese Fjord and looks over the spectacular Baffin Bay. From April to August, the sun shines throughout the day and then, after months of darkness, the sun reappears in the second week of February. The sea is frozen for ten months of the year and temperatures can fall to -30°C in the height of winter. Even today, in late April, it was bitingly cold and I was glad for the layers of clothing that I had pulled on.

On the last day of April, we took off for Qaanaaq. We were kept absorbed by the pilot who told us, among other things, that thanks perhaps to the perennial sunshine or darkness depending on the season, the local Inuit community have a different sense of time; adults think nothing of playing hooky from work to go hunting for days at a stretch, and you could often find children playing outside at three in the morning.

Ninety minutes and over two hundred miles later, we flew over the Greenland coast; large open expanses of blue water, pockets of floating ice, breathtaking icebergs and stark mountains, their faces lined by the paths of past glaciers. Qaanaaq village's multi-coloured roofs were clearly visible perched on the mountainside, and as the plane skied to a halt, it appeared that the whole town had gathered around to greet us. Before we could feel too self-important, we were told that it was a holiday and we had just interrupted a sports day on the ice. We struggled up a hill to our hotel, neat but small, with two beds per room and barely enough space to set our bags down.

The next afternoon we were treated to a ride on a dogsled – in true Arctic style. We boarded three dogsleds between us and the dogs took off, straining at their leashes with eagerness, but quickly towing the line with a sharp crack of the Inuit driver's whip. The snow-covered ground made for a bumpy ride and balancing the camera in one hand and holding on for dear life with the other, I was in an unenviable position.

All was well until, on the way back from visiting an iceberg fifteen miles away, the sled hit a bump. Camera and I rolled into the snow. I tried to struggle to my feet as the sled behind us bore down on me, the sharp edges of its runners poised to slice me into pieces. The dogs faces were almost on top of me when, at the very last moment, the driver, as though by some divine power, reined in the dogs, and the sled came to a stop inches from my face. I thanked the Lord for the driver's quick thinking and great skill.

On May 3rd, we flew back into Canada, but further north, to Eureka. When we tried to take off, the pilot found that the plane's skis had frozen into the ice. He revved the engine, dislodging the front ski and lifting the nose of the plane into the air, but the back ski refused to budge. We piled out, and after a couple of tries the rear ski came free, and we could take off.

Eureka may mean 'I found it', but in truth, it isn't so easy to find – on a map or in reality. It lies on the tip of the peninsula of Ellesmere Island that faces Axel Heiburg Island. Just six hundred miles away from the North Pole, it is a desolate place –

twenty-four tin sheds and ten people who staff a Canadian weather station constitute its only inhabitation. If the urge to climb a tree comes upon us, we were told, we would still be twelve hundred miles away from the nearest tree – the tree line had long since receded. But there was plenty of life in Eureka; summer carpets of lichen, red moss and yellow poppies; polar bears, musk oxen and caribou; thirty different species of birds. The most dramatic bird species here is undoubtedly the Arctic Tern both in colour – black-caped over the eyes with red beak and claws – and lifestyle – one that makes it migrate twenty thousand miles from the North to the South Pole every year in the quest for eternal sunshine.

More importantly, Eureka is the last stop to refuel before flying on to the pole and as we approached I spotted drums of fuel stacked near the runway. There must have been at least a hundred.

Our lodge was comfortable, with four bunk beds to a room, recreational facilities including billiards, television and video, and a reading room filled with memorabilia from past expeditions. Looking through old visitor's books dating back to 1973, I spotted the signature of Robert Swan, the first person to walk to both poles. In the billiards room stood a Steinway piano, and I speculated that at 80°N latitude, it was the northernmost site where you would hear a piano being played.

In the evening, we ventured out to search for musk oxen. We spotted through our binoculars a herd far away on the mountainside, though not close enough for photographs. The walk down the mountain along a frozen riverbed was magical, with snow glittering in the sun like precious stones and ice crystals of elegant patterns. To our left lay the forest of Axel Heiburg Island, said to be 45 million years old and extending a hundred kilometres from the Pole. The first fossil forest logs were found here, so well preserved that they could have been sawed off and burnt as they had not yet turned into stone. Sometime during the earth's history, Redwoods and water firs grew in this forest, but only dwarf willows and poppies can exist in today's harsh climate.

167

The next day we were scheduled to fly to the Pole, but to our dismay, learned that the weather was foggy and visibility poor, and we would be unable to fly out. Part of another tour group had attempted to reach the Pole on foot, returning after some members fell into the water and almost drowned. The tour leader told me tearfully that a father-daughter team and their dogs had wandered off on their own and were stranded somewhere near the Pole.

The foul weather continued and the woman in our group was getting distraught at the thought that she would not be able to make it to the Pole after all. "I told all my friends that I'll be going to the Pole!" she chided her husband. "What will they all think? Come on, you have to do something!"

Finally after much argument and cajoling, the pilot agreed to make a foray northwards to satisfy the lady. "We'll fly as far north as we possibly can, land on ice and you can take pictures for back home. Nobody will know that you didn't actually make it to the North Pole."

The lady agreed readily to this innocent deception. "Could I borrow your flag?" she asked me and I handed it over willingly. It looked as though I wouldn't be able to use it anyway. Some of our group members boarded the plane, taking along food supplies and water which they hoped to drop to the stranded father and daughter, should they be able to find them. Feeling decidedly under the weather, I chose to stay behind.

By May 6th, the last day of our trip, our last chance to touch the pole was slipping out of our grasp. Our tour leader shook his head ruefully. "We'll never make it in this weather" he said.

Having come this far, none of us wanted to leave without accomplishing our mission. After arguing about the risks, we finally decided that we would attempt to at least fly to the Magnetic Pole – the northern point at which the geomagnetic field points vertically. It would at least be a small consolation.

As we got ready to board the Twin Otter, the earlier group touched down, ecstatic with the news that they had rescued the stranded explorers and their dogs! The father and daughter team, and boisterous huskies stepped out from the plane, a little worse for wear, but in good health. An auspicious start to our journey notwithstanding, we were unable to land because of a huge cloud over the Magnetic Pole. We hovered over instead, watching as the compass seesawed out of control. Our team leader told us it would be foolhardy to attempt a landing, and I consoled myself with the thought that sometimes it takes more courage to turn back than to go forward. We returned to base, unsuccessful, but nevertheless grateful for what had been a memorable journey.

***

My hunger to reach the North Pole, however, was not satisfied. As of August 2000, only thirty-four voyages accounting for a total of 11,599 people (just 0.0002% of the world's population!) had reached the Pole and I longed to be among these unique individuals. In the summer of 2001, I decided to make a second attempt, this time by sea.

Accordingly on 1st August, I flew from Oslo to Longyearbyen, from where I was transported by helicopter, along with a handful of fellow adventurers, to our ship – the Russian icebreaker, Yamal. My first sight of the huge, bright-red Yamal against the blue green water of the Greenland Sea was exquisite, and I was very excited by the time we landed on board. The Captain and crew greeted us and we were ushered to our cabins. Mine was number 30, a cosy one with a porthole that could be opened to let in the cold arctic air.

During the following days, there were many opportunities to make friends with the other passengers. Several of them were scientists or photographers, travelling to the Arctic on work. But most of us were just nomads, travelling to the far corners of the world to satisfy our wanderlust; surgeons, newlyweds, little babies in their adventurous mothers' arms, authors, ornithologists, accountants.

The crew took great pains to entertain us. We toured the ship's engine room, spotted spouting whales and polar bears and enjoyed barbecue lunches on its deck. One evening, the crew staged a skit in which one of them, dressed as Neptune, the God of the Sea, ceremoniously handed the keys to the Pole to the Captain, amongst much applause from the rest of us. We met one of the women from the kitchen who, having sailed about twenty times to the Arctic was in contention for the world record for the most number of Arctic Polar expeditions. We participated in lectures and discussions with the ship's historian and an Arctic explorer. One evening we were even given basic lessons in Russian.

Despite these distractions, my mind was fixed on our final goal, and August 5th proved to be the fateful day. The North Pole, the northern axis of the earth's rotation, is not a fixed location; the Earth wobbles as it rotates, and the icecap drifts. The absolute proof of reaching the North Pole is when the Global Positioning System shows 90°N, and I was determined to get a photograph of the GPS monitor at this critical point. I grabbed a roll of film and positioned myself in front of a monitor in the dining room and clicked away as the readings flickered between 89° 59' 91"N and 89° 59' 98"N. I was panicking that I would run out of film by the time the GPS read 89° 59' 99"N.

And then it was 12.48 pm, and the GPS monitor showed 90° 00' N 90° 00'E. We had reached the North Pole! The ship's siren sounded in triumph, I clicked one last time, and the camera started to rewind! I had almost missed recording one of my most significant travel experiences!

I rushed to my cabin to grab more film and joined the rest of the group as we disembarked. We took turns to pose beside a sign which proclaimed 'North Pole 90N', along with a crew member who had wittily dressed up as Santa Claus! A polar bear shuffled towards us to investigate what the commotion was about, but was driven off by the Russian crew who shooed him away with flares. Some scientists in our group murmured excitedly that there had never been a sighting of a polar bear this far north – they would publish their findings on their return home. Some intrepid passengers, tied securely by ropes, took a dip in the frigid Arctic Ocean. I contented myself with the thought that I was among a select band of people who had stood at the northernmost point of the Earth. I was, literally and metaphorically, on top of the world.

If It's Ballada, It Must Be Brasil

Mathew Chandy

Spontaneous combustion: A phrase used to describe a body that inexplicably reaches its ignition point. To me, it is also an apt description of what I experienced in Bahia, Brasil. There were fires all around, of the metaphorical kind, parties breaking out everywhere and for no apparent reason. But they were easy to explain. The ballada, the party, it's in every Brasilian's blood.

Having survived a fairly traumatic transition from a carefree student in Bangalore, surrounded by the warmth of family and friends, to a 'responsible' corporate lawyer in cold and

172

grey London, I had pounced upon the opportunity to spend six months working in Brazil – or 'Brasil', as I came to think of it like everyone else there.

Many of my best memories of Brasilian balladas centre on Salvador, which I visited on a short break from Sao Paulo where I was based. Salvador is the capital of Bahia, a north-eastern state in Brasil. When the Bahia region was colonised by the Portuguese from 1500 to 1763, Salvador was the administrative and religious capital.

While Portuguese remains the language, there's a strong African influence too. Not surprising when you learn that almost 37% of all African slaves were imported to Brasil, most of them to Bahia, to sustain the sugar cultivation. Their influences are seen everywhere: in the dark skin of some of its people; in the African rhythms of the samba; in the graceful, fluid movements of bare bodies as they perform the capoeira – a beautiful, sensual dance that is actually a martial art developed by slaves.

Bahia is the perfect example of the fusion of cultures – all that's best of African and Latino culture meet in her aspect. Gorgeous black and olive skinned women, spicy and delicious food and art more beautiful than anything I have seen. A land that is truly an overdose for the senses, a celebration of life.

I spent my first evening in Bahia at the Bar O Beca, a small dingy bar, listening to an informal gathering of musicians from all corners of Brasil belting out one infectious track after another. I sat transfixed by Brasil's answer to Janis Joplin. She was plump and not particularly attractive, but with a guitar in her hand and a song on her lips, her face and body suddenly came alive. Soon she had everyone swaying and swinging to her passionate ballads and groovy tunes. Most of my fellow revellers spoke only Portuguese, a language I had started learning barely a month before. But beer and music were familiar territory.

It was here that I met Sergio, a musician with a Sanskrit tattoo on his arm and India imprinted on his heart. He

peppered me with questions: *What of the caste system, arranged marriages and bindis? So how come you haven't read* Freedom at Midnight*? How can such a peaceful nation and followers of Gandhi, resort to communal violence and hatred? Please can you organise screenings of* Lagaan *and* Monsoon Wedding*? And please translate!! Sing me a traditional Indian song?* I thought hard, the strains of Pink Floyd and Dire Straits reverberating in my mind. Finally I had to resort to singing our national anthem!

Kahlil Gibran once remarked that one needs to travel far from a mountain in order to fully appreciate its awesome beauty. Having grown up in India for twenty-three years, I took for granted the centuries of rich culture and tradition that was staring me in the face every day. But like all good expats, when I touched foreign soil I found myself clinging to my Indian roots, for fear that this almost fully-grown tree would sprout American leaves. I needn't have worried. Everywhere I went I was accosted with so many questions about my motherland, that I've learnt more about my own country in Brasil than I did living there!

India is revered in Brasil for its contribution to culture and religion – the country of art, religion, music, yoga, meditation, spiritualism and Gandhi, a counter balance to the barren and consumerist influences of American culture. Interestingly, one of the most famous schools of samba in Brasil is called Filhos de Gandhi – The Children of Gandhi.

During the annual Carnaval in Salvador (which all Brasilians know is the most inclusive in the country, the more spectacular but exclusive one in Rio de Janeiro being more of a tourist attraction), the Filhos de Gandhi parade the streets in Gandhi's traditional white robes, bang their drums and whip thousands of half-naked and intoxicated revellers into a frenzy. Sacrilege? Blasphemy? Not when you learn that schools of music and samba were once the slave's answer to oppression and tyranny. Could they have any greater inspiration than the Mahatma himself?

Later in my stay, I offered to cook a traditional Indian

174

meal for a few Brasilian friends. My offer was accepted with alacrity. They arrived with their better halves, parents, friends and friends' friends. In return, my visiting Indian friends and I were treated to 'Indian' parties thrown by my Brasilian friends – complete with colourful pictures of Shiva, Vishnu and Krishna adorning the entrance and dal-chawal for dinner!

We even had to give bhangra lessons. Feeble excuses like, "Some of us South Indians can't dance like our Punjabi brethren," were brushed aside. Some of them had even seen and been impressed by the, ahem, slightly vulgar displays of our south Indian actors like Mohan Lal, Jayalalitha and Rajnikanth! I taught them the little bhangra I knew. Yes, bhangra with a strong Malayali accent!

On that first day in Bahia I was duped out of 10 reais (around Rs 100). The guy was just so smooth and so flattering that I felt it was worth it. I was paying for the act. He singled out the 'lonely' traveller and offered to find me uma mulhere (a woman) and just couldn't understand why I wasn't interested.

"OK I eteache you capoeira?"

I feigned a back problem.

"OK I eteache you percussion?"

I knew my limitations. So he just took my money and ran.

Music is an integral part of life in Bahia. It filters through from all directions...samba, jazz, samba rock (pronounced 'samba hockey' in Portuguese), reggae (pronounced 'heggayey') and rap (yes, you guessed it, pronounced 'happy'). Sometimes it just filters through and you are conscious of it and enjoy it, but it always remains in the background. And then you hear a strain that beckons...and you follow.

On that first night, I reach the Cantina da Lua following one such strain...literally translated Cantina da Lua would probably mean 'Canteen of the Moon'. Dani (my delightful Portuguese teacher) told me never to translate. At times like this you realise it is important to think in Portuguese without translating into English.

There was a couple making beautiful music at the Cantina da Lua, if only all couples did the same. I don't even know if they were a couple. Suddenly a group of vagabondos materialised on the pavement, all gathered around the Cantina da Lua, and pretty soon they were singing louder than the lady with the mike was, but no one seemed to mind. It's part of the trip....

Talking of trips, you have to see Bahian women to appreciate what it's like to be high on beauty. The black men and women of Bahia who came across from Africa have successfully retained their art, culture, food, music and dances. There was this stunning black woman in a shop, in traditional red dress and headgear that set off her glowing skin and eyes. She had all the grace, poise and elegance of an African Queen. I had to just stop and stare.

Then somebody told me about the big, full moon party that would be held the next night. I landed up at the appointed place and time, emboldened by my ability to make friends, converse in this strange language and sway and sing along to alien but infectious melodies – only to hear that the party had been postponed as the full moon had not yet been sighted. To make things worse, the rain was pelting down – I was disappointed that my first party in Brasil was going to be a damp squib.

But I had not accounted for that typical Brasilian ballada phenomenon – spontaneous combustion!

A van pulled up with four macho Brasilians who set up their hi-fi gear in the middle of the square and lined up all the gorgeous women who were quietly enjoying their drinks in the surrounding cafes. Needless to say, the men followed suit. Soon, everybody was rocking and rolling, gyrating and swinging to some truly irresistible Brasilian rhythms – samba, forro, mambo, lambada.........we did it all.

Every now and then I would get that 'buns of steel complex'. One wouldn't normally complain about having buns of steel, at least not when you are moving them to a relentless samba

176

rhythm. But I couldn't quash the feeling that I was a great dancer on my own, but put a woman in my arms (and a hot Latino one at that) and suddenly I have two left feet and buns of steel! But soon I was having too much fun to feel self-conscious.

Looks like all damp squibs aren't damp squibs after all. I stumbled into bed at 3 am, feeling more of a man now that I could samba dance!

But the biggest ballada of them all was back in Sao Paulo. It had been building up for days, and finally peaked in a crescendo of celebration. It was 2002, and World Cup football time!

Tied up with work and classes until pretty late on a daily basis, football sessions with my office team would kick-off at eleven on Wednesday nights. This was often followed by animated discussions about the highs and lows of the game, which continued into the wee hours of the morning over beer and barbecue.

Brasilians display the flair and elegance of samba dancers in the football games that erupt on beaches, in parking lots and every deserted street. Every football game featuring Brasilian clubs or national teams play host to troops of samba dancers whipping up excitement from the stands and the celebrations invariably spill out on to the streets immediately after.

As the national team danced and dribbled their way to the finals, the rest of the nation celebrated with a vengeance. Spontaneous parties would break out after every one of Brasil's victorious matches, which, played in far away Japan and South Korea, tended to start at 2 am.

Within minutes of Brasil's famous victory over Germany in the final, thousands of people and cars, cloaked in the trademark bright green and yellow, poured into the streets of Sao Paulo (and every other city, town and village in Brasil, I am sure), chanting, "Sou Brasiliero, com muito orgulho, com muito amo…" I am Brasilian, with great passion, with great pride. Enormous buses, their roofs almost caving in under the feet of stomping musicians and

177

dancers, blockaded every major street. The revellers danced and danced and danced till they dropped. Literally.

Having been up all night indulging in some pre-victory celebrations, I crawled back home, some ten hours after the final whistle, still hoarsely chanting, "Sou Brasiliero, com muito orgulho, com muito amor..."

Midnight's Grandchildren in the Belly of the Raj

Rahul Rao

Dear Mr Rushdie,

Your *Midnight's Children* is badly in need of updating. It is a good book, but much water has flowed under the bridge since then. I was born smack in the middle of the Emergency. This entitles me to write the sequel. OK, OK, I won't steal your thunder. You can write it. But let it be about me. I've had quite close contact with more than a few major public personalities of our time, so you won't even have to rack your brains for those tangential connections between protagonist and larger historical context that you are so fond of. Here's the plug: (Granta, 2008?)

Fine, I'll admit it. Before you ferret around for my birth certificate, I was not born in the midst of the drama of the Emergency. If truth were told, I popped out into the world during the reign of a simple-living, high-

179

thinking, urine-drinking Prime Minister. But hey – I'm sure you weren't born on the 15th of August 1947 at the stroke of midnight, so we're quits. And I suppose before I begin blowing my own trumpet, I should acknowledge that I was born the great-grandson of zamindars and courtiers, the grandson of civil servants and soldiers. Native collaborators all. No freedom fighters in my genealogy, no Quit India veterans (not even a roadside Romeo great-uncle who might have seen it as the biggest bunking opportunity of the century).

Thanks to my wily ancestors, I was born with a very high quality stainless steel spoon in my mouth, so that when the time was right, I was well positioned to make that most predictable of moves for the aimless bratpack-log: Go Abroad. Between me, and the ivy-covered stone walls with their manicured lawns and Benetton-ad groups of laughing students in baseball caps that I aspired to be part of, stood a bewildering flurry of acronyms – GRE, TOEFL, USIS, I20. A significantly less complicated route – if you managed to snag it – were the Rhodes scholarships to Oxford (no acronyms, just an interview). Different destination perhaps, steeped in history, but I would still get the things that were important to me: ivy, lawns, Benetton people. Preparing for the interview, I suspected that I would have to know something about the scholarships and their Founder.

I read so much about Cecil Rhodes that, perhaps taking pity on me, in the week preceding the interview he visited me frequently. Every night he gave me a Power Point presentation outlining, in rather abrupt bullet points, his expansive vision for the world and my place in it. On the first night, he bragged about being one of the most successful British (ad)venture capitalists of all time and – like a benevolent mentor sharing business tips – divulged to me gleefully, the sordid details of how he had managed to hoodwink African chiefs into granting him concessions to mine for diamonds in the 19th century. He droned on about the vast fortune that

180

this had allowed him to amass and even offered to present the latest annual report of his beloved De Beers, but I had never been good at economics and feared that talk of non-performing assets would only make me more nervous.

On the second night, he took me on a video tour of his estates, boasting that he had virtually pioneered the system of apartheid by separating the Africans working in his mines from the outside world.

On the third night he was more intimate, chuckling blithely as he revealed that one of his favourite Sunday pastimes was to throw shilling coins into a swimming pool and watch natives dive to retrieve them for his amusement.

On the fourth night he declared, in his pompous and oratorical voice, that he had dedicated his life to re-establishing British dominion over Africa 'from the Cape to Cairo', and regretted that he had only managed to grab what are now Malawi, Zambia and Zimbabwe.

On the fifth night, he explained that he had left the bulk of his fortune to bring young men from the British Empire, the United States, and Germany to Oxford, in the hope that mutual contact between these potential leaders would facilitate understanding among the three great powers that he considered fit to run the world.

The sixth night was more of the same, but somewhere along the line he started off about the Anglo-Saxon race being 'the best, the most human, most honourable race the world possesses'; and when I looked at him quizzically, he clarified hastily that while I might never be blond and blue-eyed enough to actually be Teutonic, if I went to Oxford and did well there, I might at least be like them. Plus, I could help run the world.

On the seventh night, he wished me luck.

It should have been a perfect fit. Children of native collaborating elite go knocking on the imperial door.

181

We've done your bidding, we're almost like you, let us in, at least a little. Social climbing in the global pecking order. Essential, if one is to attain moksha from the cycle of birth and (relative) marginality and eventual nirvana.

So I'm not sure what it was – upbringing? socialisation? nationalist propaganda? self-loathing? – that led me to begin my supplication to the Rhodes Scholarship India Selection Committee with something along the following lines: 'I'm grateful that Cecil Rhodes does not sit on this selection committee. He might have listened with interest as I pontificated on the problems that the world faces today, but that interest would surely have turned to condescension – if not outright horror – if he heard what I thought ought to be done about them.' Remarkably, the head of my regional selection committee nodded empathetically, remarking that the poor (little rich) man would be rolling in his grave if he could see who they were giving his money to: women! (post-)colonials in countries he couldn't even have named! (They didn't exist at the time.)

Factoid (while we're on the subject of Cecil Rhodes' grave): In the midst of one of his lunatic and murderous outbursts against all things non-Zimbabwean – nay, against all things non-Zanu PF – Robert Mugabe demanded that Rhodes' bones be dug up from their resting place in the Matopos Hills of the erstwhile state of Rhodesia and repatriated to Britain. I often wondered how exactly the macabre handover would be effected, if it ever came to that. Would the pale-faced John Rowett – then Warden and self-styled CEO of the Rhodes Trust – simply throw open the great metal doors on the pillared portico of Rhodes House, stretch his hands out to reach for the proffered gunny sack, with a grateful 'Cheers, Bob'?

I am running ahead of me (but you do this all the time). But this is important. Because when I finally got to Oxford, no matter how many times we Rhodents were reminded in hushed and reverential tones of 'the values of The Founder', no

182

matter what moral sophistry was employed in defence of The Founder ('a man of his time' – or the quite different tack: 'if you don't like him, why take his money?'), no matter how prominent a place The Founder's portrait occupied in Rhodes House's grand Milner Hall, and no matter that a tapestry of The Founder hung opposite one of Nelson Mandela – grotesquely positing a sort of equivalence between the two men – my Selection Committee and I (nudge, nudge, wink, wink) had a contract. To be sure, the terms of that contract were vague and open-ended, but they were clear enough: be everything that Rhodes was not.

I asked to go to Balliol College, and that is where I ended up. I'm not sure why I chose Balliol, seeing as I knew very little about it at the time, beyond the fact that it was founded in 1263. Having just graduated from a thirteen-year old law school, the prospect of joining an institution that had been a going concern since about the time of Genghis Khan was strangely appealing. So it was with little information and few preconceptions that I wandered into what continues to be my academic home.

I remember flinging open the door to Balliol's dining hall and stopping dead in my tracks. I had seen it before. The same three endlessly long tables with long, backless benches on either side, arranged longitudinally in a large room with a high table at the far end about a foot above the ground, where the More Important People ate (better food?). Same, same, same as in the old dining hall of Bishop Cotton Boys' School on St Mark's Road in Bangalore. As my North American friends exclaimed at this weird and wonderful sight, using phrases like 'culture shock' and that sole adjective in their vocabulary – 'awesome' – I could only think, petulantly, "But I wanted to go somewhere different!"

There were differences of course – the spooky organ that played Jaws-like music at our Fresher's dinner, the massive stained glass windows and the general exponential increase in magnificence and grandeur. But these only made me feel more wretched, almost cheated, as if I'd had to make do with a pale imitation all these years, like the hundredth photocopy of the class topper's notes distributed the day before an exam. Then I pinched myself and thought: 'Do not become a cantankerous brown sahib like Mr Naipaul' (hee hee! I don't like him either). The only mitigating factor in all this was that the food in Balliol hall was much worse than anything I had ever had before ('chips, mash or potato wedges?', 'chips, mash or potato wedges?', 'chips, mash or...').

Munching on my forty-sixth soggy potato wedge, my eyes came to rest on Lord Curzon. Hanging on the wall. Pupil of Balliol, Partitioner of Bengal, husband of the Patron of Bowring Hospital in Bangalore). I was later to read that three successive Viceroys of India (1888-1905) had been Balliol men. 19th century India had been run by Balliol men. Of course I knew that places like this had been feeder institutions for the Raj, but the proximity to these characters, the following-in-the-footsteps-ness of the whole experience was more than slightly discomfiting. What on earth was I doing in this place? Had anything changed?

My name is George Nathaniel Curzon,
I am a most superior person.
My cheek is pink, my hair is sleek,
I dine at Blenheim once a week.

Factoid (while we're on the subject of Blenheim): Blenheim Palace is grand for daylong getaways from Oxford on rare, sunny days. On its lush, manicured grounds sits the vast, stately mansion in which Winston Churchill was born. Yes, the same Winston Churchill who, when he lived in Bangalore in 1896, described it as 'a garrison town which resembles a third rate watering place', started a butterfly collection, and left unpaid bills that you can still see proudly displayed in Bangalore Club on Residency Road, just outside the still-existing men-only bar that the Club is very proud of.

184

"Hi! I'm a Balliol trans-gendered person," someone said, digging me in the ribs and offering me his hand in greeting, jolting me out of my reverie.

"But I thought we were all supposed to be Balliol men."

"Oh no! Balliol women were invented in 1979." Seven hundred and sixteen years after its founding, I thought. So there was hope for Bangalore Club yet.

Curzon, potato wedges and Balliol men notwithstanding, I was soon to realise that Balliol was exactly the right place for me, for three very important reasons (this is, incidentally, how we are supposed to write Oxford essays – I can no longer communicate in any other way). First, it does not require one to wear academic gowns for meals – so it is possible to eat without looking like an erudite bat. Second, it allows students (indeed, all living creatures) to walk on the grass – unlike a certain Oxbridge college which permits only fellows to walk on the grass and has – to preserve the sanctity of the rule – designated all college ducks as fellows (better that than the other way around, surely). Third, it has (or had, till very recently) a tortoise called Rosa Luxembourg, which could often be seen eating its way around the college quad at the rate of a few feet a year.

Factoid (while we're on the subject of Balliol's appropriateness): When Rhodes came to Oxford to receive an honorary degree in 1899, the Master of Balliol, Edward Caird, was the lead signatory of a letter of protest to the Vice-Chancellor. Of the 92 signatures attached to the protest, 18 were of Balliol dons, more than from any other college.

So I was in the right place, but to do what? I had come Up to Oxford ostensibly to Read for a degree in International Relations, but little that I learnt in class seemed to bear any relation to events in the world outside. Inside, I was reading about World War I in the most infuriating detail (at 9:05 Bethmann-Hollweg picked up the phone and dialled the Russian Ambassador), without the faintest idea even of who was on which side. Outside, it was the best of times, it was the worst of times, it was the age of pre-emptive defence, it was the age of offence, it was the season of Us, it was the season of The Terrorists, it was post-Cold War, it was like Crusade Four, We were all going direct to Heaven, They were all going direct the other way. There was a sick king and a librarian queen on the throne in the White House; there was a slick king and a lawyer queen on the throne near Whitehall.

By day, I pondered questions of theory ('but is It empire?'), as argument and counter-argument flew between my classmates – who, incidentally, included the delightfully down-to-earth Chelsea Clinton (see? I'm much better connected than Saleem Sinai or Moor Zogoiby or any of your fictional creations). By afternoon, I read about imperial continuities in US foreign policy, including during the retrospectively halcyon presidency of one Bill Clinton (fellow-Rhodent). By night, in the company of other Rhodents such as the flamboyant and operatic François Tanguay-Renaud, the dreadlocked free radical Vincent Bouchard, the dreamy and enigmatic Bilal Siddiqi, the lithe and go-getting Oeindrila Dube, the energetic and fast-talking Elizabeth Angell and the always reliably gossipy Antara Datta, I was provoked to reach answers and practice.

And practice we did, as an entire Oxford subculture mushroomed in response to the events of the time, like the multicoloured fungus that my friend Alex Luck seemed so fond of growing over his left-over food. As war clouds gathered and the news was full of weapons inspections and Council resolutions, aluminium tubes and enriched uranium, we spawned a jargon of our own: affinity groups, non-hierarchical networks, spokes-council meetings, Direct Action. The more paranoid among us insisted that Big Brother was always watching, so that emails would only remind the faithful to meet you-know-where at you-know-what time, to disrupt you-know-which event.

 When the first missiles hit Baghdad, we were ready on Oxford's Manzil Way – demonstrating, drumming,

186

dancing, dying-in on Corn Market Street splattered with fake-blood, staging mock weddings between Bush and Blair replete with death vows. A delegation of Rhodents trooped off to meet the second-in-command at the US Embassy in London to convince him of the folly of his Commander-in-Chief, only to be entertained by an avalanche of crocodile tears as the reptilian Glyn Davies claimed fidelity to the rule of law since time immemorial on behalf of his beleaguered nation.

Back in Oxford, those who placed less store on talk offered up their bodies as traffic barricades, forming human chains and causing maximum disruption by lying down on the ever-so-narrow arterial roads that led into and out of the city. As anacondas of protesters met police cordons, one heard snatches of conversation between the two lines that only the surreally-polite British could sustain through grimaces and clenched teeth ("Sorry, but would you mind telling me when I start doing something arrestable?" "Sure luv.") Others staged acts of commercial sabotage, chaining petrol pump handles to their stations and rendering them temporarily useless, as co-conspirators distracted pump attendants with silly questions about ball bearings and phone cards to Bangladesh.

On the fifteenth of February 2003, we became part of a statistic: one in sixty people who lived in the British Isles visited London that day with the express purpose of Saying No to the then impending war on Iraq. Investment bankers and trade unionists, pink-haired punks and black burquas, bearded skull-capped Muslims and bearded skull-capped Jews made common cause.

Say hey! HEY! Say ho! HO! Bush and Blair have got to go!

At least that was better than 'No attack on Iraq!' that didn't even rhyme when I said it – given that I actually could pronounce the name of that country. I relented eventually, trying out 'No a-tark on Iraq!' and then settling on the more hegemonic 'No attack on I-rack!' No one heard me get off my high dissonant horse as my voice mingled with a million others, buoyed by whistles and samba bands and tin pots, the sound magnified a hundred-fold beneath every bridge that we marched under.

As this vast, seething mass of humanity crawled down the Thames Embankment with Big Ben looming ahead of us, I wondered if this was what the storming of the Bastille had been like. But we were (largely) British remember? So we skirted politely around Westminster and turned into Whitehall where civil servant faces peered down at us from their office windows – some, I imagine, cheered us on, while on others, upper lips quivered even more stiffly than usual. As for us, very little of the sloganeering seemed to be about 'us' – not many 'bring our boys home'; lots more 'no war for oil', and 'save the children'.

'These people built an empire?' I wondered incredulously. I might have been proud to be British on a day like this, I found myself thinking blasphemously. Walking between London's impassive public buildings, past great white palaces and museums and offices – trappings of Empire all, built on Indian indigo and Cairo cotton, on Jamaican sugar and Malayan rubber, on weaver's thumbs and opium wars – I found myself wondering, like Asya in Ahdaf Soueif's *In the Eye of the Sun*, why I felt little resentment. It wasn't simply that this was a very changed Britain – it was also that some part of me had been made in this place, even before I had arrived, even before I had been born. Overlapping geographies, intertwined histories. The contract still made sense, but perhaps its mode of performance needed to be renegotiated.

Proud to be British on February 15th. That's what I should have said to Queen Elizabeth II, when I met her several months later. It would have been the perfect thing to say: polite, even flattering, but subversive, honest. Instead, I gave a thoroughly undistinguished performance – worse, I behaved like a fawning imperial courtier.

 As part of the centenary celebration of the Rhodes scholarships, all Rhodents-in-residence had been invited

to Buckingham Palace for an audience with the Queen and Prince Philip. "Wear your sherwani!" everyone had said, but that is where I had put my foot down. I was not going to look like some miserable princeling at the Delhi Durbar, like just another ethnic pawn in Her Majesty's Commonwealth chess set. So, rather blandly attired in jacket and tie, I went, intending to blend into the background, just to...erm...see what it was like.

We stood around for an eternity in large staterooms with gilt-framed Renoirs (maybe? I know nothing about art), talking to the occasional palace official but mostly to each other and drinking copious amounts of very dilute whisky. Having walked through a succession of such rooms, I staggered around a corner and straight into QE II.

I had thought she would be at the very end of a long room on a throne and that we would have to walk down a long carpeted aisle and bow low before her, saying, "I have the honour to be, Madam, Your Majesty's humble and obedient servant." I had been practising all sorts of ways in which I might subtly avoid the bowing and scraping, but I simply had not been expecting her to stand near the door like the host at a common dinner party. She held out a white-gloved hand (was I to kiss it?) and smiled at me like out of a postage stamp, but the evening had begun on a less than graceful note.

Later she circulated, surrounded by her ladies-in-waiting. These were larger than life Barbara Cartland-like figures with dazzling smiles and coiffed hair, each of whom could have been a minor celebrity in her own right. It was hard to get a good view of anyone noteworthy as each was surrounded by huddles of chattering, gnawing Rhodents. This was going to be a case of survival of the fittest and after much manoeuvring the Canadians seemed to have made a breakthrough. Since I was often to be found in the company of these warm, friendly creatures from a cold, frigid land – and this evening was no exception – I soon found myself in the path of QE II, who was steaming inexorably towards me. I edged forward slightly so that she might dock before me. She did so and looked at me expectantly.

[Oh my god. What now?]

QE II : [after an eternity] Hello

RR : [God. She's stern.] Erm…Hello

QE II : Where are you from?

RR : [Isn't it obvious? Damn! Should have worn that sherwani.] Er…India.

QE II : [Long pause. Why oh why can I think of nothing to fill the silence?] What do you study?

RR : International Relations

QE II : [She lists to starboard, as if to hear me more clearly.] Ah! Very important subject. And you can meet people from all over, here, and talk to each other and solve the world's problems.

RR : [Oh no. She's drawing on her stock of platitudes. That must mean I'm boring and unimpressive] Yes.

QE II : [Another long, stern look. Jesus, she really thinks I'm dumb.] And what do you want to do after your studies?

RR : [Oh shit. That question again. What do I say? Pragmatic revolutionary? No. Weird. Vague. And rude? Public intellectual? Too pretentious. No one sets out wanting to be that anyway. Naipaul types, maybe. Oh come on. Say something dammit. Dimwit.] Oh…ah…Foreign Service. I want to join the Foreign Service. [I cannot believe my ears. I don't want to join the Foreign Service. I have never wanted to join the Foreign Service. I just want to say something that sounds impressive. Something that I think she thinks is impressive.]

[QE II nods and steams on.]

There is an audible collective gasp in the air and several pairs of eyebrows arch skyward. Anarchist jaws

190

drop. Tongues wag. Later, emails will fly. Allegiances will shift. Dazzled by the splendour of the state, I have sold out. I have collaborated. Liberals look at me with newfound interest. I am wishy-washy enough for them.

> *Pussycat pussycat, where have you been?*
> *I've been to London to see the queen.*
> *Pussycat pussycat, what did you do there?*
> *I was the little mouse under her chair.*

Undistinguished as it may have been, I have nevertheless had an Audience with the Queen. I am not doing too badly in Western Society. (must go easy on the upper case. danger of morphing into arundhati roy.)

What more fitting role to be cast in than Othello?

'It is the cause [vodka shot], it is the cause [vodka shot], my soul. Let me not name it to you, you chaste stars [yeah, right]. It is the cause.'

I have not shed her blood, but by the end of the cast party I have puked all over her bed sheets. I am forgiven because we have done six outdoor performances – the last one especially good – over the past week in the quad of Oriel College, thus concluding its Garden Shakespeare Summer Season.

It has been a tiring but thoroughly enjoyable experience. At least I have been able to speak in my own voice – unlike in Frank McGuiness' *Observe the Sons of Ulster Marching Towards the Somme*, where I tried, desperately, to be Northern Irish. This was accomplished with the help of an intrepid voice coach who had me say 'Hoy Noy Broyn Coy' every morning, so that slowly but surely, I acquired enough of a Protestant Northern Irish vocabulary to start a sectarian riot in Belfast.

When I wasn't reading, writing, fawning over or fighting, empire, I went to bops. (Salman: if we make this into a movie, I'd like to do a sort of anthropologist-among-the-savages bit here.) Bops are a uniquely Oxbridge institution (not even understood

191

in nearby London), where people starved of a late night social scene gather to bounce around to their parents' music. At bops, Madonna still has an American accent, Kylie is in Neighbours, Michael Jackson's black and Freddie Mercury not yet dead. (In Wadham College, every bop ends with 'Free Nelson Mandela', so I really, seriously, rest my case.) Balls are the more upscale, but less frequent, alternative to bops – guests in black tie (even at the Hindu Society's Diwali Ball), ticket prices sky-high, all manner of entertainment (jugglers, a capella singing, bouncy castles, masseurs) but always the same music (Madonna, Kylie, MJ, Freddie). Ball themes are a favourite source of controversy: the merest suggestion of a non-Western theme (Africa, 19th century Ottomania, or the Orient Express) will bring on a collective wringing of hands from hyper-compensatory white liberals and hyper-defensive post-colonials. Non-western culture becomes off limits and the only 'safe' themes end up being Anglo-Saxon. This almost always implies – you guessed it – more Madonna, Kylie, MJ and Freddie. Anyway, at least Freddie was born in Bombay.

One night after a particularly raucous bop at Trinity College in The Other Place (Cambridge), I saw Thomas Babington Macaulay stagger out past the porter's lodge. Two hundred and four years old, he insisted on attending every social event at his old college – not that he enjoyed them very much – just to see if everyone was behaving. "Lord Macaulay!" I exclaimed, "What a surprise!" He was pleased to see that I could string together a sentence in his language, though slightly perturbed that I had not set my sights on becoming a babu in the civil service. "Oh but now the best babus go to the IMF," I told him. "Now, that would really be your kind of place. They have this one-size-fits all policy to make their work really easy. It's sort of like the Penal Code you wrote that all the colonies ended up with. I should warn you, though, that we've really messed up your language," I continued. "I wish we'd done

192

the same with the Penal Code. We've still got your favourite S. 377, even though homosexuality was legalised in Britain in the sixties. It's a bit like the hunting scenes that still hang in my house, even after hunting's been banned in Britain. And the flourishing of cricket in India, even after... You should come to India now, Lord Macaulay. You'd love it!"

Come to India, come to India,
India teri hai! Hai!
Hind, hind, hind, hind...

Do I have to say something about sport? I suppose I do, though it's not a subject I tend to bring up of my own accord. It does crop up every so often though. You see, The Founder (may his bones rest in Matopos) thought it fit to require, as a criterion for selection as a Rhodes scholar, 'fondness of and success in manly outdoor sports such as cricket, football and the like'. In 1976, the word 'manly' was deleted in a move that not only paved the way for the opening of the scholarship to women, but also, I suspect, to legions of men who would not...erm...otherwise have made it. At any rate, the issue still hovers over selection committees and I was about to charge out of my interview in relief that it had not come up, only to be dragged back and questioned about my sporting prowess. This I addressed ("I run for fun") while studiously avoiding eye contact with Ranjit Bhatia (who represented India in the 10,000 m and the marathon at the 1960 Rome Olympics). For the record, I continue to run for fun, mostly in Oxford's misty, dream-like Port Meadow over fields and streams and between geese and cows, and quite recently in the 10 km Oxford Town & Gown Fun Run.

Because 'fun' is the key word, I was decidedly vague when I was questioned relentlessly over coffee the other day by a charming elderly gentleman, whom I had never met before, and who sat at my table because there were no other seats available in the QI coffee shop. Half an hour into the conversation:

?? : So, you're a Rhodes Scholar. What sports do you play?

193

RR : Er...I run.
?? : What distance?
RR : Oh...er...middle distance.
?? : Do you use the Iffley Road track?
RR : No, I don't like running round and round the same place.
?? : Where do you go then?
RR : Oh...just...here and there, really.

[Forty five minutes later, during which we have had the most wide-ranging conversation about Britain, India, politics, travel and what not –]

?? : Oh, by the way my name's Roger Bannister. What's yours?

I am clearly hopeless at this celebrity thing. That's why I'm writing to you Salman. (Gosh, I'm not sure when exactly I got on to a first-name basis with you, but you don't mind do you? I still can't call my supervisor Andy.) So do you think there's a story here? I'm not sure how it's going to end. Obviously, this is still a work in progress.

With regards and hopes for international stardom via your good self,

Rahul

PS – You may not agree with my politics – actually, I've been somewhat disturbed by some of your post-9/11 stuff. But we can agree to disagree. Remember, I'm the character. You're just the author.

PPS – You were great in *Bridget Jones' Diary*. Oscar avant le Nobel?

The Silver-Tongued Salesman of Virtual Kutch

Nikhilesh Dholakia

CG Road used to be a street with sleepy tree-shaded bungalows interspersed with low-rise office or apartment blocks, and the occasional kirana and paan shops. Then in the 1970s, Ahmedabad Municipal Corporation took an empty plot on CG Road and built a starkly simple U-shaped mall, the Navrangpura Municipal Market. Little shops ringed the U, and parking spaces filled the middle. CG Road closed the open end of the U to form an O. In the emergent two-wheeler society of the time, this market became a hit. You and your lovely could park your scooter, and the roaming waiters from half-a-dozen eateries in the market would supply you with anything from paani puri to pau bhaji.

Today, the market looks frumpy and dated, but it still does brisk business. Baskin

Robbins now competes with Rasranjan Sweet Shop and the chaat vendors. Cars have edged out scooters; the parking space overflows with Maruti Esteems and Toyota Camrys. At the shops, you can pick up knick-knacks, provisions, dresses, shoes and then indulge in pleasures of the palate with a variety of snacks brought right to your car.

Ahmedabadis like to sit and eat in their cars. The plastic chairs and tables provided by the eateries lie empty. It's probably a hangover from the days of sitting and eating with your missus and progeny on the pillion of the scooter.

As the municipal market proved its staying power, retailing on CG Road took off. Today, CG Road is a two-kilometre stretch of wall-to-wall shopping malls, big and small. Especially conspicuous are dozens of glittering jewellery stores. New malls with anchor stores such as Feminatown and Kolkata Bazaar are already in place or rising rapidly. Old malls with U-shaped or 'linear strip' formats are being spruced up, upgraded, expanded, covered up and air-conditioned. Coffee shops and restaurants have sprung up to lure in the steady streams of shoppers. CG Road has become so synonymous with retailing in Ahmedabad that the shopping area on the city's outskirts, on the highway linking Sarkhej and Gandhinagar, is now dubbed 'SG Road'.

***

The monsoon fury had hit parched Gujarat with gusto, and Ahmedabad was being pelted by heavy showers alternating with light drizzle. Ruby and I were dodging puddles on CG Road, looking for 'dangly' silver earrings for our daughter Nishita. She is a student at Wesleyan University, an institution whose funky ways have led Newsweek to dub it the 'hottest school in USA in terms of diversity'. Nishita wanted a dorm room décor and sartorial ensemble from India that would not let Wesleyan slip from this exalted 'diversity' perch. We had already bought 'jungle green' (not just any green, she insisted; it has to be 'jungle green'), ethnic bedspreads from a Kutch handloom store. Now, we were hunting for 'dangly' silver earrings. Well, okay… Ruby was hunting for 'dangly' silver earrings and I, dutiful husband and father, was tagging along.

Stepping out of one silver store, where the marble floors were dangerously slick from rain, we were walking on CG Road towards the tourist taxi parked in one of the angled parking strips. Through the corner of her eye, in a nondescript mall of about six small stores, Ruby spotted the word 'silver'. On closer scrutiny, we discovered that the full sign read: 'Harilal Handicrafts Museum – Antique Silver Crafts from Kutch'. A somewhat crumbling open staircase led to the second floor where the shop was located.

As we entered, the store clerk turned up some of the lights. We were to learn that the more we shopped, and the more the storeowners became enamoured of us, more lights kept coming on!

"Do you have any silver earrings?" asked Ruby in her cute, whimsical Gujarati. She knows a lot of Gujarati, but is befuddled by the gender endings. In her native Bengali, there are no gendered prepositional forms or verb endings. Ruby learnt Spanish, a gendered language, for two years, but she finds the gendered usage of Hindi and Gujarati maddeningly frustrating.

"How can my nose be feminine while my ears are masculine?" she queries in exasperation. When reminded about gendered usage in Spanish, she retorts that in Spanish there is logic to gender – the words ending in 'ah' sounds are feminine and those ending in 'oh' sounds are masculine, for example.

Harilal Handicrafts carried silver antique stuff from Kutch. By and by, the store clerk inquired and divined that we were visiting the famous B-school; and that off and on, I had long-standing associations with Ahmedabad.

In inventory management courses in B-schools, we learn about A, B and C categories of items. C items are routinely ordered in bulk, a bit more attention is paid to B items, but the real art of inventory control lies in showering management attention on the expensive A items. The store clerk quickly classified Ruby and me as A items. He phoned the owners' home, which must have been nearby. Soon enough, Vinodbhai – one of the two brothers owning the place – showed up.

Vinodbhai was ebullience personified. He started pulling out things from under the glass counter and from various corners of the dozen glass display cases lining the store walls.

"Look at this... it must to 70-80 years old... it is a payal, for the feet, but it is so perfectly made with interlocking silver links that we have put strings on both sides and made it into a necklace... see how perfectly it hangs..." Ruby tried it on, looked in the mirror, and loved the way it draped.

"Do you know what this is?" Vinodbhai asked, showing us a silver neck ornament with a tiny, ice pick-type object as well as a tiny spoon-like thing. "This is an old-time Kutch toothpick and ear-cleaner...people carried them strung on a chain around their neck...just look at the size of these...people don't have such big teeth and ears anymore!"

"And this," he pulled out a silver flower with a winding stem, "is a perfume holder." He unscrewed the flower and showed how some drops of perfume can be stored in a tiny chamber. Visions floated before our eyes; of Kutchi royal couples, idly sauntering the corridors of palaces and havelis, indulgently sniffing perfume from silver flowers.

"Oh... and these are the anklets that Kutchi women wore on their feet" he said. These were huge rings of solid but carved silver. If they had been iron with chains attached, they could well have belonged in a dungeon.

"We had this American customer... he bought thousands of rupees worth of stuff... he gave us this idea," exulted Vinodbhai. Adding a base and attaching silver wire tripod legs converted the massive anklet into an ashtray.

 "These look enormous, but they are so well made that they fit perfectly and you don't feel the weight at all!"

Vinodbhai showed how the huge armlets and anklets unclasped. Ruby tried on one of the armlets. Unless she was considering a role as a she-warrior in a Bollywood-Hollywood C-movie, this was not her style!

We were late for an appointment, so we bought one pair of earrings, and prepared to leave. Vinodbhai insisted that we revisit, when we had more time on our hands. We exchanged cards and phone numbers, and promised to come after the weekend, on Monday evening when Ruby's class at the B-school ended. It took a good fifteen minutes just to say goodbye.

On Monday, we persuaded our friend Shyla to drive us in her car to the Kutch silver store. This time, the Kutch store folks were prepared. The younger owner, Mukeshbhai, was at hand, as also the original lanky store clerk. There were also two women behind the counter, who did not say anything but just lent their presence and smiled faintly. We figured they were family members too. Almost all the lights were turned on!

Mukeshbhai was a younger, less stocky version of Vinodbhai, with an equally broad grin, but minus the infectious ebullience. He pulled out various things and showed them to us. A phone call was made and special Kutchi tea was ordered from the owners' house. Ruby took one sip and winced. She has become used to the English brew and the rich, milk-and-masala laden Gujarati concoction is not, you may say, her cup of tea. She gave me a furtive, beseeching look and whispered, "Please drink mine too." I obliged – the rich brew was a stimulating foil to the gathering monsoon grey outside.

As Ruby and Shyla examined various earrings, chains and trinkets, I sat on a chair and sipped the tea. My eyes wandered to the upper edge of the wall behind the counter. There were several photos of Vinodbhai and Mukeshbhai with celebrities: Sam Pitroda – India's telecom wizard; a German-Indian model bedecked with Kutchi jewellery; ex-PM Narasimha Rao; ex-PM Chandrashekhar; various high brass of the armed forces.

The lanky store clerk came by me and said, "I got to shake Bill Clinton's hand when he was in India."

"Wow!" I exclaimed, "Any photos?"

"There was an official photographer taking pictures, but I have not been able to locate him," said the clerk.

Just then, Vinodbhai showed up, donning a natty hat and looking like a seasoned Bollywood comic. He took charge of the 'showing' and the rate at which merchandise was pulled out and displayed jumped up several notches. Unlike Mukeshbhai, he was not content that only Ruby and Shyla looked at things... I was made to get up, fondle the silver goodies, and nod in appreciation also.

"You are so lucky," he turned to Ruby, "to have married this man."

"Uh..oh," I thought. Ruby is going to lecture Vinodbhai on who the lucky one was... to have nabbed the Bengali aesthete with two Berkeley degrees and a Northwestern doctorate.

But Vinodbhai's smile and manner was just too disarming.

"I guess so," she said, "But don't you think Nikhilbhai is lucky to have married me?"

Vinodbhai smiled some more and agreed readily.

There was a lot of good banter about the glory of Kutch, the fabulous quality of Kutchi silver cutting and carving, the famous celebrities of Kutchi origin that Vinodbhai and Mukeshbhai had dealt with.

"You folks have taste...you know about arts and crafts...Please take our merchandise and market it abroad...People here don't understand the value of these antiques and the fine Kutchi silver workmanship. When I get the occasional American or German buyers, they buy out nearly the entire store..." on and on went Vinodbhai.

We had made our selections and wanted to leave. Not so easy, given Vinodbhai's bubbling enthusiasm. Another round of tea? We had to refuse, firmly.

Vinodbhai's mobile rang. After a short conversation, he

200

informed us that in a couple of days a shipment of delicious Kutchi dry dates would arrive, and that we must return to taste this delicacy.

"We will try," we muttered insincerely.

A guest book was brought out. Vinodbhai asked me to figure out where one of the signatories was from. It was a doctor from Bavaria, in Germany. I guessed correctly.

He opened a fresh page. We wrote messages of goodwill in English, Hindi, Gujarati, Bengali, Malayalam, German and Spanish, and signed our names. The jewellery and trinkets were ready to be wrapped up. No, we did not want the gift boxes – just a simple plastic bag would do.

I pulled out whatever cash I had in the wallet, and promised to send the balance later. Shyla had bought a chain that needed fixing, so she was planning a return trip anyway. I said I would send the remaining money with her.

Warm handshakes, another set of visiting cards thrust in our hands. Two hours after we had entered, in delicious exhaustion, we plunked ourselves back into the seats in Shyla's car. If shopping in Virtual Kutch was so much fun, we wondered, what would it be like in the real Kutch?

…When and if we ever made our way to it.

The Whiz of Aus

Alex Joseph

It's been twenty-one years since I migrated to Australia, and by now I consider myself to be something of an, albeit unofficial, authority on its culture. However, I continue to be surprised by the enormous differences between India and Australia. One has a large

and relatively poor population with a rich cultural heritage, whereas the other has a small and rich population with almost no heritage worth mentioning!

The one aspect of Australia that really strikes me as different is the Australian attitude towards religion. India is a deeply religious country. India and the US are perhaps the only large countries in the world today where religion plays such a dominant role in social life and in politics. Except for the name of the deity, and the language used, the prevailing philosophy is the same: God rules. It is almost impossible to imagine an avowed atheist becoming President of the US, at least in our lifetimes. Similarly, can you imagine what society's attitude would be towards any public figure in India who flaunted his atheism?

Australia is totally different. Though nominally a 'Christian' country, most Aussies simply do not practise any religion. Attendance at services, conducted by all major Christian denominations, has fallen dramatically and Australia can almost be called a 'post-Christian' society. Several churches have been closed; many sold off to real estate developers. Fewer bums on pews means less money in the collection plate. And that means the front-line troops of the churches – the priests, pastors, vicars and deacons cannot be paid as well as they should. As a result, lay people are compelled to take on more and more of the jobs involved in running a parish.

And yet, Christianity is not dead in Australia. The fastest growing Christian denominations are the evangelical ones. These groups often don't have priests. The church leaders are lay people, usually professionals with some other full-time employment. Other groups that are increasing rapidly are what some would label 'pseudo-Christian' congregations, like Mormons, Seventh Day Adventists, Jehovah's Witnesses and so on. But the fastest growing religious groups in Australia are the Hindus, Muslims and Buddhists. These are increasing mainly because of migration – whereas a white migrant is likely to be somewhat ambivalent about his Christianity, migrants from Asian and African countries tend to be quite religious, at least for the first two generations! The wealthy Hindu community (mainly Indians and Sri Lankans) have constructed very beautiful temples in Melbourne and Sydney – these are so large and so elaborate that there is talk of making them tourist attractions!

I have not come across any Indian who is totally indifferent towards religion. I do not know a single person in India, who, when pressed on this point, would declare himself an atheist. Australians are just the opposite. The majority are actually atheists. They may not consciously think of themselves as such, but their level of indifference towards God and religious practices is so high, that for all practical purposes this is an atheistic society. Almost all my Aussie colleagues, fellow teachers at the school where I teach, and most of my students, have absolutely no hesitation in admitting that they do not believe in any God, never pray, never go to a church and that they do not consider themselves Christian.

Living and working among so many atheists does have an effect on you. Though it is unlikely that I will ever become an atheist myself, I do have a great deal of respect for my atheistic colleagues. In Australia, a person may be deeply spiritual, even if he is not religious. I feel the basis for their moral and ethical behaviour is in some way superior to mine. After all, my morality is partly based on fear – fear that I would anger my God by doing something wrong and that He would punish me or that I would go to hell or suffer some such awful fate. But my atheist friends do not fear any God; they do the right thing out of personal conviction. I sometimes suspect that both my children have become 'post-Christian'; I am not quite sure how I will react if my fears are confirmed!

Australia's egalitarian ethos is probably the best-known characteristic of its society, probably having roots in its convict past. The nation started off in 1788 as a dumping ground for criminals from overflowing jails in the UK, and prisoners continued to be sent to Australia till the mid 1800's. Obviously, these unfortunate wretches hated their masters. Over the past 200 years, this hatred has mellowed into today's irreverence and healthy disregard for wealth, inherited or otherwise, and any form of authority or power whether parental, religious, political or even in the workplace.

An interesting side issue – it is a mark of honour if one can trace one's background to a convict who was transported to Australia! For me, this is truly amazing. As an Indian, I would be ashamed to admit it, if one of my ancestors was a criminal. Strangely, modern-day Australians have a completely different attitude!

Everyone knows that bosses are called by their first names in the US, and that it is normal for subordinates to keep sitting when the boss is standing next to them. Well, all that is true of Australia also, but they go much further. Even the Prime Minister and the State Premiers are treated with the same casual familiarity. In fact, even such high officials sit in the front seat with their drivers. This is not insignificant – is there any country on earth where the head of government routinely sits in front with his driver?

The same applies to taxis also; most Australian taxi drivers would be offended if a single male person passenger sat at the back. The philosophy behind all this is simple – everyone is equal as an individual in society and should be treated with equal dignity and consideration. Another example – there is generally no tipping in Australia. You do not have to tip waiters, hotel staff, taxi drivers, lift-operators, hairdressers and so on. One probable reason is that minimum wages are relatively high and minimum wage legislation is rigidly enforced. But I feel the real reason is the egalitarian ethos.

Australia's egalitarianism also finds voice in industrial and public policy. Consider the low salary differential, even in large organisations. The biggest employer is the federal government, headed by the Prime Minister. After tax, he earns only about eight times the salary of the lowest paid federal government employee. And, excluding a few highly paid executives, similar low multiples apply in the private sector also.

In the social welfare arena, minimum wages and unemployment benefits are perhaps the highest in the

world, much higher than in richer countries like the US and Japan. You may see an occasional beggar, but it's probably because he has blown his unemployment benefit or his wages on drink or drugs.

However, high minimum wages are driving a lot of industry to low wage countries. It is now cheaper to import some fruit products from as far away as Brazil than to produce them locally. Also, the dole is so generous that industry is finding it difficult to get workers to perform a wide variety of menial and unpleasant tasks. As a result, we have started seeing 'guest workers' in Australia for the first time. The federal government is under a lot of pressure from industry to tighten the eligibility criteria for the dole, to reduce the need for large numbers of guest workers. Some of the more radical people in industry are even calling for the abolishing of minimum wages, but that is not likely in the near future.

There are no urban ghettos in Australia. Despite having a lower per capita income than the US and many European countries, Australian public housing is much better. In any case, only a small fraction of the population needs to rely on public housing – the rate of private home ownership is the highest in the world.

Public health services in Australia are superior to those in much richer countries. Even as a tourist you are far better off, health-wise, to suffer an emergency in Australia than in the US. If you collapse on a street in the US, the hospital you are taken to may be more interested in who will pay the bill than in saving your life. In Australia, the first concern is treatment; the bill is mentioned only when you are well and healthy.

New migrants to Australia are delighted to find the relatively classless nature of its society. Being a Keralite, I am a member of the local Malayali Association. We have four or five functions every year, of which the Onam dinner is perhaps the most popular. After the dinner, there is a job to be done – cleaning the floor, indeed a messy job, but it is often the doctors and other professional types who do this menial task while the nurses and clerks stand around sipping tea and chatting. It is perhaps only in Australia that one can see a neurosurgeon cheerfully clean the floor while his nurse gossips with her friends!

I have often seen the Principal of the school where I teach sweeping the entrance area when it gets badly littered. For the head of any organisation to perform such a demeaning job publicly is unthinkable in India. Professional Aussies are not seriously concerned if one or more of their children decide to go into a manual trade such as carpentry or plumbing. Indian migrants are of course devastated if one of their kids drop out of school or decide not to go to university. Perhaps things will change after two or three generations!

Australians hate putting anyone on a pedestal; cutting down 'tall poppies' is almost a national pastime. It is the absolute antithesis of the hero worship that Indians indulge in, almost deifying those who achieve great success in sports, entertainment, business or politics. In the U S too, success is almost a state religion. Successful people in Australia, however, are almost ashamed of their success. It is not that success is looked down upon in Australia; it is just that successful people are expected to be modest. One great benefit for successful people in Australia is that they may be recognised but are largely left alone without being mobbed by fans and paparazzi.

A somewhat related issue is the Australian attitude towards work itself. Most people have heard the American joke about not buying a car made on a Friday or Monday. (Cars made on Fridays are of poor quality because everyone is busy planning for the weekend and cars made on Mondays are of poor quality because of hangovers from the weekend!). I have not yet heard that joke in Australia, but Aussies are extremely casual about work. People do not live to work here; they live only for the holidays. Top executives in Australia, like top executives world-wide, may slave long hours, but the average Joe Bloggs won't be seen dead in an office or factory after the official closing time. I was surprised to hear that computer whiz kids in Bangalore practically live in their offices. They ought to keep in mind that their counterparts in Australia go home promptly at 5 pm if not earlier! And yet, in spite of the seemingly laidback attitude to life, Australians are very productive and innovative. Per capita, Australia is a nation with one of the highest numbers of Nobel Prize winners and inventors. As for sports, it is undoubtedly the world champion if all sports are considered! The country is living proof of that old dictum – it is much more important to work smart rather than work hard.

It is very rare to see a three-generation household in Australia, except among migrants from Asian countries and some South European nations like Italy and Greece. It is almost expected that kids move out of the family home when they finish their studies, or if they stay on at home, parents expect them to contribute – there is no 'free lunch'! Old Aussies do not feel comfortable 'being a burden' to their kids – they move into nursing homes or old folks' homes.

A cause for the poor family ties (or may be a consequence?) is the very high divorce rate in Australia. Nearly half Australia's marriages end in divorce. Re-constituted families are very common, of the 'yours, mine and ours' variety.

As a teacher, I have had interesting (and often sad) experiences relating to family break-ups and reconstitutions. One common example: John Smith suddenly becomes John Brown, because his mother has re-married. Then, after a few months, the mother splits from the new hubby, so John Brown goes back to being John Smith again! Another example, thankfully less common: John Smith's girlfriend is Jane Jones. Suddenly their lives are thrown into confusion, because John's mother has married Jane's father, so now technically John and Jane are stepbrother and stepsister, living under the same roof. Both John and Jane may have been 'going steady' (or as wags would euphemistically say – 'shaking hands vigorously') for a long while. Now both John and Jane need to find a new girlfriend and boyfriend respectively. Single women with small children to look after are particularly hard hit when their husbands walk out on them. Occasionally I get this excuse from a student for not doing homework: "I was helping Mum entertain her new boyfriend."

Because of the high marriage-failure rate, youngsters are often unwilling to marry – they continue to live together in de-facto relationships, for years and years. Australian family law recognises de-facto relationships as marriages for property, child-custody, and inheritance matters. Till I came to Australia, I had never heard the term 'de-facto marriage'. It took me quite a while to get used to it! It also took me quite a while to learn never to say 'wife' or 'husband', just 'partner'!

This lack of permanence in relationships has another side effect – the falling birth rate. Of course, birth rates are falling for a variety of reasons, but it is generally agreed that the growing unpopularity of marriage as an institution is one of its main causes. In India the youth are increasing in numbers, but in Australia, it is just the opposite! I sometimes joke with my Australian friends that they better be nice to me, because twenty years down the track there will be too few Aussies left, and it would be young Indians who would be running the place!

Strong family ties in Australia among Indian migrants create problems in terms of sporting loyalties. For the adults it is simple, we always barrack for India. But, for the youngsters who grew up in Australia, there is a question of divided loyalties. As my son said many years ago when he was very young, "I am happy to cheer for Australia. But, when Australia plays India, I am confused. I don't know for whom to cheer. And in the end I don't know whether we have won or lost!"

If there's one thing that I don't like about this wonderful country it is the Australian passion for gambling. On a per capita basis, Australians gamble more than any other society on earth. Some say it is because Australian society does not have an aversion to risk, especially financial risk. As proof, they point to the very high level of share ownership in Australia, second only to the US, and likely to overtake the US very soon. Others say the high incidence of gambling is proof of the innate optimism of Australians. The wide-open spaces and the abundant sunshine seem to foster a feeling of perpetual optimism. And, being optimists, they continue to pour their money into various lotteries, poker machines, horse races, bingo parlours and casinos. Social workers are very concerned at the rising number of 'problem gamblers,' but no state government wants to legislate against gambling. Taxes on gambling are high and these taxes are a very important source of revenue for all Australian states.

Despite all the differences, India and Australia share much more than a love of cricket and a common colonial heritage. Both are true democracies and the press in both countries is genuinely free. This is truly remarkable, because in our part of the world, democracy and a totally free press are the exception and not the rule – can you name even five countries, east of Suez, that fit the bill? Both India and Australia have very similar traditions in the military, the judiciary, in education and in business.

I was in my late thirties when I migrated here, so I'm still very much 'Indian' at heart, I still feel more comfortable in India, notwithstanding all the irritations of life in a third world, country. After all, this is *my* third world country, the place where my heart will always be. Sometimes I think it is because of the similarities with my native place that I love Australia so much. But it is the differences – in attitudes, values and systems – that make me love and appreciate both countries even more.

Whispers of the Past

Vidya K Baglodi

I was returning to Bangalore from the UAE after a gap of nearly ten years. I was taken aback by the changes that had transformed this gracious garden city into a suave silicon city! The gentle green of my remembered childhood had given way to the uncompromising grey of steel and concrete.

Driving from the airport to the house made me wonder if my memory was playing tricks on me. The development was astonishing – as was the increased pollution and congestion. Chrome and glass on either side of the road reflected my bewilderment, while the chaotic traffic had me tearing my hair in despair. I was left rueing the loss of beloved childhood haunts that had disappeared overnight without a trace.

During my school days (in the 70's) we lived in Koramangala in a house that had no electricity. We had two dogs, a cow and a lovely garden of roses (no less than 58 varieties!). I studied for my examinations under the light of a hurricane lamp. The nocturnal peace would be interrupted from time to time by the howling of foxes and wolves. King cobras were frequent and inescapable visitors. The snake charmer would come all the way from Adugodi to entice these majestic but unwelcome visitors and draw them away to even greener pastures.

Our home was surrounded by miles of wilderness and the only signs of habitation were the buildings of St John's Hospital, John Fowler and the Survey of India.

My sister, a student of Mount Carmel College had just one bus she could catch in the morning. To miss that bus meant an inevitable holiday for there were no buses after that. But it was not so easy to miss the bus: the drivers would stop and honk in a friendly but determined manner to inform us of their arrival. They were also indulgent enough to wait – something quite unheard of in today's world. Of course, missing the bus meant walking all the way from Koramangala to Adugodi.

Today's Koramangala is unbelievable! I was unable to recognise Sarjapur Road, Madivala and Adugodi that have been transformed radically. Everywhere we saw evidence of the technology boom, hoardings for innumerable new consumer products, fancy eating-joints and of course more malls and super-malls.

I decided to take a full-day sightseeing trip. I started out from the Jayanagar shopping complex, along with a busload of other tourists, at 8.30 am. Our first stop was the ISKON temple, Rajaji Nagar. I was dumbfounded to find that the shrine was scrupulously clean, meticulously maintained and complete with self-explanatory boards that obviated the need for tour guides.

After admiring the view from the top, we proceeded to the Bull Temple and then to Tipu's Summer Palace. The roses were in full bloom and the fragrance heady, as we walked to the palace with its pillars of teak, and the gallery where men and women once sat segregated. Hushed by the sense of history, we listened to the guide desperately trying to recreate the wonders of the past – if only the walls could have whispered their secrets!

Everything else passed by in a confused but exciting blur despite the valiant efforts of the tour guide who limped along with his mixture of English interspersed with Kannada. The

Visweswarya Museum with the early aeroplanes and the first sewing machine; the famous Mysore Sandalwood Factory; the architectural magnificence of the Vidhana Soudha; the Urvasi theatre belonging to Jayapradha (did you know that?).

Most of my fellow tourists began to lose interest as the day wore on. But I persevered, mindful of my daughter's school project. The grateful tour guide, deciding I was the most diligent, turned his complete attention to me.

"He seems to be more interested in you than us," my co-passengers teased.

We arrived at Bannerghatta National Park in time for the last safari of the day. The lions and tigers were magnificent but the only recurring thought in my mind, I must confess, was, "What if one of them decided to attack us?"

We then visited the zoo where I collected a few feathers from each birdcage (not bird – please note all animal-bird lovers) for my daughter's holiday homework.

On our return to the city we stopped at the sprawling Lalbagh Park, famous for its glasshouse and flower show. For a minute I felt I was in Holland. I went on a shopping spree to pick up some seeds. In spite of my knowledge of Kannada (learnt in school), I was fleeced mercilessly by the vendors. But I guess that's the price you pay for being a tourist and letting it show through dress, accent or attitude.

But now that the hollyhocks and cockscomb have started to sprout in my balcony garden in Sharjah, I feel it was worth it, even if everyone at home insisted it was an exorbitant price to pay.

Having splurged quite a bit on many things I really did not need, and having paid much more than I should have for the same, I did not have enough money to buy some more souvenirs, but the shop owner was kind enough to send the salesman home to pick up the money. He told me that he could even send the card machine home. Where but in India would you get that kind of service?

Later I visited Kemp Fort and Bangalore Central to shop

till I was ready to drop. Then, I stopped to gorge on red guavas from roadside carts and dropped into Woodys to eat those incredibly crisp and delicious dosas. I ate bravely and greedily without a thought of possible belly upsets. Those, if any, would come in the future, while I was living in the present – or should I say the past? For here were all the flavours from my childhood, and in an instant I was a child again.

Maaza Baala

Mahendra Rathod

My mother was just nineteen when I was born. She brought me at two-weeks-old to Bombay – a world that still, after three years, was a new universe. My father, the eldest of a large family in Rajkot, a then very colonial city in Gujarat, had migrated to Bombay to take up work as an accountant with a tannery. He had moved to Bombay as a bachelor to make money, lend support to an extended family and to save for his future wife and child.

He had found an affordable room; but the room was part of a common shared universe, which was then a hallmark of middle-class affordability. It was an open-door-all-day kind of an environment but he did not resent the intrusion and unwritten requirement to share one's life. He was a friendly soul. He found that he had nice neighbours on either side – that was a big comfort.

Having just come into a big city; he was willing to take any advice and support that came his way. The Kadams were his neighbours on

one side. Rukminibai Kadam, the wife, was a formidable woman –
standing tall and upright, invariably wearing a kashta – a 9-yard sari
typical of the Konkan area in Maharashtra – and chain-chewing
paan. Her loving nature was all but invisible under her stern gaze and
rich baritone.

When my father first moved in, he must have looked helpless and
simple. So she, as was her wont, took over the role of an elder
sister. She eased him into city life. And when he had the premarital
jitters she gave him a lot of advice and sent him off to his own
wedding with joy and anticipation in his heart.

They say some special bonds are designed up there and there is
not much you can do about it. One look at my teenage mother and
the wrinkled up two-week-old was enough for Rukminibai. She took
us both under her wing. Though my mother spoke no Marathi,
language was never a barrier between them. My father thought it
was just wonderful. I have never asked my mother what she thought.
I guess as a nineteen-year-old uprooted from a village and plonked
into a city she might have been relieved to have any support.

Rukminibai took charge of our lives and gave her advice on
everything – from baby feed recipes to how to cure various
illnesses. She took a particular liking to me – this odd bundle that
kept everyone awake with loud bawling at all hours. And not even
pretty or cuddly at that, I am told. I was scrawny with very curly
hair. Maybe it was the hair.

She never had any problems raising her own daughter who was
four years old then. She mistakenly thought I would be docile too. As
my mother got more fretful, Rukminibai took upon herself this
challenge of managing me. My mother was relieved and grateful.
One worry less for a few hours. It was hard enough with so many
new things to cope with: languages, social mores, city dwellers'
double-talk and her husband's fragile new corporate life.

 Rukminibai knew no fairy tales, so history it was. She
started telling me stories of brave warriors who defeated the

Mughals. Less than a year old, it must have been her voice that put me to sleep. Later, as a small boy her stories of Marathas and Mughals fascinated me.

I started speaking early. I was quick at giving ad-hoc names to everything and everyone. By then, Rukminibai was very much a part of our life. I would spend half a day in her room playing on their high four-poster bed that was my den. One day, my Father told me that Rukminibai was my Faiba, meaning paternal aunt in Gujarati. The name soon stuck and very soon the whole neighbourhood slipped into calling her Faiba. Even her husband and daughter found it convenient to call her Faiba to others.

Soon it was all play and no study. I would fly kites, spin tops, play marbles, tennis-ball cricket and cotton-ball hockey; try my hand at cards, chess and checkers. Rukminibai, from her wooden bench outside her room, kept an eagle eye on me; rushing to pick me up every time I fell and scraped my knees. She always had a bottle of tincture-of-iodine ready. When I was not playing, I was asking her questions and making her retell stories of her native land – Sawantwadi in Maharashtra.

Faiba developed every mother's ultimate myopia – she thought I was the handsomest, smartest, nicest boy who could do no wrong. She was the local judge and jury to whom the boys went with complaints about me, whenever I bent the rules in my favour at games, which was often, since I owned the bat and the ball. But it was truly a blind justice – she could never ever see or believe that I could do any wrong. It was all the boys' fault – so she sent them off either with a twist to the story – a justice that seemed to satisfy them; or she rebuked them for thinking I could ever do such a thing! Soon the boys realised the futility of this kind of a justice system and I was left alone.

I came from a vegetarian family but soon learnt to eat fish and chicken at Faiba's house. My parents were broadminded about it. And she was a superlative cook so my high point of

217

happiness was when I smelt the spicy red chillies being fried and the fragrance of cooking fish wafting across the veranda.

Curiously I don't remember her hugging or cuddling me. Her love and affection was transmitted through her big, smiling eyes and her evident joy at my company.

As I grew up, our games took an adolescent turn. It involved curiosity about girls; it involved wrestling and causing pain in the name of non-sissy games. We dared not cry or complain. Gone was Faiba's totally biased protection to her baala (young boy). I was also unhappy with her cry of "Where is Maaza Baala? Where is my boy?" I was a man now, not her baala. I resented her interventions. But everything was forgotten including the intense group-preoccupation with girls as soon as Faiba called me for FISH – she made the best fish curry in the world. All the fish dishes I have eaten since in over twenty countries, have been measured against her dishes and found wanting.

When I was about eleven we moved house. It was a large apartment on the third floor not far from where we were living before, but a totally different universe. Doors were closed the whole day and opened occasionally to exchange milk or sugar between neighbours. My contact with Faiba dwindled dramatically (such is the selfishness of youth) and the only times I met her was when she would bring me a large dish full of fish to our apartment building and would stand down below and cry out, "Mahendra Baala!" She could not climb as she had very high blood pressure. I would go dashing down, taking three steps at a time with youthful nimbleness. I would give a brief response to her questions about my studies and my family. And then I was gone.

Then I moved to residential dormitories at IIT and then IIM. I did not get to see her except a few times. I did not make the effort – I was busy dreaming about a future and already afraid of losing it. I then moved abroad and did not see her again. On some of my short trips home, she would come to know and would send over my favourite dish. I would invariably be out on business, but ate the fish with relish when I returned home. I remember tossing, on several occasions, an offhand question over the shoulder, "How is Faiba keeping?"

My trips to India became less frequent and then one day when I made my usual fortnightly call to my mother, I heard that Faiba had passed away. For a brief moment, guilt singed my core. I spent a moment in prayer for her well being in the next world. I thanked God for giving me Faiba and a very happy childhood. Then I was back in my own world.

My life abroad was comfortable and the eye-popping novelty of the western world lasted for over twenty-five years. However among the pot-pourri of life's emotional baggage that one collects, something kept gnawing away at my heart – Faiba's memory. I had not done enough to repay her with the one currency she craved for: love. I took and took but did not give.

I tried to share this feeling with my mother but she was no help – she defended me (as always, my siblings complain) by saying that I had been busy and that Faiba had felt my love across the distance of space and time. My wife in her deep wisdom, felt my pain and coaxed me to go find Faiba's daughter and to make my peace.

I took the decision to travel to Faiba's village – the place that she loved as a child. I was sure that just the soil there would allow me to reconnect. I wanted it as a journey of closure. I knew her daughter had moved back to the village. I would go and visit her and talk to her about Faiba and the missing years. I would help her if she needed help.

I had known that Faiba came from a village near Sawantwadi in Maharashtra, close to the Goa border. I decided to go to Sawantwadi and to start from there. I flew into Bombay on an early morning flight and took a taxi straight to Dadar bus station. I had decided to go by road, as that would allow me to reflect and to see the countryside – get a feel for the place where Faiba grew up.

219

My long stay abroad had made me too soft – I could not travel by local buses or trains, only by air-conditioned taxi. I felt a trip like that to honour Faiba's memory would be hollow. I decided to travel by an ordinary non-A/C, State transport bus. The long uncomfortable journey was a part of my expiation.

As you leave Bombay and travel the coastal road, the surrounding landscape is quite refreshing; majestic hills in the distance stand proud as if retelling the history of the Mughal defeats at the hands of the Marathas; lush green carpets the countryside. Once you leave the city, the countryside comes upon you very suddenly and this India is very different from the India of cities. The landscape is unbroken for miles. There is acceptance of the destined. There are no super dreams being chased unto despair.

I had trouble soaking in the wonderful sights of rural India – my bus was jam-packed, full of country folk – shepherds and farmers. The shepherds I could instantly identify; the smell of sheep and goat travels well and is not something that you can wish away. The farmers had strong, callused hands and red soil under their nails. The villagers wore their traditional khadi and Gandhi caps. Some were barefoot; others had rough slippers on. All of them were chewing paan or tobacco. There were only two ladies, both in kashtas. I stood out with my neatly tailored clothes, Italian shoes and well-groomed appearance. There was no way I could have made myself belong there: my discomfiture was plain to all. The bus rolled on with a mind of its own, swaying from one side to another as if it was born to disco. I hung on to the handrails of the seat in front of me. After a few hours I began wondering if I had made the right decision. Would I even survive the journey?

After what seemed like an eternity, the bus stopped at a large town for a tea break. We were told to be back in twenty minutes otherwise the bus would leave without us. Several buses were parked at the shop and passengers were busy washing themselves, eating snacks, drinking tea, smoking and making

220

phone calls. Loud music blared from the speakers mounted on various walls and the songs were – what else? – the latest Hindi film hits.

I had to choose something to eat. I knew Sawantwadi was a long way off and I would starve if I didn't eat now. After a good look I chose batata wada, fried potato snacks. I reasoned the boiling oil would kill all the bacteria and other bugs. I stopped myself from speculating on what kind of oil it was and how many times it had been reused. I bought a large bottle of mineral water but the look and the taste of it made me uneasy. I drank a Coke for safety's sake – although the newspapers were saying even that was not safe. There were large puddles of water in several places and people rinsed their mouths and spat into the puddles. They ate the cold food and drank the local water. None keeled over. I wondered: is there an upper limit to immunity or can you beat the bacteria?

My co-passengers could not contain their curiosity and asked me if I was a doctor. I said no, I was visiting an old relative near Sawantwadi. They asked me questions about my job but I could not convey 'business manager'. When I said bank manager it clicked. I had respect. I told them I had travelled from a foreign land but that held no meaning for them. But when I told them I was going to look for a lost relative, they looked at me with sympathy and wished me luck. I asked them on the off chance but none had heard of the Kadam family. I knew my task was almost futile – to search for someone in modern India was asking for a lot!

The bus took off again. I was very tired and I dozed off. The smells, the noise, the lurching, all made me want to turn back and vanish back into my world. But I decided to sleep it out. It worked – I slept. When I woke up it was time to eat again. I decided to stick to my routine of wada and Coke. I added some bread to the wada to fill up my stomach. A couple of Cokes did the job. God bless America and its colas!

I reached Sawantwadi late at night. My bones were jostled

221

beyond repair and my posterior had never seen such hardship. I got off and collected my backpack. I found a small, family-run hotel where I bathed and then set out to look for a place to eat. I remembered from some strange depths of my childhood memory, that Faiba used to talk of Khanavals – family-run eating houses where the food was clean and really tasty. I asked for a Khanaval. It was a rarity in these days of chrome and polish, and melamine tableware. The hotel tried to dissuade me – you'll have to sit on the floor, you'll get only veg food and so on. I found one and asked the owner to give me local food. He served me on banana leaves with rice and varan – cooked lentils and potato dishes. Thrilled, I sat cross-legged and ate. That night, I slept like a log.

After a local breakfast, I caught another bus. I had to draw upon the furthest reaches of childhood memory to remember Faiba had mentioned a village called Nivati. I asked about it and yes, it was only a few hours away. I took the bus to Nivati. This bus was half-empty. After a few hours we arrived at Nivati, a village smack on the seashore. I remembered Faiba describing her childhood days playing on the shores of Nivati as I listened with wonder – children are often surprised that adults were children once.

I walked up from the bus stop to a nearby cliff. I could see the surf and the fisher-folk preparing to cast to the sea. There were lush jackfruit and mango trees as far as the eye could see. The red fertile soil seemed to say: farming is easy. On one side of the cliff there were cashew trees laden with fruit. The cashew fruit looks very odd but very pretty too. I remembered Faiba telling me that if you eat the fruit when it is raw you will have a ruined throat.

I got back to the bus stop and asked if any Kadam family from Bombay lived there. All shook their heads. I knew this was the village but could they have moved? It was, after all, more than twenty-five years. I asked at the small shops near the bus stop. I asked the rickshawallas. No use. I wandered further and finally found a post office. The postmaster knew a Kadam

222

family but didn't know if they were from Bombay. He called a small boy and asked him to show me to an address.

I followed the boy up and down several alleys and finally we were in front of a door. He pointed silently. My heart beat rapidly. I didn't know what I was doing or what I was going to do. I asked the boy to knock instead of me. He did. The door opened and it was darkish inside. Outside was bright light and I was bathed in light. I saw someone look at me askance and then the door opened fully.

It was Baby – Faiba's daughter – grey and tired-looking. I was expecting to find her so it was not difficult to recognise her. But she was not expecting me. She took half a minute and asked in amazement, "Arre, Mahendra what are you doing here?" The bond of childhood camaraderie had survived the test of time and physical changes.

I went in and she shooed away the curious boy who still hung around. The house was small – a one-person house. On one wall was a large framed photo of Faiba. There was a family portrait on the other wall with all three of the Kadams. Her father was quite diminutive and even in the photo Faiba looked imposing.

Baby knew I had come a long way – it showed on my face, I guess. Soft city dwellers! She made some tea and as we drank she tried to work out my sleeping arrangements. Practical person that she always was! I could not stay there and there was no hotel. She went to a neighbour and had him move over to his brother's for the night. I could sleep in his bed for the night.

We sat, awkward at first, and exchanged life histories. She was very keen to know about me and it did not take long for me to delve into my complete life story. It was as if I carried it on my sleeve. I then asked about their life after I left for abroad. She said there wasn't much to tell. Faiba became increasingly ill in later years and the medical costs were high. Baby had never married and was the sole family Faiba had. She had a decent job and could manage the household on the income. Later, after Faiba passed away she decided that she had had enough. So she came here and with some savings from some inherited land that she sold, she was living a comfortable life.

We spoke for hours. She was flabbergasted to see me and kept looking at me with a curious but happy look.

She revealed for the first time how she was resentful as a child at the attention and special treatment I got in her own house. She would try and tattle to my mother to make me look bad (that explained the inexplicable caning I got sometimes from my mother!). But everyone was so taken in by my charm (her words not mine) that she gave up and accepted me as a nuisance that couldn't be wished away. Fortunately our floor had eleven daughters, so she had enough company to forget me. She did say she got to eat lovely dishes more frequently because of Faiba lavishing all that attention on me. We laughed: I, self-consciously.

She also revealed how Faiba used to be thrilled at my progress through school and later through IIT and IIM. She would tell anyone and everyone how 'Maaza Baala' had done so well. Baby would shush Faiba and tell her not to call me that anymore – after all, I was all of twenty! "Mahendra would be annoyed," she would tell her. But that made no difference. Baby recounted these stories without any residual rancour. I was moved.

I asked Baby if Faiba had ever expressed disappointment that I had never come to see her at all. She thought for a moment and said slowly, "No never. She knew you were there for her as she was there for you."

I slept well that night. Next day we spoke some more. But in some deep sense we both felt that a chapter had been properly closed. I was happy that I had actually found the house and Baby. I kept looking at the large picture of Faiba on the wall. Maybe I was trying to weld together two memories: one kept hidden and one recounted. I brought in some fresh flowers from the garden outside and prayed at Faiba's photograph. I asked for her

224

forgiveness. I felt quite at peace; as if I had revisited my old home and met Faiba. And I was pleased that Baby was happy and well settled.

The next day I left for Bombay, feeling light as air.... a faint 'Maaza Baala' coming out of the woods somewhere.

Authors

An alumnus of IIT Madras and IIM Ahmedabad, **Alex Joseph** worked in Bombay in manufacturing and project management for ten years before moving to Indonesia where he worked as a management consultant. He then joined an industrial group in East Java as General Manager. After migrating to Australia in 1983, he opted out of the rat race by becoming a schoolteacher.

Alex lives with his wife and two sons, all Aussie citizens, on the outskirts of Melbourne. They frequently visit India to meet friends and relatives. Alex has been writing on and off over the years – he was the editor of his school's newsletter, wrote prize-winning stories for the IIT magazine, was one of the founder-editors of the IIM campus newspaper and has also been published in magazines and technical journals. In 1995, in a national essay writing competition on immigration policy, Alex came second.

Anthony Koithra's writing has been described as a series of words, often with spaces between them interspersed with punctuation, line breaks and spelling errors, arranged into paragraphs of varying length. His work has appeared on several major grocery lists, lavatory walls and bail application forms. He dabbles in graphic design, painting, animation and film, and frequently subjects anyone nearby to the results – this has earned him an odd mixture of accolades and restraining orders, in a proportion he would rather not disclose. He talks too much, sleeps too little, reads and watches garbage, is distinctly lacking in taste and common sense, and is exceptional only for a preternatural ability to

226

pour perfect Rusty Nails. He works at Deutsche Bank in the island nation of Singapore and has been known on occasion to litter, although very surreptitiously and in minute quantities. Don't tell anyone.

 Handicapped by degrees in engineering from VJTI, Mumbai, and Financial Management from NMIMS, Mumbai, **Aruna Nambiar** found that she was the proverbial fish-out-of-water, while working as a Relationship Manager in a multinational bank. After peddling loans to consumerist yuppies and wheedling fixed deposits from rich old ladies for five years, Aruna finally came to her senses and turned her back on retail banking to focus on writing.

She now works as a freelance writer and editor and has written for the *Times of India, Economic Times, Indian Express, Deccan Herald* and *India Today-Travel Plus.* Some of her short stories can be read in our collection *Curtains: Stories by 9 Women.*

Having suffered many an uncomfortable voyage, and enjoyed the occasional magical one, she is now settled in Bangalore with her husband, and partner in peregrination, Raghu. She spends her spare time avoiding housework and stoutly denying that she either watches American Idol or reads Glamour magazine. Send her bouquets (no brickbats) at anambiar2005@yahoo.com

Deepa Ravi was born in 1972, and grew up mostly in Chennai. After graduating in English Literature, followed by a Diploma in Journalism, she pursued a career in advertising spanning 11 years. Writing has been her hobby since childhood, and she enjoys writing short stories, drawing inspiration from personal experience. Deepa regards RK Narayan as her Guru and her family as her main support.

Living in the Middle East for the last 8 years, she is now in Dubai with her husband and little daughter.

227

 **John Mathew** proclaims that he is a self-made man – and has little doubt that his family, teachers and probably God Almighty himself would approve of this statement as it absolves them of an embarrassing responsibility. John's literary career was launched at the age of six, when he was commissioned by a group of older classmates to paint graffiti on the school walls. His depiction of female anatomy (based on the imaginative and wholly inaccurate descriptions from his nine-year-old schoolmates) with complementary and exhaustive synonyms in Malayalam alongside, did not, sadly, win him many accolades.

Armed with a degree in Financial and Portfolio Management, like any normal Keralite of the 70s, he migrated to Bahrain, and subsequently moved to Abu Dhabi where he has lived happily since, with his wife, daughter and son, whom he adores but not necessarily in that order. He has been working for the Abu Dhabi Government for 24 years.

John writes regularly for the annual magazines of Indian associations, and is a regular contributor to the Letters to the Editor columns of several newspapers. His preferred epitaph would be, "For someone who started life drawing dirty pictures on school walls, he did not do too badly."

 **Mahendra Rathod** considers himself to be the eternally curious kid. He showed precocious talent as an artist, but pursued Indian Ivy League education. An alumnus of IIT and IIM he has happily merged his strong scientific-rational bent with eclectic explorations. Interests range from quantum physics, cosmology, Zen, psychiatry and of late, religion and its power to unify.

He was the CEO of a chemical company in Dubai for twenty-five years and now advises a multinational company on business development. His travels to more than 23 countries on work and pleasure have provided him with a rich treasure trove to draw from for his writings. He has published several short stories and hopes to make films someday as he thinks film is the most complete art form. He is peacock-pleased with his unique molten wax technique of painting and to complete the confusing picture of this kid: he shares his passion for golf with his wife Naina. They have made Dubai as their home

Twenty-six year old **Mathew Chandy** works in London as a corporate lawyer with Linklaters, an international law firm. He grew up in Bangalore and was the Vice President of the Students Union at the National Law School, from which he graduated in 2001. His many passions include music (closely involved with Bangalore's Strawberry Fields Music  Festival, he says he would have become a famous rock star if only he had an iota of musical talent), animals and travelling, all of which were an integral part of his recent travels in Brasil and South Africa. His other pursuits are sport (football, squash, tennis, cycling and running), cooking (an interest developed to avoid eating dull English food) and teaching.

After obtaining a medical degree from Madras University, **MR Shetty** practised Medical Oncology in Arlington Heights Illinois. He has now retired and lives in Bangalore.
His hobbies include travelling, writing and photography. His photographs have appeared in several publications. Some, taken on his visit to the North Pole, are exhibited at the Scott Polar Research Institute, UK. His first book, *Wildlife Adventures*, was published in 1997. He reached the geographic North Pole on August 5th, 2001.

229

Nikhilesh Dholakia's interests in writing date back to his childhood days in Delhi when he self-published an illustrated magazine for the private reading pleasure of his family and friends. Later, he continued these literary interests by making contributions to college publications.

At present, Nikhilesh is a professor at the College of Business Administration in the University of Rhode Island, USA. He also teaches as a visiting faculty at the Indian Institute of Management, Ahmedabad (IIMA). When he is not teaching or researching patterns of globalisation, Nikhilesh writes poetry and fiction. Some of the writings by Nikhilesh and his erstwhile classmates from IIMA appear on the weblog Vista-71. Nikhilesh lives with his scholar-professor wife Ruby Roy Dholakia in Rhode Island. He siezes every chance to travel.

After a degree in Chemistry, Botany and Zoology from Bangalore's Mount Carmel College, and a post-graduate degree in Molecular Biology from the University of Hertfordshire UK, **Preethi D'Sa** now works in the Communication Field in Abu Dhabi. She continues to update her skills with ongoing education in graphic design, technical and medical writing and quality management.

When she is not occupied with Technical and Business Writing, Corporate Communications, Desktop Publishing and Web/Graphic Designing, Preethi writes articles for magazines and websites, and volunteers her skills for editing newsletters. Preethi enjoys playing the piano and guitar, and is an enthusiastic traveller.

For 23 years, **Rahul Rao** lived in Bangalore. After obtaining a degree in law from the NLSIU, he was awarded a Rhodes scholarship in 2001 to study International Relations at the University of Oxford, where he is currently reading for a D.Phil. and teaching.

In his spare time, he enjoys reading fiction, drama and film, and runs for fun. He can also occasionally be seen drinking heavily and winning madly at Russian roulette. His winnings have financed much travel – to Italy, Spain, Turkey, the United States and Brazil in the recent past. He lives in Oxford and Bangalore in the temporal – but not emotional – ratio of about 11:1. Indeed, on his annual visits home he eats like a camel filling its hump before it returns to the gastronomic Sahara that is the rest of the year. He is also known to boost the December prices of Nilgiris' coffee. He wants to make a living from writing (hint: give him work at rahulrao78@yahoo.co.in).

Raja Ramanathan first travelled, at 90 days old, from Calcutta to Singapore. He lived in England for seven years and returning to India at the age of eight, worked his way through school, university, business school and jobs in Indian industry. Then wanderlust struck again. He moved to Bahrain, and nine years later to Canada, where he now lives. For him, India continues to remain like the other woman, always full of wonder and dark fascination. Canada lives with him as his partner...

Raja struggles with the beliefs of any system, but has been influenced by Hinduism, and the teachings of the Christ and Buddha. He has a commitment to Vipassana meditation, and enjoys listening to J Krishnamurti. Raja loves good food. Once unable to make a decent cup of tea, today he enjoys cooking and is happy to report that his wife Lakshmi, daughter Geetanjali and son Siddhartha are fans of his culinary skills.

231

Sarita Mandanna is from Coorg and was fortunate enough to be raised all over India, from Secunderabad to Srinagar. She has also variously lived in Hong Kong, Dubai and the US. All this moving around has perhaps set the stage and travel is now a deep-rooted, undeniable itch.

A graduate of the Shriram College of Commerce and IIM Bangalore, Sarita has an MBA from the Wharton Business School and now works and lives in New York City.

Vidya K Baglodi completed her schooling in Bangalore, but returned to Chennai for further education. Heartbroken after failing to obtain the requisite marks by just one percent for entrance into an engineering course, she pursued a degree in Economics, Commerce and Statistics from Stella Maris, Chennai. Her fascination for meeting people led her to complete a secretarial course, after which she joined the hospitality industry, where she worked in various capacities in administration and public relations.

She has been blessed with a wide circle of friends who have nicknamed her Chilly for the sharpness and bluntness of her talk, and her openness in all situations. At the age of 41 she found the man of her dreams and blessed with a daughter a year later, she is now a homemaker settled in the UAE. Her interests include music, interiors, gardening, travelling and writing.

 **N.C.Unni** (Illustrator): His halcyon childhood in Trivandrum consisted largely of cutting classes, dismantling car engines (and wondering how to reassemble them) climbing trees and roofs, and dabbling in sketching and painting against the express wishes of his mother, who did not want a 'painter' for a son (she was convinced that all artists are Bohemians). After graduating in Mathematics from University College Trivandrum he completed a post-graduation in Textile Technology & Engineering in faraway Bhiwani. He worked for an MNC in Mumbai, indulging his artistic side only during cartoon competitions at office Christmas parties, or while completing his daughters' graphs and diagrams through their school and college years, and on regular jaunts to Jehangir Art Gallery to look wistfully at the paintings.

He is now retired and lives happily in Bangalore with his wife Jayam. He enjoys reading, watching five news channels simultaneously, debating politics, and spending time with his two daughters and their husbands.

233

ABOUT UNISUN PUBLICATIONS

Everyone has to start somewhere, sometime and so do we. What better place and time than here and now!

A new publishing house for original, quality work in English in India... Unisun Publications, a division of Unisun Technologies [P] Ltd.

We have a panel of distinguished patrons, experienced editors and designers.

And we make this promise to every writer...

If you are a writer worth reading, we are a publishing house worth approaching. We offer you quality publishing and higher royalties.

And to our readers another promise...

We give you writers worth reading at prices worth considering.

Unisun Publications,
a division of Unisun Technologies [P] Ltd
Kodava Samaja Building, Ist Floor,
#7, Ist Main Road, Vasanthnagar,
Bangalore 560 052. INDIA.
Phone 080-22289663 Fax 080-22289294
e-mail: info@unisun4writers.com
website: www.unisun4writers.com